When revelation comes athlete and sage are merged.

W. B. Yeats, *A Vision*

THE ROCKET THE FLOWER THE HAMMER AND ME

EDITED BY
DOUG BEARDSLEY

POLESTAR
BOOK PUBLISHERS

Published by

Polestar Press Ltd., R.R. 1, Winlaw, B.C., V0G 2J0, 604-226-7670

Acknowledgements

"The Hockey Fan Came Riding" printed by permission of Birk Sproxton; "My Career With the Leafs" from the book *My Career With the Leafs and Other Stories* © 1982 Brian Fawcett, Talon Books Ltd., Vancouver, Canada; "Hockey Night in Canada" from the book *Hockey Night in Canada*, © 1987 Diane Schoemperlen, Quarry Press, Kingston, Ontario; PP. 31-34, 37-40, 98-100, 145-146 from *King Leary*, by Paul Quarrington, copyright © Paul Quarrington, 1987, published by Doubleday Canada Ltd., reprinted by permission of Doubleday Canada Ltd.; "Signing Up: The Larry Robinson Story" printed by permission of Jim Smith; excerpts from *Peckertracks* © 1978 Stan Dragland, Coach House Press, printed by permission of Stan Dragland; "Goalie" printed by permission of Rudy Thauberger; "Iron Man" printed by permission of Mark Jarman; "Competition" printed by permission of Barbara Novak; "The Return of Aurel Joliat" printed by permission of David Gowdey; "Teeth" by permission of Fred Stenson; "The Puck Artist" by permission of Levi Dronyk; "Blue Moon" printed by permission of Lionel Kearns; "The Drubbing of Nesterenko" by permission of Hanford Woods; excerpt from *The Last Season* by Roy MacGregor © 1983, reprinted by permission of Macmillan of Canada, A Division of Canada Publishing Corporation; "Wives" from *Night Driving* by Peter Behrens © 1987, reprinted by permission of Macmillan of Canada, A Division of Canada Publishing Corporation; excerpt from *The Loved and The Lost* by Morley Callaghan © 1951, reprinted by permission of Macmillan of Canada, A Division of Canada Publishing Corporation; excerpt from *Two Solitudes* by Hugh MacLennan © 1945, reprinted by permission of Macmillan of Canada, A Division of Canada Publishing Corporation; excerpt from *The Bus Ride* © 1974, printed by permission of Don Gutteridge; "The Hockey Game" by Wes Fineday, printed by permission of Fifth House Publishers, Saskatoon, Saskatchewan; excerpt from *The Saxophone Winter* by Robert Harlow © 1988, published by Douglas & McIntyre Ltd., reprinted by permission; "Truth" from *The Fencepost Chronicles* by W. P. Kinsella © 1986, reprinted with permission from The Colbert Agency, Toronto, Ontario; "I'm Dreaming of Rocket Richard" from *Tribal Justice* by Clark Blaise © 1974, reprinted by permission of Clark Blaise.

The Rocket was produced by Polestar Press in Winlaw, B.C. and printed by Gagne Printers in Louiseville, Quebec in November 1988.

Cover illustration by John Hodges.

CONTENTS

To all shinny players everywhere,
and to the immortal hockey men of Mount Royal,

and especially for my brother David Beardsley,
who, on ice, personifies Hemingway's "grace under pressure."

Forward

All the young Canadian hockey players that sweep over the blueline generation after generation carry with them something more than a puck and a burning desire to score; they also bring the mannerisms of their heroes, whether the immortal Rocket Richard, or the recently regenerated Guy Lafleur, known affectionately in English Canada as "The Flower." As added ammunition, they may be followed by the occasional winger or two who drops his blade at the slightest provocation (real or imagined) to engage in fisticuffs. These skaters have heroes of a different sort — heroes like the Flyers' Dave "The Hammer" Schultz, mayhem-maker and hockey enforcer supreme. In the world of fiction, Schultz becomes Felix Batterinski in Roy MacGregor's ambitious novel *The Last Season* and Danulchuck in Don Gutteridge's *Bus Ride*.

Young hockey players emulate the style of these three heroes, and of Howe, Beliveau, Messier, Lemieux, or "The Great One," Wayne Gretzky.

One way to play beyond yourself is to pretend that you are one of these hockey heroes when you're on the ice. It's what pairs author Hanford Woods "alongside Dallas Smith" on the Bruin defence, or allows Batterinski to imagine he's Tim Horton. Whoever you play against is disadvantaged if he isn't pretending to be anybody but himself. It is not that he is limited in what he can do; it is simply that he's playing against two — one a boy his age, the "other" an NHL star. This fantasizing about stardom and becoming the other player is common among those who've played the game since childhood. We all want to be Paul Quarrington's "King of the Ice," all of us dream of doing what Brian Fawcett lives out in "My Career with the Leafs": "Young, we all want to be hockey's ace" ... "beserkers taking care of each wing" as Mark Jarman puts it in "Iron Man." Is this what gives us our sense of spirit that sets us apart from the Russian national team players?

The twenty-three stories in *The Rocket, The Flower, The Hammer, and Me* reflect the synthesis of spirit and skill, both real and imagined, that make the game what it is in our country—an extended metaphor for the shaping experience of what it means to be Canadian. "So you see," says Billy the Kid Semeniuk in Levi Dronyk's story, "any kid without an instinctive understanding of the game is genetically un-Canadian." In an essay, John Metcalf has written: "A great hockey player emerges from *a hockey world*." Rudy Thauberger's "Goalie" keeps it on the same line: "What choice do I have? What else have I ever wanted to do?"

The game further serves Canadians as a metaphor for lost innocence, a wistful nostalgia best exemplified by Lionel Kearns' "Blue Moon," where Harvey Santini plays hockey with a self-confidence he is unable to emulate in the "teasing and ridicule" of "real" life. As Diane Schoemperlen writes: "Hockey, like stamp collecting, (is) a world apart, immune to the regular prejudices...."

We may agree with Morley Callaghan's McAlpine, who says of the game: "It used to look wonderful," and the priest from the same novel who comments, "It's a different game today...more of them can't hold on to the puck"—but we are all involved, invisibly related, pro or con to the game, whatever our background or upbringing. Judging from the Schultzs, Dave Browns, Batterinskis, or whomever, some of us had early childhoods that would obviously have benefitted from the motto burned into the wood above the entrance of the Bowmanville Reformatory: "TO KEEP A BOY OUT OF HOT WATER, PUT HIM ON ICE."

All hockey players—indeed, all athletes—believe they will go on forever like Aurel Joliat endlessly skating back and forth on the Rideau Canal. As one of the players in Gutteridge's *Bus Ride* intones: "When it went well it was like a dance ... such moments were reserved for our dreams." Our hero dreams of applause "falling endlessly like snow" around him, dreaming, too, "of a real arena where every shift, every glistening shot, was rewarded with cheers, was recorded and sent winging on air-waves over all the snows of this country's towns and hamlets."

Finally, it is with regret that we were unable to include Roch Carrier's short story "The Hockey Sweater," and a piece entitled "The Sportive Center of Saint Vincent de Paul" by Hugh Hood.

But we feel certain that the stories in this anthology— selected from 99 submissions received over the year— best capture the spirit, grace, and beauty of the game, and show Canadians and Canadiens alike as puck artists in an "icedream heaven."

As editor, I'd like to thank Julian Ross and the people at Polestar Press, Jim Brennan, Brenda Hornby, Stephanie Judy, and Donna Macdonald, for their continued encouragement, help, and patience. And I'd particularly like to thank the writers who said an enthusiastic yes to *The Rocket, The Flower, The Hammer, and Me.*

Doug Beardsley
Montreal - Vancouver Island, October 1988

I'm Dreaming
of Rocket Richard

Clark Blaise

We were never quite the poorest people on the block, simply because I was, inexplicably, an only child. So there was more to go around. It was a strange kind of poverty, streaked with gentility (the kind that chopped you down when you least expected it); my mother would spend too much for long-range goals—Christmas clubs, reference books, even a burial society—and my father would drink it up or gamble it away as soon as he got it. I grew up thinking that being an only child, like poverty, was a blight you talked about only in secret. "Too long in the convent," my father would shout—a charge that could explain my mother's way with money or her favors—"there's ice up your cunt." An only child was scarcer than twins, maybe triplets, in Montreal just after the War. And so because I was an only child, things happened to me more vividly, without those warnings that older brothers carry as scars. I always had the sense of being the first in my family—which was to say the first of my people—to think my thoughts, to explore the parts of Montreal that we called foreign, even to question in an innocent way the multitudes of unmovable people and things.

I'm Dreaming of Rocket Richard

When I went to the Forum to watch the Canadiens play hockey, I wore a Boston Bruins sweatshirt. That was way back, when poor people could get into the Forum, and when Rocket Richard scored fifty goals in fifty games. Despite the letters on the sweatshirt, I loved the Rocket. I loved the Canadiens fiercely. It had to do with the intimacy of old-time hockey, how close you were to the gods on the ice; you could read their lips and hear them grunt as they slammed the boards. So there I stood in my Boston Bruins shirt loving the Rocket. There was always that spot of perversity in the things I loved. In school the nuns called me "Curette" — "Little Priest."

I was always industrious. That's how it is with janitors' sons. I had to pull out the garbage sacks, put away tools, handle simple repairs, answer complaints about heat and water when my father was gone or too drunk to move. He used to sleep near the heating pipes on an inch-thick, rust-stained mattress under a Sally Ann blanket. He loved his tools; when he finally sold them I knew we'd hit the bottom.

Industriously, I built an ice surface, enclosed it with old doors from a demolished tenement. The goal mouth was a topless clothes-hamper I fished from the garbage. I battered it to splinters, playing. Luck of the only child: if I'd had an older brother, I'd have been put in goal. Luckily there was a younger kid on the third floor who knew his place and was given hockey pads one Christmas; his older brother and I would bruise him after school until darkness made it dangerous for him. I'd be in my Bruins jersey, dreaming of Rocket Richard.

Little priest that I was, I did more than build ice surfaces. In the mornings I would rise at a quarter to five and pick up a bundle of *Montreal Matins* on the corner of

Van Horne and Querbes. Seventy papers I had, and I could run with the last thirty-five, firing them up on second and third floor balconies, stuffing them into convenient grilles, and marking with hate all those buildings where the Greeks were moving in or the Jews had already settled and my papers weren't good enough to wrap their garbage in. There was another kid who delivered the morning *Gazettes* to part of my street—ten or twelve places that had no use for me. We were the only people yet awake, crisscrossing each other's paths, still in the dark and way below zero, me with a *Matin* sack and he with his *Gazette*. Once, we even talked. We were waiting for our bundles under a street lamp in front of the closed tobacco store on the corner. It was about ten below and the sidewalks were uncleared from an all-night snow. He smoked one of my cigarettes and I smoked one of his and we found we didn't have anything to say to each other except *"merci."* After half an hour I said "paper no come" and he agreed, so we walked away.

Later on more and more Greeks moved in; every time a vacancy popped up, some Greek would take it—they even made sure by putting only Greek signs in the windows—and my route was shrinking all the time. *Montreal Matin* fixed me up with a route much further east, off Rachel near St-Andre, and so I became the only ten-year-old in Montreal who'd wait at four-thirty in the morning for the first bus out of the garage to take him to his paper route. After a few days I didn't have to pay a fare. I'd take coffee from the driver's thermos, his cigarettes, and we'd discuss hockey from the night before. In return I'd give him a paper when he let me off. They didn't call me Curette for nothing.

I'm Dreaming of Rocket Richard

The hockey, the hockey! I like all the major sports, and the setting of each one has its special beauty—even old De Lorimier Downs had something of Yankee Stadium about it, and old Rocky Nelson banging out home runs from his rocking chair stance made me think of Babe Ruth, and who could compare to Jackie Robinson and Roberto Clemente when they were playing for us? Sundays in August with the Red Wings in town, you could always get in free after a couple of innings and see two great games. But the ice of big-time hockey, the old Forum, that went beyond landscape! Something about the ghostly white of the ice under those powerful lights, something about the hiss of the skates if you were standing close enough, the solid *pock-pock* of the rubber on a stick, and the low menacing whiz of a Rocket slap shot hugging the ice—there was nothing in any other sport to compare with the *spell* of hockey. Inside the Forum in the early fifties, those games against Boston (with the Rocket flying and a hated Boston goalie named Jack Gelineau in the nets) were evangelical, for truly we were *dans le cenacle* where everyone breathed as one.

The Bruins sweatshirt came from a cousin of mine in Manchester, New Hampshire, who brought it as a joke or maybe a present on one of his trips up to see us. I started wearing it in all my backyard practices and whenever I got standing room tickets at the Forum. Crazy, I think now; what was going on in me? Crying on all those few nights each winter when the Canadiens lost, quite literally throwing whatever I was holding high in the air whenever the Rocket scored—yet always wearing that hornet-colored jersey? Anyone could see I was a good local kid; maybe I wanted someone to think I'd come all the way from Boston just to see the game, maybe I liked the good-natured kidding from my fellow standees ("'ey, you, Boston," they'd shout, "oo's winning, eh?" and I'd snarl back after a period or two of silence, *"mange la baton, sac de marde..."*). I even used to wear that jersey when I delivered papers and I remember the pain of watching it slowly unravel in the cuffs and shoulders, hoping the cousin would come again. They were Schmitzes, my mother's sister had met him just after the War. *Tante* Lise and Uncle Howie.

I started to pick up English by reading a *Gazette* on my paper route, and I remember vividly one spring morning — with the sun coming up — studying a name that I took to be typically English. It began *Sch*, an odd combination, like my uncle's; then I suddenly thought of my mother's name — not mine — Deschenes, and I wondered: could it be? Hidden in the middle of my mother's name were those same English letters, and I began to think that we (tempting horror) were English too, that I had a right, a *sch*, to that Bruins jersey, to the world in the *Gazette* and on the other side of Atwater from the Forum. How I fantasied!

Every now and then the Schmitzes would drive up in a new car (I think now they came up whenever they bought a new car; I don't remember ever sitting in one of their cars without noticing a shred of plastic around the window-cranks and a smell of newness), and I would marvel at my cousins who were younger than me and taller ("they don't smoke," my mother would point out), and who whined a lot because they always wanted things (I never understood what) they couldn't get with us. My mother could carry on with them in English. I wanted to like them — an only child feels that way about his relatives, not having seen his genetic speculations exhausted, and tends to see himself refracted even into second and third cousins several times removed. Now I saw a devious link with that American world in the strange clot of letters common to my name and theirs, and that pleased me.

We even enjoyed a bout of prosperity at about that time. I was thirteen or so, and we had moved from Hutchison (where a Greek janitor was finally hired) to a place off St-Denis where my father took charge of a sixteen-apartment building; they paid him well and gave us a three-room place out of the basement damps. That was *bonheur* in my father's mind—moving up to the ground floor where the front door buzzer kept waking you up. It was reasonably new; he didn't start to have trouble with bugs and paint for almost a year. He even saved a little money.

At just about the same time, in the more spacious way of the Schmitzes, they packed up everything in Manchester (where Uncle Howie owned three dry-cleaning shops) and moved to North Hollywood, Florida. That's a fair proportion: Hutchison is to St-Denis what Manchester is to Florida. He started with one dry-cleaning shop and had three others within a year. If he'd really been one of us, we'd have been suspicious of his tactics and motives, we would have called him lucky and undeserving. But he was American, he had his *sch*, so whatever he did seemed blessed by a different branch of fate, and we wondered only how we could share.

It was the winter of 1952. It was a cold sunny time on St-Denis. I still delivered my papers (practically in the neighborhood), my father wasn't drinking that much, and my mother was staying out of church except on Sunday—it was a bad sign when she started going on weekdays—and we had just bought a car. It was a used Plymouth, the first car we'd ever owned. The idea was that we should visit the Schmitzes this time in their Florida home for Christmas. It was even their idea, arranged through the sisters. My father packed his tools in the rear ("You never know, Mance; I'd like to show him what I can do..."). He moved his brother Real and family into our place—Real was handy enough, more affable, but an even bigger drinker. We left Montreal on December 18 and took a cheap and slow drive down, the pace imposed by my father, who underestimated the strain of driving, and by my mother, who'd read of speedtraps and tourists languishing twenty years in Southern dungeons for running a stop sign. The drive was cheap because we were dependent on my mother for expense money as soon as we entered the States, since she was the one who could go into the motel office and find out the prices. It would be three or four in the afternoon and my father would be a nervous wreck; just as we were unloading the trunk and my father was checking the level of whisky in the glove compartment bottle, she'd come out announcing it was highway robbery, we couldn't stay here. My father would groan, curse, and slam the trunk. Things would be dark by the time we found a vacancy in one of those rows of one-room cabins, arranged like stepping stones or in a semi-circle (the kind you still see nowadays out on the Gaspesie with boards on the windows and a faded billboard out front advertising "investment property"). My mother put a limit of three dollars a night on accommodations; we shopped in supermarkets for cold meat, bread, mustard, and Pepsis. My father rejoiced in the cheaper gas; my mother reminded him it was a smaller gallon.

Quietly, I calculated the difference. Remember, no drinking after Savannah, my mother said. It was clear: he expected to become the manager of a Schmitz Dry Kleenery.

The Schmitzes had rented a spacious cottage about a mile from the beach in North Hollywood. The outside stucco was green, the roof tiles orange, and the flowers violently pink and purple. The shrubs looked decorated with little red Christmas bulbs; I picked one — gift of my cousin — bit, and screamed in surprise. Red chilies. The front windows were sprayed with Santa's sleigh and a snowy "Merry Christmas." Only in English, no "Joyeux Noel" like our greeting back home. That was what I'd noticed most all the way down, the incompleteness of the signs, the satisfaction that their version said it all. I'd kept looking on the other side of things — my side — and I'd kept twirling the radio dial, for an equivalence that never came.

It was Christmas week and the Schmitzes were wearing Bermuda shorts and T-shirts with sailfish on the front. *Tante* Lise wore coral earrings and a red halter, and all her pale flesh had freckled. The night we arrived, my father got up on a stepladder, anxious to impress, and strung colored lights along the gutter while my uncle shouted directions and watered the lawn. Christmas — and drinking Kool-Aid in the yard! We picked chili peppers and sold them to every West Indian cook who answered the back doorbell. At night I licked my fingers and hummed with the air-conditioning. My tongue burned for hours. That was the extraordinary part for me: that things as hot as chilies could grow in your yard, that I could bake in December heat, and that other natural laws remained the same. My father was still shorter than my mother, and his face turned red and blotchy here too (just as it did in August back home) instead of an even schmitzean brown, and when he took off his shirt, only a tattoo, scars, and angry red welts were revealed. Small and sickly he seemed; worse, mutilated. My cousins rode their chrome-plated bicycles to the beach, but I'd never owned a two-wheeler and this didn't seem the time to reveal another weakness. Give me ice, I thought, my stick and a puck and an open net. Some men were never meant for vacations in shirt-less countries: small hairy men with dirty winter boils and red swellings that never became anything lanceable, and tattoos of celebrities in their brief season of fame, now forgotten. My father's tattoo was as long as my twelve-year-old hand, done in a waterfront parlor in Montreal the day he'd thought of enlisting. My mother had been horrified, more at the tattoo than the thought of his shipping out. The tattoo pictured a front-faced Rocket, staring at an imaginary goalie and slapping a rising shot through a cloud of ice chips. Even though I loved the Canadiens and the Rocket mightily, I would have preferred my father to walk shirtless down the middle of the street with a naked woman on his back than for him to strip for the Schmitzes and my enormous cousins, who pointed and laughed, while I could almost understand what they were laughing about. They thought his tattoo was a kind of tribal marking, like kinky hair, thin mustaches, and slanty eyes—that if I took off my shirt I'd have one too, only smaller. *Lacroix*, I said to myself: how could he and I have the same name? It was foreign. I was a Deschenes, a Schmitz in the making.

On Christmas Eve we trimmed a silvered little tree

and my uncle played Bing Crosby records on the console hi-fi-shortwave-bookcase (the biggest thing going in Manchester, New Hampshire, before the days of television). It would have been longer than our living room in Montreal; even here it filled one wall. They tried to teach me to imitate Crosby's "White Christmas," but my English was hopeless. My mother and aunt sang in harmony; my father kept spilling his iced tea while trying to clap. It was painful. I waited impatiently to get to bed in order to cut the night as short as possible.

The murkiness of those memories! How intense, how foreign; it all happened like a dream in which everything follows logically from some incredible premise—that we should go to Florida, that it should be so hot in December, that my father should be on his best behavior for nearly a month...that we could hope that a little initiative and optimism would carry us anywhere but deeper into debt and darkest despair...

I see myself as in a dream, walking the beach alone, watching the coarse brown sand fall over my soft white feet. I hear my mother and *Tante* Lise whispering together, yet they're five hundred feet ahead ("Yes," my mother is saying, "what life is there for him back there? You can see how this would suit him. To a T! To a T!" I'm wondering is it me, or my father, who has no future back there, and *Tante* Lise begins, "Of course, I'm only a wife. I don't know what his thinking is—"), but worse is the silent image of my father in his winter trousers rolled up to his skinny knees and gathered in folds by a borrowed belt (at home he'd always worn braces), shirtless, shrunken, almost running to keep up with my uncle who walks closer to the water, in Bermuda shorts. I can tell from the beaten smile on my father's lips and from the way Uncle Howie is talking (while looking over my father's head at the ships on the horizon), that what the women have arranged ("It would be good to have you so close, Mance...I get these moods sometimes, you know? And five shops are too much for Howie...") the men have made impossible. I know that when my father was smiling and his head was bobbing in agreement and he was running to keep up with someone, he was being told off, turned down, laughed at. And the next stage was for him to go off alone, then come back to us with a story that embarrassed us all by its transparency, and that would be the last of him, sober, for three, four, or five days...I can see all this and hear it, though I am utterly alone near the crashing surf and it seems to be night and a forgotten short-wave receiver still blasts forth on a beach blanket somewhere; I go to it hoping to catch something I can understand, a hockey game, the scores, but all I get wrenching the dial until it snaps is Bing Crosby dreaming of a white Christmas and Cuban music and indecipherable commentary from Havana, the dog races from Miami, *jai alai*.

That drive back to Montreal lasted almost a month. Our money ran out in Georgia and we had to wait two weeks in a shack in the Negro part of Savannah, where a family like ours—with a mother who liked to talk, and a father who drank and showed up only to collect our rent, and a kid my age who spent his time caddying and getting up before the sun to hunt golf balls—found space for us in a large room behind the kitchen, recently vacated by a dead grandparent. There were irregularities, the used-car dealer kept saying, various legal expenses involved with international commerce between Canadian

I'm Dreaming of Rocket Richard

Plymouths and innocent Georgia dealers, and we knew not to act too anxious (or even give our address) for fear of losing whatever bit of money we stood to gain. Finally he gave us $75, and that was when my father took his tools out of the back and sold them at a gas station for $50. We went down to the bus station, bought three tickets to Montreal, and my father swept the change into my mother's pocketbook. We were dressed for the January weather we'd be having when we got off, and the boy from the house we'd been staying in, shaking his head as watched us board, muttered, "Man, you sure is crazy." It became a phrase of my mother's for all the next hard years. "Man, you sure is crazy." I mastered it and wore it like a Bruins sweater, till it too wore out. I remember those nights on the bus, my mother counting the bills and coins in her purse, like beads on a rosary, the numbers a silent prayer.

Back on St-Denis we found Real and family very happily installed. The same egregious streak that sputtered in my father flowed broadly in his brother. He'd all but brought fresh fruit baskets to the sixteen residents, carried newspapers to their doors, repaired buzzers that had never worked, shoveled insanely wide swaths down the front steps, replaced lights in the basement lockers, oiled, painted, polished... even laid off the booze for the whole month we were gone (which to my father was the unforgivable treachery); in short, while we'd sunk all our savings and hocked all our valuables to launch ourselves in the dry-cleaning business, Real had simply moved his family three blocks into lifelong comfort and security. My father took it all very quietly; we thought he'd blow sky-high. But he was finished. He'd put up the best, and the longest, show of his life and he'd seen himself squashed like a worm underfoot. Maybe he'd had one of those hellish moments when he'd seen himself in his brother-in-law's sunglasses, running at his side, knowing that those sunglasses were turned to the horizon and not to him.

Truth

W. P. Kinsella

No matter what they say it wasn't us that started the riot at St. Edouard Hockey Arena. The story made quite a few newspapers and even got on the Edmonton television, the camera showing how chairs been ripped out of the stands and thrown onto the ice. There was also a worried-looking RCMP saying something about public safety, and how they had to take some of the 25 arrested people all the way to St. Paul to store them in jail. Then the station manager read an editorial about violence in amateur hockey. None of them come right out and say us Indians was to blame for the riot; they just present what they think are the facts and leave people to make their own minds up. How many do you think decide the white men was at fault?

There was also a rumor that the town of St. Edouard was going to sue the town of Hobbema for the damages to the arena. But nothing ever come of that.

Another story have that the trouble come about because my friend Frank Fencepost own a dog named Guy Lafleur. Not true either. Frank do own a dog named Guy Lafleur, a yellow and white mostly-collie with a question mark for a tail. And Guy Lafleur the dog *was* sitting on a seat right behind our team players' box. That dog he bark whenever our team, the Hobbema Wagon-burners, get the puck. And every time he bark Frank would shout the same thing, "Shut up, Guy Lafleur you son of a bitch." A lot of heads would turn every time he said it, because, as you maybe guessed, St. Edouard was a French Canadian town. But it was something else that started the riot.

We never would of been there anyway if Frank hadn't learned to read and write. Someday, I'm going to write a story about the time Frank go to an adult literacy class. Now, just to show off, he read everything in the *Wetaskiwin Times* every week, even the ads. One day he seen a notice about a small town hockey tournament that offer a $1000 first prize.

"I think we should enter a team, Silas," he say to me.

"What do we know about hockey?" I say back. Neither me nor Frank skate. I played a little shinny when I was a kid, but I don't much like ice and snow up my nose, or for that matter, hockey sticks.

"Let's go see Jasper Deer," say Frank, "there's a $200 entry fee to be raised."

Jasper is employed by Sports Canada. All the strings on Sports Canada are pulled from Ottawa. Jasper he have an office with a grey desk big as a whale, in the Consolidated School building. About fifteen years ago Jasper was a good hockey player. I'm not sure what Sports Canada is, but I know they figure if they give all us Indians enough hockey sticks, basketballs and volley-balls, we forget our land claims, quit drinking too much, get good jobs so we can have the weekends off to play games.

Jasper is glad to have anybody come to see him. He

was Chief Tom's friend, was how he come to get this cushy job, though he would rather be trapping, or cutting brush than sit in an office. He is already bleary-eyed at ten o'clock in the morning.

"You want to enter a team in a tournament, eh?" he say to us, pushing his desk drawer shut with his knee, the bottles rattling.

Hobbema has a team in the Western Canada Junior Hockey League, so once guys turn 21 and don't get signed by any NHL team, they got no place to play.

"It'll be easy to get some good players together," Frank say, "and playing hockey keep us young people sober, honest and religious."

By the time we leave Jasper is anxious to put his head down have a little sleep on his desk, but he agree to pay for uniforms, loan us equipment, and rent us a school bus to travel in. I write down all those promises and get him to sign them.

Trouble is, even though a thousand dollars sound like a lot of money to me and Frank, the guys we approach to play for us point out it don't even come to $100 each for a decent sized team. So the players we end up with is the guys who sit in the Alice Hotel bar bragging how they turned down NHL contracts ten years ago, plus a few of our friends who can stand up on skates, and a goalie who just got new glasses last week.

The uniforms are white as bathroom tile, with a bright red burning wagon on the front, with HOBBEMA in red letters on the back. Some people complain the team name is bad for our Indian image, but they just ain't got no sense of humour.

Frank is team manager. I am his assistant. Mad Etta, our 400 lb. medicine lady is doctor and trainer, and

Truth

Guy Lafleur is our mascot.

St. Edouard is way up in north-east Alberta, a place most of us never been before. Gorman Carry-the-kettle drive the bus for us. We have a pretty rowdy trip once we get Etta all attended to. She squeeze sideways down the aisle and sit on the whole back seat.

"I'm surprised the bus didn't tip up with its front wheels about three feet off the ground," say Gorman.

"Don't worry, you'll balance things out," we tell Gorman. He is about 280 lbs. himself, wear a red cap with a yellow unicorn horn growing out of the crown.

We stop for lunch in a town called Elk Point, actually we stop at the bar, and since most of the team is serious drinkers, it is 3:00 p.m. before we get on the road again. I have to drive because Gorman is a little worse for wear. When we get to St. Edouard, a town that have only about ten houses and a little frame hotel gathered around a wine-coloured elevator as if they was bowing down to it, we find we already an hour late for our first game. They was just about to forfeit us.

The game played in a hoop-roofed building what is a combination curling rink and hockey arena. It sit like a huge haystack out in a field half a mile from town. Being February it is already dark. All I can see in any direction is snow drifts, a little stubble, and lines of scratchy-looking trees wherever there's a road allowance. The countryside is not too different from Hobbema.

Soon as our team start to warm up, everybody, except maybe Frank, can see we is outclassed. We playing the St. Edouard Bashers. Their players all look as if they drove down on their combines. And they each look like they could lift a combine out of a ditch if it was to get stuck. Most of our players are hung over. And though most of them used to be hockey players, it easy to tell they ain't been on skates for years.

The St. Edouard Bashers is young, fast and tough. Someone mention that they ain't lost a tournament game in two years. There must be 4,000 people in the arena, and they all go "Booooo," when our team show itself.

"I wonder where they all come from," says Frank. "There can't be more than fifty people in the town; sure must be some big families on these here farms."

They sing the national anthem in French, and after they done with that they sing the French national anthem. Then about a half a dozen priests, and what must be a bishop, he got a white robe and an embroidered quilt over his shoulder, come to centre ice where they bless a box of pucks. The priests shake holy water in each goal crease. The players all cross themselves.

"We should of brought a thunder dancer with us," says Frank. "Make a note of that, Silas. We do it next time."

I don't bother to write it down. I'm already guessing there won't be a next time.

Right after the puck is dropped St. Edouard take hold of it, carry it right in on our goal. They shoot. Our goalie don't have any idea where the puck is; by pure luck it hit him on the chest and fall to the ice. The goalie, Ferd Tailfeathers, lose his balance fall forward on the puck.

About that time a half-ton St. Edouard defenceman land with a knee on Ferd's head, smash his mask, his face and his glasses about an inch deep into the ice.

Guy Lafleur stand up on his seat and bark like a fire alarm.

"Shut up Guy Lafleur you son of a bitch," says Frank. Then looking out at the rink where Ferd lay still as if he been dead for a week or so, he say, ''That fat sucker probably broke his knee on Ferd's head.''

But the St. Edouard defenceman already skating around like he scored a goal, his stick raised up in the air, his skates making slashing sounds.

It is Ferd Tailfeathers get carried from the ice.

''Who's buying the next round?'' he ask the referee, as we haul him over the boards.

''They take their hockey pretty seriously up here, eh?'' says Frank to a long-faced man sit next to Guy Lafleur. That man wear a Montreal Canadiens toque and sweater, and he have only four teeth in front, two top, two bottom, all stained yellow, and none quite matching. I notice now that almost everybody in the arena, from old people, like the guy next to Guy Lafleur, to tiny babies in arms, wear Montreal Canadiens sweaters. Somewhere there must be a store sell nothing but Montreal uniforms.

''You think this is serious,'' the old man say, ''you ought to see a wedding in St. Edouard. The aisle of the Catholic Church is covered in artificial ice, at least in the summer, in winter it freeze up of its own accord. The priest wear goal pads and the groom is the defenceman,'' he go on in a heavy French accent.

''I didn't see no church,'' says Frank, ''only big building I seen was the elevator.''

''You seen the church,'' say the old man, ''elevator got torn down years ago. You guys should stick around there supposed to be a wedding tomorrow. The bride and bridesmaids stickhandle down the aisle, careful not to be off-side at the blue-line; they get three shots on goal to score on the priest. If they don't the wedding get put off for a week.''

Another old man in a felt hat and cigarette-yellowed mustache speak up, "We had one priest was such a good goaltender there were no weddings in St. Edouard for over two years. Some of the waiting couples had two, three kids already—so the bishop come down from Edmonton and perform a group ceremony."

Knocking Ferd out of the game was a real unlucky thing for them to do. I'm sure they would of scored ten goals each period if they'd just been patient. In the dressing room we strip off Ferd's pads, look for somebody to take his place.

Frank tell first one and then another player to put on the equipment.

"Put them on yourself," they say to Frank, only not in such polite language.

"You're gonna have to go in goal," Frank say to me.

"Not me," I say. "I got some regard for my life."

"Put your goddamned dog in the goal," say the caretaker of the dressing room. We can hear the fans getting restless. They are chanting something sound like "Alley, alley, les Bashers," and stomping their feet until the whole building shake.

"You guys should go home now," the old caretaker say. "They just looking for a bad team to beat up on. The way you guys skate it will be like tossing raw meat to hungry dogs."

"I think he's right," I say. "Let's sneak out. We can fend off the fans with hockey sticks if we have to."

We are just about to do that when Frank get his idea.

"It's why I'm manager and you're not," Frank say modestly to me that night when we're driving back toward Hobbema.

We hold up the game for another fifteen minutes

while we try to find skates big enough to fit Mad Etta.

Etta been sitting in the corner of the dressing room having a beer. Her and Frank do some fast bargaining. End up Frank have to promise her $900 of the thousand dollar prize money before she'll agree to play. Frank he plunk a mask on Etta's face right then and there.

"Not bad," say Etta, stare into a mirror. The mask is mean looking, with a red diamond drawed around each eye and red shark teeth where the mouth should be.

When we ask the Bashers to loan us a pair of BIG skates, they tell us to get lost.

"We've got to default the game then," we tell them, "guess you'll have to refund all those fans their money."

That make them nicer to know.

"Yeah, we didn't bring them all the way up here not to get in a few good licks."

"Besides, the fans are in a mean mood. They want to see some blood. We're going to get even for what happened to Custer," say their biggest defenceman, who is about the size of a jeep and almost as smart. He give us his extra skates for Etta, then say, "We'll score four or five goals, then we'll trash you guys for a full hour. Get ready to bleed a lot."

We sat Etta on a bench with her back to the wall. Me and Frank get one on each side of her and we push like we was trying to put a skate on a ten pound sack of sugar.

"I'm too old for this," puffs Etta. "What is it I'm supposed to do again anyway?"

"Just think how you'll spend the $900," says Frank, tie her laces in a big knot, "and everything else will take care of itself."

Three of us have to walk beside, behind, and in front,

in order to steer Etta from the bench to the goal. The fans are all going "Oooh," and "Ahhhh."

I get to walk behind.

"If she falls back I'm a goner," I say.

"So keep her on her feet," huffs Frank. "I figure you value your life more than most, that's why I put you back there."

"That's one big mother of a goaltender," say one of the Bashers.

"More than you know," says Etta, but in Cree.

"Alley, alley, les Bashers," go the audience.

Once we get Etta to the net she grab onto the iron rail and stomp the ice, send chips flying in all directions, kick and kick until she get right down to the floorboards. Once she got footing she stand with an arm on each goal post, glare fierce from behind that mean mask what painted like a punk rock album cover.

Soon as the game start again the Bashers get the puck, pass it about three ways from Sunday, while our players busy falling down, skate right in on Mad Etta and shoot... and shoot...and shoot. Don't matter where they poke the puck, or how often, there is always some part of Mad Etta blocking the goal.

After maybe ten shots, a little player zoom in like a mosquito, fire point blank; the puck hit Etta's shoulder and go up in the crowd.

"That hurt," shout Etta, slap with her goal stick, knock that little player head over heels as he buzz by the net. She get a penalty for that. Goalies can't serve penalties, but someone else have to. The Bashers take about twenty more shots in the next two minutes.

"You're doin' great," Frank yell from the bench.

"How come our team never shoot the biscuit at their

goal?'' Etta calls back.

"We're workin' on it," says Frank, "trust your manager."

Things don't improve though, so Etta just turn her back on the game, lean on the net and let the Bashers shoot at her backside. There is more Etta than there is goal; even some shots that miss the goal hit Etta. I think it is a law of physics that you can't add to something that is already full.

There is no score at the end of the first period. Trouble is Etta assume the game is only one period long.

"I got to stay out there how long?" she yell at Frank. "I already earn more than $900. That little black biscuit hurt like hell," she go on. "And how come none of you guys know how to play this game but me?"

The players is all glassy-eyed, gasp for air, nurse their bruises, cuts, and hangovers.

As we guide Etta out for the second period, Guy Lafleur go to barking like a fire siren again. He always hated Mad Etta ever since one day he nipped at her heels while she huffing up the hill from Hobbema General Store, and Etta punted him about forty yards deep into the mud and bullrushes of the slough at the foot of the hill.

When she hear the dog Etta spin around knock a couple of us to the ice, make Frank afraid for his life, and go "Bow-wow-wow," at Guy Lafleur, sound so much like a real dog that he jump off his seat and don't show his nose again until after the riot.

The way we dressed Etta for the game was to put the shoulder pads on, then her five-flour-sack dress, then tape one sweater to her chest and another to her back.

Soon as she get to the goal she have to guard for the second period, she don't even stomp the ice, just fumble in the pocket of her dress, take out a baggie with some greenish-looking sandy stuff in it, sprinkle that green stuff all across the goal line. Frank rush off the bench, fall twice on the way 'cause he wearing slippery-soled cowboy boots.

"What are you doin'?" he yell at Etta, who is waddling real slow, force each skate about an inch into the ice every step, and is heading for the face-off circle to the left of her goal.

"If I stay in front of that little closet I'm gonna be so bruised I'll look polka-dotted. I've had enough of this foolishness."

"But the goal," cries Frank.

"Hey, you manage the team. I'll do what I do best," and Etta give Frank a shove propel him on his belly all the way to the players' gate by our bench.

As the referee call the players to centre ice, Etta sit down cross-legged in that face-off circle, light up a cigarette, blow smoke at the fans who stomping their feet.

The St. Edouard team steal the puck on the face-off, sweep right over the defence and fire at the empty goal. But the puck just zap off to the corner as if there was a real good goalie there. After about ten shots like that the Bashers get pretty mad and the fans even more so. It is like Etta bricked up the front of the goal with invisible bricks.

The St. Edouard Bashers gather around the referee and scream at him in both of Canada's official languages, and all of Canada's swear words.

The referee skate to the net, test with his hand, but there is nothing to block it. He stick one skate into the net. He throw the puck into the net. Then he borrow a stick from one of the Bashers and shoot the puck in, several times.

"Stop your bitchin' and play hockey," he say to the St. Edouard players.

"I bet I could sell that stuff to Peter Pocklington and the Edmonton Oilers for a million dollars an ounce," Frank hiss into my ear. "You're her assistant, Silas. What do you think the chances are of getting hold of a bag of that stuff?"

"It would only work when Etta stare at it the right way," I say.

"Hey, Edmonton Oilers could afford to buy Etta too. She's more valuable than Wayne Gretzky. And we'd be her agents..."

"Forget it," I say. "You can't buy medicine."

Les Bashers keep shooting at our goal all through the second period and into the third, with no better luck.

It a fact of hockey that no matter how bad a team you got you going to score a goal sooner or later. At about fifteen minutes into the third period, Rufus Firstrider, who skate mainly on his ankles, carry the puck over the St. Edouard blue-line, try to pass to Gorman Carry-the-kettle, who been wheezing down the right wing.

The goalie see the pass coming up and move across the goal mouth to cover it, and there's a Mack truck of a defenceman ready to cream Gorman if the puck even gets close to him. But Rufus miss the pass entirely, fall down and accidentally hit the puck toward the net and score. That is all the goals there is: Hobbema Wagon-burners 1, St. Edouard Bashers 0.

It was them and their fans who started the riot. We all headed for the dressing room, except for Frank, who jump into the stands looking for Guy Lafleur, and suffer a certain amount of damage as a result.

After the RCMP cooled everyone off and escorted us to our bus, Frank show up with a black eye and blood on his shirt, while Guy Lafleur have a notch out of one ear but a big mouthful of Basher hockey sweater to make up for it.

They got carpenters screwing the seats back in place and men busy resurfacing the ice. The Bashers decide to start the tournament over the next day, playing against teams they can beat. They agree to pay us $2500 to go home and never enter their tournament again.

And that's the truth.

excerpts from the novel

The Last Season

Roy MacGregor

Even in the forty below weather of Pomerania, I always had to be the first one to the rink. And I kept it up in Vernon. Coach Bowles — to me he deserved being nick-named Sugar — he got so tired of seeing me standing around the side entrance when he arrived to set up that he slipped me my own key so I could come and go as I pleased. The day Poppa came to watch I left Riley's about noon, even though we weren't playing until seven. I'd told Poppa I'd see him after the game, that I needed the time before to unwind and get ready, and he seemed to understand. And I took the same crazy route to the arena I've followed since we won our opening game of the season against Orillia, shortcutting across the curling rink parking lot, hopping the chainlink fence around the war memorial — wreaths just now starting to wilt after a week in the cold and rain — then over across the field back of the Legion Hall, through the lane between the houses, down the slope by the river and up again to the rink. Someone down toward the docks was burning wet leaves and the smoke was rolling along the river, sharp and delicious. For some reason it made my stomach growl.

Sugar was already there, sharpening in the skate room. I could hear the stone and smell the dry grind, and though I loved to watch him work, I passed and went directly to the dressing room. The lights were on over the ice and I could hear Bull Tate tripping the tank levers as he began his first flood. Usually I loved to watch that too, the water spreading wet and glimmering behind him, the steam rising from the spread rag and the taps, but this I passed on too.

It was not a matter of trying to be first, I *had* to be first. And far worse in Vernon than back home. At our very first skate in Vernon we all dressed together, and Tom Powers, who had already been made team captain by Sugar, stopped right in front of me, pointed straight at my drawers and shouted: "Christ, if you're going out there in *that*, forget the equipment—no one's going to come near *you!*"

No one had ever said anything like that in Pomerania. I'd been expecting to be called "Polack," had even specially remembered the great line Jaja's hero, Wally Stanowski, had when he played for the Leafs, so I could use it, too: "I train on Polish sausage, the breakfast of champions." But they weren't laughing at my heritage— it was my underwear! I couldn't just jump up and paste Powers, so I leaned over and pretended I'd lost something in my duffle bag, scrounging around till I felt some of the burn leave my face. So I didn't have nice, new, bright white insulated underwear—big goddamned deal! I was angry and I couldn't shake it. I carefully checked out Powers during the warm-up, the way he'd skate in over the blueline and then let the puck drop back from the blade to his skate, kick off over onto the other skate and then kick the puck back up to the blade, the illusion being that he had lost it. I skated around memorizing his move and gathering myself, enjoying the season's first waft of arena air on my face, giving my little extra kick as I rounded the net so I came out of the turn with pants hissing and the ice behind me making a sound like I'd just been withdrawn from a scabbard. And then, when scrimmage began, I simply waited for Powers to try that little suck move on my side, aiming for his head rather than the puck, and I put him up so high he did a complete somersault in the air and came down so hard on his brand-new Tackaberry skates that the left blade bent and Sugar, smiling rather than angry, had to go off with him into the skate room and pound it straight with a mallet.

After that I never had a moment's trouble from Tom Powers. After that, though, I never failed to be the first one dressed either. Not that I had to any more. At the very next practice I arrived to find a brand-new cellophane-wrapped set of Stanfield longjohns resting on my seat. The only other person in the rink was Sugar Bowles, sharpening, but he never said a word about the underwear, and I never mentioned it either. But it had to be him.

I could hear Sugar coming along dragging a new bundle of sticks and I got up and caught the door for him. I'd been imagining I was Tim Horton sitting there yakking up a storm with Stanley and Bower before we took to the ice. But it was hard to think of Sugar as Punch Imlach. Sugar had more hair sticking out one ear than Punch had on his entire head, I swear, about an inch above his eyebrows, hair like Poppa's, black and thick and dry-looking like he'd just washed it, though I doubt Poppa and he had had a half-dozen washes between

them over their lifetimes. Punch looked like a bank
teller; Sugar like the holdup man. Sugar had this huge
scar on his face running from the corner of his right eye
down across the cheek and sliding off his jawbone. The
right eye seemed to look at you but was cloudy, the left
one nearly as black as his hair. Tom Powers put it about
that Sugar had lost his eye in a hockey fight, kicked by a
skate when he was down, but Sugar hadn't verified this
story. Powers also said Sugar was once a prospect himself, but when Danny pressed him on the way back from
a North Bay game, Sugar denied he'd even played the
game and told us all to shut up and try and get some sleep.

"Batterinski."

"Yah," I said, looking up. The cloudy eye seemed to
have me fixed. Sugar was still taping, but not thinking
about it.

"What do you think of Fontinato?"

"He's okay."

"You ever hear of Sprague Cleghorn?"

It sounded like a disease to me. "No. Why?"

"Cleghorn'd eat Fontinato for breakfast."

"He played?"

Sugar nodded and spit. "Five times they arrested him
for hurting players. Five times."

I shook my head. I didn't know what else to do.

"Newsy Lalonde," he said, letting it hang.

I looked at Sugar, unsure.

"Sent more'n fifty guys off the ice on stretchers."

Sugar finished taping the first stick, bit off the tape
and picked up another, his head turning so the left eye
could catch me directly. "Who do you like in the NHL,
Batterinski?"

"Horton," I said.

"You take a look at Fontinato," he said. "And maybe even this new guy Eddie Shack. You understand?"

I didn't. Sometimes no one could figure out Sugar or his crazy riddles. Talking with him was always like breaking an oar halfway across the lake. But I did like some of his sayings. He really pissed Powers off one practice when he said: "You don't have enough talent to win on talent alone," and when Powers came up after practice and asked Sugar if it was meant for him in particular, Sugar just said: "If you have to ask, you must have a question." Beee-utiful.

One of the sayings was meant for me in particular, and I knew that for certain because he gave it only to me, all folded over and placed in an envelope with my number on it. "The unforgiveable crime is soft hitting," it read. "Do not hit at all if it can be avoided, but *never* hit softly." Underneath was this name, Teddy Roosevelt, which sounded vaguely familiar to me, but I didn't have the nerve to ask.

The other guys straggled in, Terry LeMay, the goaltender, Powers and his sidekick, Bucky Cryderman, then Danny.

"Hey, Bats," Cryderman said, laughing, "you want I should call your old man in here to tighten your skates?"

"Screw off," I said, closing the issue. Danny was a loudmouth.

Ten minutes before warm-up Sugar was ready for his talk and slammed a stick into the equipment box for our attention. "All right, then," he began. "We should be ready. You all remember Parry Sound from the exhibitions, so you forwards know if you get a chance you shoot. Goalie's weak on long ones to the stick side; but don't try to suck him because he's good in tight and flops well. So keep it simple and make your first shots count. I'll be juggling lines to keep Powers' line away from their checkers, so if I touch your shoulder that means *you* are on, not necessarily your line, so just keep track of yourselves, okay?

"These guys like to carry the puck and they like to make the pretty play, but they don't seem as keen when the going gets rough. Batterinski?"

"Yah?"

"You set the pace, you understand?"

"Uh huh."

"Sprague Cleghorn, remember. Now the rest of you are going to be seeing a very small player out there and though he's a defenseman they'll probably play him up front 'cause he's only peewee age."

"A *peewee?*" Powers said, falling into giggles.

"Laugh once and get it out of your system," Sugar said, eyeing Powers with the black left ball. "His name is Orr and I've seen him and he's already a better player at twelve than any of you are at fifteen. Understand that? Don't let his size fool you and watch him. Defense, I want you to stick to him like snot to an oven door, understand?"

All around the room we grunted that we did.

"Cryderman," Sugar called, kicking at Bucky's skates stuck out in front of him like he was about to take a nap. "What's the toughest fish in the ocean?"

"Huh?"

"Come on. You guys think you're all big fish in a little pond. What is it?"

"I dunno," Bucky said. "A shark, I guess."

"That's very good, Cryderman. Now there's something special about sharks that I want you all to consider.

There's one thing that makes sharks different from all other fish...anyone care to guess what it is?''

"The fin," said Powers.

"Nah."

"The teeth," Danny shouted, showing his.

"No."

Sugar waited, scanning the room, then he smiled. "A barracuda's teeth are just as nasty, maybe worse. What makes a shark truly unusual is what he *doesn't* have. And that's a swim bladder."

Someone laughed. Powers, probably. Or Bucky.

"Go ahead," Sugar said. "Laugh. But let me tell you first what it means. A shark has to keep moving constantly. A shark does not float, like other fish. A shark can't float. He has no swim bladder, see. He can't let up for a minute and that's what makes him top dog. You think about that awhile, okay?"

Sugar walked out the door and closed it silently and no one said a word. No laugh, no burp, no fart. No one would dare destroy Sugar's pregame silences because they worked. We were leading the league.

Danny and I could hardly believe it when we first got here. We were used to Father Schula's prayers that no one got hurt, but so far this year we had had Sugar read aloud from *Tom Sawyer*, quote John Kennedy and Winston Churchill and some Chinese guy I'd never heard of and give lectures on everything from why water droplets scoot on a hot pan ("Keep the puck away from the traffic") to how vultures in Egypt break open ostrich eggs by dropping small stones on them ("You can't do it all yourself").

By tradition, I went onto the ice first. Number seven was the first sound in the arena always, first scrape on the ice, first slice of the corner, first stick on a puck, first crash of puck against the boards. In a way I created the game, just as I so often finished the game. With my hands.

I didn't see Poppa until "God Save the Queen." The record always skipped slightly and Al Willoughby, the arena manager, had piled so many pennies on the arm the record had slowed to a near growl. But no one sang along anyway, so it didn't matter. I quickly scanned the seats, skinny Wilemena Bowles, Sugar's wife, in her usual seat, clutching the gong of her cow bell so it wouldn't sound, and behind her a plastic golf hat held over a heart. *Poppa.* And he was singing along, or trying to. The only one in the arena fool enough to even try.

Powers won the first face-off and got it straight back to me. I circled slowly, shifted, then doubled back and cut across ice when the winger charged me. At their blueline I hit Powers with a perfect pass and he stopped, a give-and-go play. I followed through, slipping up the far wing and into the clear, and Powers put on the shift I figured he would, a shoulder dip, but when he tried to thread the pass through the defenseman's skates the puck was suddenly stopped and Powers was standing there looking like a fool.

It was the *kid!* They'd *started* him for Christ's sake, and on defense too. He looked like a mascot out there, but suddenly the puck was sailing off his stick high through the air and perfectly into the glove of the winger who'd originally rushed me. I was caught up ice. Parry Sound came in two on one, a deke, a flick pass and a stab and poor old Terry didn't have a prayer. Parry Sound 1, Vernon 0.

Sugar let into us on the bench. What had he said in the dressing room about floating? Why did Powers stop?

What made me so sure I could just walk away from my position? We took it all, heads down, not saying a word. Sugar waited through ten minutes of stopped time before he tapped my shoulder again.

At the start of the second period Danny got the puck back to me at the point and I slammed a low, hard one, and Danny, just like we used to practise back home, skated in front and let his stick dangle so it just ticked the shot straight down onto the ice and suddenly it was 1-1. I slapped Danny's pads and went straight back toward the face-off circle, skating bent over, stick riding both knees, looking up from the ice just once to see how much time was left. I wanted to look at Poppa, but couldn't. But I could imagine what he must have felt hearing his family name crackling out over the P.A. system. Had a Batterinski ever before known such glory?

A minute left in the second period and I was last man back with the blond kid breaking over center, intercepting a bad Bucky pass over to Powers. He looked like an optical illusion coming in on me, too small, too compact, rushing in a near sitting position, but still accelerating too fast for me to simply ride off into the corner. I forced him slightly to my left, then stepped right, where he came, and stopped and thrust out my hip with a little bit of knee I hoped the referee wouldn't catch. I had him clean. But then I didn't. All I felt was the wind from his sweater on my face as he somehow stepped yet another way and was gone. I turned and lunged, sweeping his feet out from under him, but even that was too late. The red light came on even as he flew through the air past Terry, and before he landed I could see him smile and raise his hands in victory, as if he'd somehow had control even as he sailed through the air.

The Last Season

*   *   *   *   *

I knew it wasn't right, but it felt great. I could feel my defenseman on my knuckles and when I touched them they stung with his jaw, just as I knew when he moved this week he would feel me and I would be with him, his better, for weeks to follow. He had my mark on him. I too had swelling and redness, but on the knuckles it shone with pride. Where his swelling made him less, mine made me more. I tried to feel his fear of me, and in trying this, my respect for myself grew. I went to the half-shattered mirror but saw no pimples. Just *Batterinski*, hulking in his pads, solid from blade to brushcut, a man oddly at ease while others about him panic.

Danny always talked about how quickly things take place. "He never even saw the puck," he'd say. But it was never so with me. I was like Willoughby's recording of "The Queen." When attention was on me, time slowed down. In a fight, I relaxed. I could sit in the dressing room in the hours before a game and twitch so bad sometimes a foot would jump right off the floor. But when my defenseman charged I was aware even of my own breathing. He came in flailing, but to me it was like watching someone swim toward me doing the crawl. I could sense his intention and I could feel his blind fury. When I had him about the waist it almost felt as if I was comforting him. That I didn't just keep squeezing until his insides poured out his mouth was an act of charity. I put him down and I ended his humiliation quickly for him, even hiding his face under his sweater when it happened. He should have thanked me.

The horn went to signal the end of the game and

Danny was first in to confirm what I already knew.

"Ugga-bugga!" Danny shouted. His victory call. "Five-four for us, Bats."

I smiled. The rest poured in, shouting, slapping, tossing sticks and gloves. As they passed by they looked with the respect of the leeches but had no fear in touching, which I was glad for. I felt their hands and their sticks praising me.

"You fucking near killed that twit, Bats!"

"I heard the ambulance."

"Best check of the season."

"You turned it around, Bats old fart."

I said nothing in return. I sat there, completely dressed but for my gloves at my feet and felt no different than if I was lying in bed on a Saturday morning. The trainer, Biff, came in with a tray of Pepsi and made sure I got mine first. Then came Sugar, making like he was scribbling the final score down on his clipboard in case he'd somehow forget. He stopped, looked with the good black eye and winked it.

"Teddy Roosevelt," he said.

I said nothing, just smiled and looked down and began undressing slowly. Not undressing, more like dismantling: sweater, elbow pads, shoulder pads, lift off the braces, take off the skates, pants, undo garter, socks, shin pads, jock. Each piece dropped off with reluctance. If only the people who saw me on the street could see me in uniform, the big "A" over the heart, the number "7," the tuck of my sweater into the back of my pants. I knew the uniform spoke better for me than I did myself.

Coming out of the shower Sugar reached out and caught my arm, turning me toward him. He whispered:

"That your dad waiting out there?"

Danny! The son-of-a-bitch.

"Yes."

"You want me to call him in?"

I shook my head. Sugar hung his thick lower lip out and nodded his understanding.

When I was dressed though, Sugar insisted on leaving the dressing room with me. Poppa was outside, leaning on the nearest edge of the snack counter, chewing on a Coffee Crisp like a little kid. There were chocolate and wafer crumbs all over his chin and front.

"Mr. Batterinski?" Sugar said before I could say a word.

Poppa looked like he was about to get into trouble with the law. "Yes?"

"I'm Ted Bowles, sir. Felix's coach. Delighted to meet you."

Poppa took Sugar's hand like it was some sort of trick. I began praying he would say nothing with "th" in it.

"How'd you like the game?" Sugar asked.

"Yes." Poppa said, brushing the crumbs off his chin like he hadn't properly heard the question. "Some of it."

"Your boy here," Sugar said, smiling, "he turned it around for us."

Poppa looked startled. "He did?"

"Sure he did. We were flat as pancakes before he shook things up." Sugar smacked me on the back of the head, reaching up to rub his knuckles into my brushcut. I knew I was turning red. "You got any more like this back home, Mr. Batterinski?" Sugar asked.

*   *   *   *   *

In hockey it is called a "rep," short, of course, for

"reputation." Mine grew out of North Bay: one game, one moment, the clock stopped, the game in suspension—and yet it was this, nothing to do with what took place while clocks ran in sixty-eight other games, that put me on the all-star team with more votes than Torchy. Half as many, however, as Bobby Orr. But still, it was Orr and Batterinski, the two defensemen, whom they talked most about in Ontario junior.

Bobby Orr would get the cover of *Maclean's*. I almost got the cover of *Police Gazette* after the Billings incident. My rep was made. The *North Bay Nugget's* nickname for me, Frankenstein, spread throughout the league. I had my own posters in Kitchener; there were threats in Kingston and spray-paint messages on our bus in Sault Ste. Marie; late, frantic calls at the Demers house from squeaky young things wanting to speak to the "monster."

They didn't know me. I didn't know myself. But I loved being talked about in the same conversations as the white brushcut from Parry Sound. Orr they spoke of as if he was the Second Coming—they sounded like Poppa praising the Madonna on the church in Warsaw; for me it was the same feeling for both Orr and the Madonna—I couldn't personally see it.

Orr had grown since I'd seen him first in Vernon, but he was still only sixteen in 1964 and seemed much too short to be compared to Harvey and Howe, as everyone was doing. He'd gone straight from bantam to junior, but Gus Demers still said he was just another in a long list of junior hockey's flashes-in-the-pan. Another Nesterenko, another Cullen.

We met Oshawa Generals in that year's playoffs, and the papers in Oshawa and Sudbury played up the Batterinski-Orr side of it. "Beauty and the Beast," the Oshawa

Times had it. The *Star* countered with "Batterinski's Blockade," pointing out that the Hardrocks' strategy was to have Batterinski make sure Orr never got near the net, though no one ever spoke to me about it. I presume it was understood.

On March 28 we met on their home ice, the advantage going to them by virtue of a better record throughout the season. I said not a single word on the bus ride down, refusing to join Torchy in his dumb-ass Beatles songs, refusing even to get up and wade back to the can, though I'd had to go since Orillia. My purpose was to exhibit strength and I could not afford the slightest opening. I had to appear superhuman to the rest of the team: not needing words, nor food, nor bodily functions.

If I could have ridden down in the equipment box I would have, letting the trainer unfold me and tighten my skates just before the warm-up, sitting silent as a puck, resilient as my shin pads, dangerous as the blades. The ultimate equipment: me.

I maintained silence through the "Queen" and allowed myself but one chop at Frog Larocque's goal pads, then set up. Orr and I were like reflections, he standing solid and staring up at the clock from one corner, me doing the same at the other, both looking at time, both thinking of each other. We were the only ones in the arena, the crowd's noise simply the casing in which we would move, the other players simply the setting to force the crowd's focus to us. Gus Demers had advised me to level Orr early, to establish myself. Coach Therrian wanted me to wait for Orr, keep him guessing. I ignored them all. They weren't involved. Just Orr and me.

His style had changed little since bantam. Where all the other players seemed bent over, concentrating on something taking place below them, Orr still seemed to be sitting at a table as he played, eyes as alert as a poker player, not interested in his own hands or feet or where the object of the game was. I was fascinated by him and studied him intently during the five minutes I sat in the penalty box for spearing some four-eyed whiner in the first period. What made Orr effective was that he had somehow shifted the main matter of the game from the puck to him. By anticipating, he had our centers looking for him, not their wingers, and passes were directed away from him, not *to* someone on our team. By doing this, and by knowing this himself, he had assumed control of the Hardrocks as well as the Generals.

I stood at the penalty box door yanking while the timekeeper held for the final seconds. I had seen how to deal with Orr. If the object of the game had become him, not the puck, I would simply put Orr through his own net.

We got a penalty advantage toward the end of the period and coach sent me out to set up the power play. I was to play center point, ready to drop quickly in toward the net rather than remaining in the usual point position along the boards and waiting for a low shot and tip-in. Therrian had devised this play, I knew, from watching Orr, though he maintained it was his own invention. I never argued. I never even spoke. I was equipment, not player, and in that way I was dependable, predictable, certain.

Torchy's play, at center, was to shoulder the Oshawa center out of the face-off circle while Chancey, playing drop-back left wing, fed the puck back to me, breaking in. A basketball play, really, with me fast-breaking and Torch pic-ing. The crowd was screaming but I couldn't hear. I was listening for Orr, hoping he might say something that would show me his flaw, hoping he might show involvement rather than disdain. But he said nothing. He stared up at the clock for escape, the numbers meaningless, the score irrelevant. He stood, stick over pads, parallel to the ice, back also parallel, eyes now staring through the scars of the ice for what might have been his own reflection. Just like me, once removed from the crowd's game, lost in his own contest.

The puck dropped and Torchy drove his shoulder so hard into the Generals' center I heard the grunt from the blueline. Chancey was tripped as he went for the puck, but swept it as he fell. I took it on my left skate blade, kicking it forward to my stick, slowing it, timing it, raising back for a low, hard slapper from just between the circles. I could sense Orr. Not see him. I was concentrating on the puck. But I could sense him the way you know when someone is staring at you from behind. I raised the stick higher, determined to put the shot right through the bastard if necessary. I heard him go down, saw the blond brushcut spinning just outside the puck as he slid toward me, turning his pads to catch the shot. His eyes were wide open as his head passed the puck; he stared straight at it, though it could, if I shot now, rip his face right off the skull. He did not flinch; he did not even blink. He stared the way a poker player might while saying he'll hold. Orr knew precisely what my timing was before I myself knew. I saw him spin past, knew what he was doing, but could not stop; my shot crunched into his pads and away, harmlessly.

The center Torchy had hit dove toward the puck and it bounced back at me, off my toe and up along the ankle, rolling like a ball in a magician's trick. I kicked but could not stop it. The puck trickled and suddenly was gone. I turned, practically falling. *It was Orr!* Somehow he'd regained his footing even faster than I and was racing off in that odd sitting motion toward our net.

I gave chase, now suddenly aware of the crowd. Their noise seemed to break through an outer, protective eardrum. There were no words, but I was suddenly filled with insult as the screams tore through me, ridiculing. It seemed instant, this change from silently raising the stick for the certain goal, the sense that I was gliding on air, suspended, controlling even the breath of this ignorant crowd. Now there was no sense of gliding or silence or control. I was flailing, chopping at a short sixteen-year-old who seemed completely oblivious to the fact that Batterinski was coming for him.

I felt my left blade slip and my legs stutter. I saw him slipping farther and farther out of reach, my strides choppy and ineffective, his brief, effortless and amazingly successful. I swung with my stick at his back, causing the noise to rise. I dug in but he was gone, a silent, blond brushcut out for a skate in an empty arena.

I dove, but it was no use. My swinging stick rattled off his ankle guards and I turned in my spill in time to see the referee's hand raise for a delayed penalty. I was already caught so I figured I might as well make it worthwhile. I regained my feet and rose just as Orr came in on Larocque, did something with his stick and shoulder that turned Frog into a lifesize cardboard poster of a goaltender, and neatly tucked the puck into the corner of the net.

The crowd roared, four thousand jack-in-the-boxes suddenly sprung, all of them laughing at me. Orr raised his hands in salute and turned, just as I hit him.

It was quiet again, quiet as quickly as the noise had

first burst through. I felt him against me, shorter but probably as solid. I smelled him, not skunky the way I got myself, but the smell of Juicy Fruit chewing gum. I gathered him in my arms, both of us motionless but for the soar of our skates, and I aimed him carefully and deliberately straight through the boards at the goal judge.

Orr did not even bother to look at me. It was like the theory you read about car accidents, that the best thing you can do is relax. Orr rode in my arms contentedly, acceptingly, neither angry, nor afraid, nor surprised. We moved slowly, deliberately, together. I could see the goal judge leaping, open-mouthed, back from the boards, bouncing off his cage like a gorilla being attacked by another with a chain. I saw his coffee burst through the air as we hit, the gray-brown circles slowly rising up and away and straight into his khaki coat. The boards gave; they seemed to give forever, folding back toward the goal judge, then groaning, then snapping us out and down in a heap as the referee's whistle shrieked in praise.

I landed happy, my knee rising into his leg as hard as I could manage, the soft grunt of expelled air telling me I had finally made contact with the only person in the building who would truly understand.

If it would stop there, the game would be perfect. But I knew, having taken my best shot, I would have to deal with the rebound. My hope was to clear it quickly. I pushed Orr and began to stand, only to be wrapped by the linesman trying to work a full nelson around my shoulders. I went to him gratefully, shifting with false anger, yanking hard but not too hard, according to the unwritten fighter-linesman agreement. He was talking in my ear the way one does to calm down a dog who has just smelled porcupine.

"Easy now, fella. Just take it easy now, okay?"

I said nothing. I pulled hard; he pulled back hard. He twisted me away; I went with him, scowling, delighted.

"Get the trainer!" I heard the referee shout to one of the Generals.

I twisted back. Orr was still down on the ice. The other linesman stood above, waiting to embrace him, but Orr just lay there, eyes shut, face expressionless.

"Chickenshit!" one of their larger players yelled at me and then looked away quickly, afraid to own up to his words. I lunged toward him, but gratefully let the linesman reel me in.

"Just easy now! Easy, easy, easy," he said in my ear. I felt like barking, just to throw him off.

The referee signalled to the linesman to get me to the box, and I let him wrestle me over with only a few stops and twists. Some of the crowd was hanging up over the glass and screens, throwing things, spitting, screaming. They looked like the muskrat Danny had once taken on a tip trap and failed to drown; we'd put it in a box and stabbed cattail stems through the cardboard at the little fucker until it ran at the screen we'd placed over top, screeching and spitting at us as if it would have torn us to pieces if it hadn't been blocked from us. These rats seemed voluntarily caged. Unlike the muskrat, they welcomed their confinement. If they broke through and got to me they'd have trouble finding the courage to ask for my autograph.

Orr did not return to the game. We won 4-1 on Torchy's hat-trick. I scored the fourth on a desperate empty-net attempt by Oshawa, and the slow slider from center was booed all the way into the net, making it as sweet as if I had skated through the entire team and scooped it high into a tight corner as the last man back slashed my feet out from under me. I even asked the linesman for the puck, just to rub it in.

But such sweetness never seems to last. The X-rays went against us, Orr returned for game three and after six we were out of it, retired for the season. Orr scored or set up seventeen of the Generals' twenty-two goals over this stretch. I scored twice, set up three and spent sixty-two minutes in the penalty box, twelve of them for boarding him. But Orr and I did not make contact again until May 19, 1974 when Eddie Van Impe, Moose, the Watsons and I set up the defensive minefield that even the Great Orr with perfect knees couldn't have penetrated. Philadelphia 1, Boston 0. The Flyers take their first Stanley Cup in six games.

excerpts from the novel

King Leary

Paul Quarrington

I was found guilty in the juvenile court of arson (I wasn't charged for killing the chicken) and sentenced to spend time at the Bowmanville (Annex) Reformatory for Boys. My crime was judged a serious one, and the judge shook his jowls somberly and said he thought it would be best if I stayed at the reform school until my sixteenth birthday. The judge kind of implied that when I turned sixteen he'd throw me into a real grown-up slammer.

Clay Clinton attended the court proceedings, dressed in a blue suit with short pants. He nodded judiciously throughout and seemed to think the judge's verdict was a wise one.

So they took me on the train down to Bowmanville, Ont. I was accompanied by a correctional officer, a fat man who smoked cigars and didn't say a solitary word to me. The general feeling was that I'd turned out bad, but this fellow seemed to think I was headed for the gallows. When he noticed people staring at us, and quite a few people did, the correctional officer would say to them, "Arsonist," and tip his head in my direction.

The first few times I tried to say, "I didn't know Rex's

dung would explode!'' but every time I said that, the correctional officer would give me a cuff on the side of the head.

At the Bowmanville train station, I was turned over to my new keepers. I thought things had gone from bad to worse.

They were *monks*.

There were four of them, all dressed in long black robes like they were waiting for a funeral to pass by. And as if them being monks wasn't bad enough—if the old man saw a monk he'd cross his fingers and wouldn't uncross them until he'd seen a horse sneeze—they were the oddest assemblage of monks the world has ever seen.

One was a great big cusser, ugly as all get-out. He looked like what dogs are dreaming about when their back legs start twitching. Another of the monks looked like a fireplug, short and squat, even to the extent of having a bright red face with a little yellow top, that being his blond hair. If this man of the cloth marched into any seaside groghouse, the drunken sailors would back out politely. The third monk was just barely there, that's how slight he was. He looked like something was eating him up from the inside. The skin on his face looked as thin as tissue paper.

The fourth was a regular enough goom, except for his eyes. They were crossed and bossed and weird in every way, a strange milky blue color. This was Brother Isaiah, about whom there were two schools of thought. The most popularly held position was that Brother Isaiah was blind as a bat. The other school (Brother Isaiah himself being practically the only adherent) had it that Brother Isaiah could see perfectly well. To add fodder to this case, Isaiah was always saying sentences that

began, "I see..." or "You look...." That's what he did
now. He leant in real close to me and rested those egg
blue eyes on my chest for a few seconds and then said,
"I see you have arrived safe and sound, Mr. Leary."

I grunted, my old mother's admonitions of politeness
be damned.

The ugly one made a big show of puckering his mouth.
Speech took some preparation in his case. "Did you
have a nice trip?" the monster demanded.

Next the tough little fireplug monk wanted to know if
I was tired, and the skinny one asked, "Are you hungry?"

I didn't say anything. I was thinking of asking the
correctional officer if he might be interested in adopting
me.

The monks lined out (they couldn't walk to the icebox,
I was to find out, without forming into a single file), and
they led me to an old cart that was full of farming equipment, groceries, and gewgaws. There were two old
horses hitched up front, and they seemed to get uneasy
on our arrival, snorting and shifting their trembling legs
around. I found out why. The blind monk, Brother
Isaiah, climbed up onto the box. It took him upwards of
two minutes to even find the reins, him groping with
his hands, those two bossy-milk eyes of his no use at all.

Then the monk made a sharp chicky sound with his
tongue and the side of his mouth. The old nags started
moving forward and this Brother Isaiah started steering.
If you want to call it steering. The wagon kept going
back and forth across the road, and a few times we came
within an ace of tumbling into the ditch. I was the only
one who seemed to notice or care. One time the blind
monk drove the horses straight for an old oak tree. I
watched the two ancient beasts exchange glances, and I

guess they decided that the time had finally come for rebellious action, because they pulled away just in time.

The three others sat with me in the cart and paid this wagoneer no mind. They kept trying to make conversation, but I wasn't having none of it. Instead, to keep myself occupied, I started digging around in all the junk, looking to see if there was anything interesting.

I found a hockey puck. It seemed a strange thing to find in a cart full of monks. I rooted around some more and came up with a pair of skates and a couple of sticks.

The ugly one, who'd told me that his name was Brother Simon, puckered up his face truly gruesome in order to ask, "Do you play hockey, Percival?"

I shrugged juvenile delinquent-style, but managed to sneak a little nod into it.

The fireplug, Brother Andrew, grinned and said, "Most excellent." He had a nice smile, except for the lack of teeth. He had the same amount of teeth as I do now, approximately one.

The skinny one — sunlight passed through the man — whose name was Brother Theodore, he asked, "What position do you play?"

"Mostly the centerman, but I can play the point or the cover-point. I can play the rover. I could play the wings. It none of it makes any difference to Little Leary. You could stick me in goal for all of that."

Brother Isaiah all of a sudden swung around and aimed his strange wally eyes somewhere in my general vicinity. "Mr. Leary," he said, "your new home."

Ahead of me, sitting at the end of a road and the top of a hill, was a castle. It looked like a picture ripped out of one of my brother Lloyd's storybooks, *The Knights of the Round Table*. The first time I saw it, the reformatory was

golden in the autumn sun, all covered by clouds and ivy.
It had turrets and round windows and even a moat,
except for the moat was just an ambitious ditch. We
had to cross a small bridge to get over, and then we had
to pass under a gateway. I looked up and saw that someone had burned these words into the wood:

TO KEEP A BOY OUT OF HOT WATER, PUT HIM ON ICE

*   *   *   *   *

It was sometime in late October when the brothers
started putting together the boards. They were usually a
quiet bunch, but they got even quieter, all of them
rushing around with hammers in their hands and nails
sticking out of their mouths. The only thing us lads
heard from them was pounding out in the playing field,
pounding and the occasional grunt. I personally thought
the monks were crazy, and I'll tell you why: they laid
out the boards in a circle. A huge and, as far as I could
tell, perfect circle. I even asked Brother Isaiah about it.
He just grinned and fastened his strange eyes on my left
shoulder. "Have ye not known?" he asked me. "Have
ye not heard? It is he that sitteth upon the circle of the
earth that bringeth the princes to nothing." That's the
kind of answer I used to get from Brother Isaiah. So anyway, they laid out the boards in a circle, and around the
beginning of December they raised them. The monks
took the old horses off the cart. It took the horses and
sometimes six or seven brothers to raise each section of
board. The weather stayed pleasant for a week or two,
the sun all biting and bright even though the trees were
naked as firewood. We all waited; the monks prayed.

On Christmas Eve the temperature fell about forty

degrees. The brothers rushed out with buckets and hoses. They stayed out there all night, and to keep themselves amused they sang. They sang strange songs with words I didn't understand. All night long the monks watered the world, and the winter air turned the water to ice. Blue-silver ice, hard as marble. On Christmas morning the round rink was ready. Brother Simon was out there skating, his face even uglier, reddened by lack of oxygen, his carbuncles polished by the stinging wind. For a huge, monstrous man he sure could dance out there on the ice! He had some figure-skating moves, dips and twirls, his arms raised slightly, the hockey stick acting as a balancing pole. And as I watched him, Brother Simon the Ugly became airborne. It seemed he was up there for a whole minute, and during that time he pirouetted lazily. This stunt robbed me of my breath and made my knees quiver. I determined right then and there to learn how to do that. It would be some months before I did, and it would take a couple of years for me to refine it and come up with the spectacular St. Louis Whirlygig.

Brother Andrew, the one who looked like both the fireplug and the bulldog that might employ it, was streaking up and down, dodging invisible opponents. Whatever he was doing, it made my hardstep look like a cakewalk. I said to myself, if you could do that, no one could ever stop you. It took me some months to learn to skate like Brother Andrew the Fireplug. I call it Bulldogging. Miles Renders, who is currently coaching the Toronto Maple Leaves, calls it "achievement through perseverance and mental imaging," and I say that one of the reasons the Leaves are faring so poorly is that Renders would call Bulldogging something like that. All it is, is, you are at point one. You want to be at point two. The shortest distance, as every schoolboy knows, is a straight line, but there are no less than four big johnnies blocking the way. The secret is, don't give a tinker's cuss, just go, man. Just go.

Brother Theodore the Slender, who seemed on the verge of evaporation with all the rink-building activity, stood in the center of the round rink, his eyes half-closed, his pale lips moving slightly in silent prayer.

And some of the other monks (there were twenty-odd monks at the reformatory, regular fellows, especially in comparison to the four I knew best) were taking shots on Brother Isaiah.

I have never in my life seen such a good goaler as Brother Isaiah, and I have seen everyone from the Chicoutimi Cucumber to that tall slender fellow who looked like a schoolteacher and played so well for the Montreal Canadiens in the seventies. Yet I am convinced to this day that Brother Isaiah was blind as a bat, though he denied it. Isaiah might occasionally admit to being "a tad shortsighted," but you'd have to catch him walking into a brick wall. But the other monks couldn't get a shot by him. Isaiah would just reach out and grab them in his glove (and gloves back then didn't amount to much), or else he'd get the toe on them, or the chest in front of them, or bang them away with his stick. Brother Simon the Ugly tried to jimmy one by him, dancing right up to the goal crease, flipping the puck off his backhand as he made one of his ballerina twirlabouts. Brother Isaiah flicked it away with his wood. Then Andrew the Fireplug comes barreling along the wing, taking out a couple of bystander brothers just for style, and he unleashes a slapshot even though the damn thing isn't even invented back then! Brother Isaiah the Blind raises his left shoulder maybe a quarter inch and the rubber is dancing harmlessly behind the net.

But there was Brother Theodore standing in the center of the huge silver circle, and his eyes were popped open all the way and his mouth had ceased working. In front of him was a puck. Brother Theodore the Slender brought his stick back real slow, and then, with a motion that cut the air like a knife, Brother Theodore whacked the rubber. I swear to Jesus he hit that puck harder than Bobby Hull ever hit one, and it didn't even look like he was trying. Brother Isaiah didn't hear it or feel it, or however else he detected pucks, as I believe with all my heart that the man couldn't see the sun if it tumbled into his backyard.

There was a small smile on the face of Theodore the Slender.

I learnt how to do that, too. Some people (like scrawny Hermann over on the next bed) say that shooting was the weakest part of my game, but in my prime I could whistle the rubber like nobody's business. I scored on every goaltender there was in my day, and they'll tell you that I had one of the hardest shots going. Unfortunately you can only ask Hugo "Tip" Flescher, because he's the only one still breathing. What's more, you better hurry. But Theodore the Slender gave me the gam on shooting, which is this: shooting is more mental than physical. You just practice so much that you can feel the puck, like the blade of your lumber was the palm of your hand, and then you just inner-eye that puck into the back of the net. "Set it there first," Brother Theodore was wont to say, "and then put it there." In other words, *wham, bingo.*

The monks left off playing long enough to tell us that there were plenty of skates in the recreational hall cupboards, so us puppies ran off to lace up. I had my own pair with me, of course. I'd brought them from By-town, even though I'd had to leave out most of my clothes to get them into my suitcase. I was the first one on the ice with the Brothers of St. Alban the Martyr, and I commenced to hardstep. I flew around the circle. I got my speed up so that ice formed in my eyebrows. When I finally stopped, I saw that all of the other delinquents, and all of the black-robed monks, were staring at me.

Brother Simon the Ugly puckered hideously and made the following pronouncement. "It would seem," he said, "that Percival is something of a natural!"

The phrase just tickled me. One time I even asked my wife, Chloe, to put that on my grave marker: PERCIVAL H. LEARY, SOMETHING OF A NATURAL. But Chloe died many years back, done in by more diseases and ailments than I could count. I can't recall what it says on her gravestone.

Andrew the Fireplug divided us boys into two teams, and we had some shinny scrimmages. Periodically Isaiah would stop us and give us such coaching tips as, "Who through faith wrought righteousness, he quenched the violence of fire and waxed valiant in fight!" We quickly learnt how to nod politely (us little boys nodding at a blind man!) and then we'd get back to playing. I was the best pup on the ice, scoring four or five goals in as many rushes. Then I stole the puck from a boy named Billy and smashed him into the boards. Theodore the Slender rendered a two-finger toot that almost ripped the ears off my head.

"Leary," he intoned somberly. "Expulsion!"

"What?" I screamed.

All of the monks droned "Expulsion" in unison. It sounded like their strange singing.

"You mean I can't play anymore?"

Theodore the Ugly said, "You *weren't* playing."

I was mortified. I threw away my stick and left the ice.

You see what they were trying to tell me, don't you — that hockey is a team sport. I had forgotten that, because I was so damn much better than anybody else.

*　*　*　*　*

It was in Montreal, March 13 of one-nine one-nine, that I made my first move to become the King of the Ice. I did that by deposing the previous King, Lalonde. He was called Newsy, although his right name was one of those French affairs with too many vowels. Lalonde looked like God wrought him out of stone — except really Lalonde looked like God had thought better of the idea halfway through and gone out to a movie. In the middle of Newsy's face were two eyes, as black as a nun's habit, and when Lalonde was angry — all of the time — they acquired a distinct lunatic sheen. Many a player was beaten just by a look at those eyes. Mind you, Newsy Lalonde could play. He was what you might call a talented and sound hockey player, and when you combine that with largeness and the ability to scare the holy bejesus out of people, then you got something. In 1919 he was thirty-two years old, and that's when I went after him.

I was Little Leary, the heart and soul of the Ottawa Paddies. I wore the Letter *C* over my heart, captain of the shinny-playing Irishters. I had the ginger back then, brother.

We were tied up in overtime.

Patty Boyle called for a time-out. The Paddies crowded around him at the bench.

Manfred looked at me and smiled that long crooked grin of his. "Let's do it, Percy," he said with a wink. "I'm getting hungry."

I nodded, stuff stirring in my guts.

"Here," said Manfred, and he stuck something in my gloved hand. It was his crucifix, the huge one. I noticed that Our Savior was not dying, He was stone dead. "Carry that," said Manny.

"You figure that's gonna help, do you?"

"You know what Brother Isaiah would say."

Manny had an uncanny knack for remembering the blind monk's drivel. I shrugged.

"Brother Isaiah would say, 'It couldn't hurt.'" Manfred winked again. "The Magic Stone, Percy."

"The Magic Stone?"

"Percival!" shouted Clay from the stands. He was sitting in the front row, having used some of his Bytown timber baron connections to get the ticket. "Score a goal, my prince! We're wasting valuable drinking time!"

"Go, you Lucky Number Seven!"

I dropped the crucifix inside my jersey. The metal felt cool and soothing on my belly.

We set up for the face-off. Newsy Lalonde was staring at me.

"Hey, newsboy," said I, "don't stand there. That's where I mean to skate with the puck."

"You are horsemeat, O'Toole." Lalonde always

affected to disremember my name, or maybe he really did, and he just used any Irish monicker that popped into whatever he was using for a mind.

"Come on, guys," said Manfred, "let's not fight."

"Mind your own business, chief," said Lalonde.

Manny crossed himself.

I crossed myself, too, and I touched the crucifix.

The rest is historical.

I heard Clay Clinton shout "Yes!" with all of his heart and soul. Clay had just won a lot of money—this was the start of what is commonly referred to as his "vast financial empire"—but his shout had a lot more to it than that. And I heard Manny cry, "Hey!"—that big delighted bellow of his. I realized that I'd scored, that we'd won the Stanley Cup. For that instant, we were three young men alone in the universe.

* * * * *

The rink that the Brothers of St. Alban the Martyr built was round. Hockey rinks are curved in the corners, as you likely know, but basically they should be squared. Our rink was a circle.

One night, I couldn't sleep. I didn't usually have that problem (I do nowadays, in my dotage—I have actually snoozed for periods of seven seconds and been wide awake for the rest of the night) but that evening, there in the reformatory, I was restless. There was a full moon, and it filled the window across from my cot, and for some strange reason I could make out all the mountains and craters. The moon was a strange color, too, a silver like a nickel had been flipped into the sky.

Then I heard the sounds, the soft windy sweeping of hockey sticks across ice. At first I thought I was dreaming, but then I recalled that I never did dream to speak of. I moved across to the window, soft on my feet so as not to wake the other delinquents. The moon was so bright that I do believe I squinted up my eyes. I have never seen it like that since.

I could see the rink, and I could see the shadows moving on it. The monks were playing a little midnight shinny. It quickened my heart. I threw on some clothes and flew outside.

There were five of them. I watched from a distance at first. I couldn't understand what sort of game they were playing. The action would move erratically within the circle, and sometimes the five would split so that three men would rush two, or four would rush one, and then sometimes the five of them would move in cahoots, the idea seeming to be to achieve a certain prettiness of passing. Then a man would break from the pack, and another man would chase him around the circle, and as quick as that happened they'd rejoin the three in the center. There were no goal nets on the ice. Just five men, a puck, and a lot of moonlight. They played in silence. I moved closer.

Simon the Ugly was the easiest to pick out, because he was the biggest. He was dancing, jumping into the air, and sometimes I could see his monstrous frame silhouetted against the trout silver moon. Theodore the Slender cut a shadow so fine that it was hard to pick out, but I could tell him from the quick, precise movements of his twiggy arms as he took a shot. And Andrew the Fireplug, it was he who was likeliest to make a break for the boards, to drift like gunsmoke around them. I

watched him scoot off with the puck, and then I watched a man slip up easily behind Andrew and relieve
him of the rubber. That was Isaiah the Blind. I could
scarcely credit it. Playing goaler is one thing—I mean,
at least Isaiah was standing still between the pipes, and
you could always convince yourself that he was simply
the luckiest son of a bee *ever*—but here he was skating
around like a madman, stealing pucks, passing and re-
ceiving, and the moonlight was sitting on his dead eyes
like it does on the still surface of a lake. I crouched
down behind the boards. Brother Isaiah had an aerial
maneuver that made the Whirlygig look like tumbling
down a flight of stairs, he had dekes and fakes that
would have baffled God! Whatever the hell game they
were playing—and I never did come close to figuring
it—Brother Isaiah was the best. In fact, Brother Isaiah
was the best I've ever seen, bar none. That includes
me, Duane Killebrew, and the fifth man out on that
moon-washed rink, Manny Oz.

excerpts from the novel Peckertracks

Arena

Stan Dragland

The arena is dimly lit and cool inside, and smells of new lumber. The shell of the arena has been up for three years, but it's been used as a huge granary to help pay the cost of construction. The last of the wheat was only trucked out three weeks ago, and already the boards of the new rink are in place. There are player's boxes at one side, and a penalty box at the other. Percy hops over the boards and gives the door of the penalty box a push. It's locked from inside so he reaches over and slides out the bolt. The door swings open. The two by six top of the gate has been cut diagonally where it meets the two by six of the boards, so it won't be able to put any strain on the hinges, or swing out onto the ice. Percy slams the door. It closes with a chunk, like the doors of the Pontiac. *Body by Fisher.* Percy notices that the edges of the two by six that runs all around the rink have been chamfered and sanded smooth. There's a one by twelve baseboard that sweeps around the bottom of the boards. *Get most wear there, I guess.* Percy wonders how the men of the town found out how to build a rink. They don't seem to have left anything out. Everything is incredibly solid. It makes Percy feel really good.

'That you, Perce?' Percy looks around. He can't make out where the voice came from.

'Over here.' Percy locates Ben at the north end of the rink, where some men are working on the dressing rooms and the waiting room. He walks over.

'Really sumpin, eh?'

'Jeez, I'll say.'

'Makes Excelsior's look pretty rickety. Say Perce, didja know the Merchants're gonna be playin Intermediate C next year?'

'No, ya mean in a league?'

'That's right, with playoffs, the whole works. There's, lessee, there's gonna be Excelsior, Bures, Credit and ... one other, oh yeah, Kuziar. N Depot.'

'Ya don't mean the Credit Hornets.'

'No, they're still Intermediate A, but there's gonna be another team.'

'Hey, should see some good hockey.'

'Merchants're gittin new uniforms too. Ya know, green n white, with sweaters that lace up in front. Really sharp.'

'Zat right? Howja find out?'

'I wuz over't the Cockshutt n Art Darby n Al Goring wuz lookin through a catalogue.'

'God, makes ya sorta wish it wuz winter already, doesn't it?'

Ord and the Merchants

Fairview is in town for an exhibition game against the Merchants. They play in a Saskatchewan league. Intermediate B, but, as Art Darby says, they're 'suckin the hind tit' in their league, and the Merchants are on top of their own, so it could be a good game.

It gets around that Fairview has brought a player called Ord, who's been suspended from play in their own league. Nobody knows what for, but the Depot fans take a dislike to him during the warm-up. For one thing, he's obviously a good player. He skates with style. But also he looks uppity. As soon as the game starts the fans start to ride him.

Depot scores first. Art Darby. *One of his patented slap shots.* The Fairview goalie fishes the puck out of the net with his stick and slaps it at the boards in disgust. He leans on his pads a minute, looking down at the ice. Then he looks up and says 'fuck!' Nobody can hear him for cheering, but Percy's been watching his face.

'See that?' he says to Ginny, who's standing beside him.

'Yes.' She's half-smiling. It's their own joke. Percy feels as bold as if he'd said fuck himself. It's great to have Ginny next to him, pushing close. Against the cold? Bob Raft isn't with her. Does that mean something?

It isn't long before Ord starts to respond to the crowd. He smiles at them satirically and spits towards the boards at faceoffs. Once he takes off a glove and blocks one nostril, then the other, and fires a couple of gobs on the ice.

'Well the *fil*thy! Ja ever see anything so dis*gus*ting!'

'BOO! Wipe the ice withim!'

Halfway through the second period Ord gets into a

fight with Paul Craig. He goes wild, hitting like a windmill, and Paul can't do much more than cover up. Ord has to be dragged away by his own players. Is there something wrong with this guy? Percy starts to watch his face as he skates by. Now that he's stopped smiling he only looks about half there.

Ord is getting all the razzing now, which is even kept up after the whistle blows and play stops. The Merchants start to get the message, if they needed any. The bigger ones, like Neely, are starting to lay for Ord. The game is getting rough. There are a lot of penalties. In fact Percy sees that the Merchants are getting dirty. Nobody seems to care. Neely skates behind the Fairview net and conks the goalie on the head with his stick. A cheer goes up from that end of the rink. The goalie bellows and starts out of his crease after Neely, who's following the play up the ice, looking innocent. The referee and most of the crowd are watching the play, so there's nothing the goalie can do but skate back to his net, one glove off, testing his head for blood. After that he starts to take swipes with his stick at any Merchant who gets near him, trying to get them across the back of the legs.

Things are getting out of control. Percy isn't much for hollering, so he notices that some of the people who were shouting are quiet now, just watching. There's still plenty of noise though. Some people are yelling 'Killim!' at Ord. A few are slapping the boards with pieces of broken hockey stick.

Ord gets cross-checked against the boards where Percy is standing. As he starts to skate away somebody grabs the end of his stick. He whirls around and chops as hard as he can into the crowd, hitting Ginny on the side of the arm. She falls against Percy, then to the concrete. Some people bend over her. Percy is speechless, torn between helping Ginny and watching what's going to happen on the ice. Some of the Merchants skate over to see who's been hurt. Somebody says 'My God! He coulda killed somebody!' Neely says 'Alright boys, let's gittim.'

The noise has built to a howl. Ord is skating around with a neutral expression on his face, like nothing happened. Now some of his own players grab him and start to shove him toward the dressing room. He tries to push them off. Neely crashes through and takes a swing at Ord, missing and falling down with his momentum. Paul Craig, right on his heels, sits on him till he cools off. A Fairview player has Ord's arm twisted behind him, and two or three more are forcing him out through the gate and down the walk to the dressing room. The spectators there are silent as he passes. Nobody wants to taunt him. He could get loose and go for anybody.

The game is held up. The players are all on the ice, standing in groups and talking. Paul Craig is talking to a Fairview player. *Good old Paul*. He's the oldest player on the ice, nobody knows how old, and still the best puck handler. He keeps his hockey pants up with a belt and makes it look natural. Art Darby is flipping shots at the net. Neely is skating around, looking hard at the dressing room door. Now it opens, and Ord comes out in street clothes. His teammates escort him out the side door, to hoots and jeers. Word comes around the boards that they've put him in a car and told him to get the hell out of here.

Finally the game resumes. There's still most of a period to play, and the hockey is very clean. But the spark is gone out of the game. Nobody has much to holler. Nobody cares much that Depot wins 5-2.

Percy walks home by himself. News of the game gets there ahead of him.

'What in Heaven's name goes on at those hockey games? Somebody hit Ginny with a stick? Her mother's really up in arms. Grown men! If that's what hockey's all about you'd better stay home from now on.'

'How's Ginny?'

'Well there's nothing broken apparently, but really!'

There's not much use trying to explain. His mother never goes to hockey games, so she doesn't understand how the emotions get involved.

Percy tries to read, but he can't concentrate. He prowls around the house. Then he goes to the basement, gets his trapper mitt and a rubber ball. He throws it against the wall, catches it, throws it against the wall.

'Stop that Percy! Everybody's going to bed.'

Percy's a long time getting to sleep.

Blue Moon

Lionel Kearns

Whenever Harvey hears the song he thinks of Sybil
Chalmers, who in 1949 came into the grade seven class,
and sang it, astonishing them all.

"We have a new face with us this morning," the
teacher had said. "This is Sybil." She was a middle size
girl with her red hair in a kind of page-boy perm, a
common style in those days. "Sybil wants to sing us a
song," added the teacher.

This was something out of the ordinary. No one sang
songs to the class. It was unheard of. It was unthinkable.
Even so, it might be better than getting into the morning's
social studies lesson. So the boys did not jeer at this
point, as they might have done, had they had more time
to consider what was happening.

"What are you going to sing, Sybil?" asked the teacher.

"*Blue Moon,*" said Sybil, and after a little pause, she
began to sing: "*Blue Moon/ You saw me standing alone/
Without a dream in my heart/ Without a love of my own/*"
and so on, right through the whole song, including
the choruses.

Sybil belted it out in a deep, rich, sexy, crooning voice
that should have been coming over the radio or out of

the mouth of a movie star, but should definitely not be occurring here in this time and place. The class was stunned. What was happening? One of themselves, even though she was a newcomer, was standing there revealing herself to be something very strange and threatening—a non-child, a young woman, a sexual being, or was it a kind of parody? No one knew how to respond, so they stared at her, noticing her small breasts pushing out her sweater front as she sang with all that husky-throated self-assurance and conviction about the unmentionable, about romantic love.

When she finished there was silence. The class was in a state of shock. Even the teacher was upset. She had agreed to Sybil's suggestion, thinking that it would be a children's song, executed in the customary thin high pitch of a school-girl. But Sybil's rendition of *Blue Moon* seemed almost obscene. After a long pause someone began to clap, and then there was general applause. But that grade seven class was never the same again.

Three years later Harvey is on a train with the other members of his Midget B hockey team. They are headed for Regina, the site of a minor hockey tournament. Walking through the train with some of his team-mates on the way to the diner, Harvey sees Sybil Chalmers. Wam! He passes her without speaking, pretending he does not recognize her. She is sitting with her mother. *"Blue-moon-blue-moon-blue-moon,"* the words race through his mind's ear as he moves quickly on through the door at the end of the train car. His friends behind him have also noticed her, and one of them gives a whistle before Harvey can close the door and move quickly on through the next one into the diner.

"Did you see that cutie?" someone says, as they are shown to their seats by the dining car steward.

"Hey, Stupid, that's her mother she's with," says one of the others.

"Let Harvey have her mother," says someone.

Harvey, of course, does not let on that he knows her, though he can feel his cheeks turning hot. He has a sudden moment of terror, thinking the others will notice his blush, but this passes. While he eats his lunch he tries to convince himself that he has been mistaken. The girl in the next coach is much too beautiful to be Sybil Chalmers. But the song is going through his head. *"Blue moon/ You saw me standing alone..."*

"You watch me," says Ed. "I'm going to make a date with her when we go back through her coach. I'll bet she's getting off at Regina too."

"Bet she ain't," says someone.

"Five bucks says you don't even speak to her," says somebody else.

"Ten bucks she doesn't speak to him!" says one of the others.

Harvey is feeling a bit sick. What should he do? He is not participating in the merriment of his team mates. "The stupid bunch of jerks," he thinks to himself. "If I was alone I'd speak to her for sure."

When they finish their lunch Harvey is the first one up and through the door at the end of the diner. He knows that Sybil and her mother are facing the other way, so if he walks through fast enough she won't have a chance to recognize him. He can hear the laughter and loud remarks of the others behind him.

"Excuse me, do you know the time?" Ed is saying, trying to sound serious.

"What's the matter with your watch, Ed?" someone shouts.

"Hey Lady, you have to watch this guy. He's got lover's nuts," someone is hooting amongst the uproar.

Harvey is at the end of the train car and shutting the door on their noise and laughter. Sweating and cringing, he is relieved to be out of that space and finally into the safety of his own seat. He sits there alone, asking himself why he is such a chicken. If he played hockey like that he certainly would not be on this team or this trip. By now the others are coming through the door and down the aisle in quick succession.

"Boy, did she ever tell Ed," says one of them, a little subdued.

"That's five bucks you owe me anyway," says Ed.

"Bull Shit! You didn't talk to her. You talked to her mother! Ha ha ha, and did her mother ever put you down," says one of the others.

"You're a bunch of jerks!" says Harvey.

For the next two hours Harvey sits looking out the window at the monotonous prairie landscape. The train comes to several stops, once at a siding, twice at small prairie towns that seem to have no more than a few empty box cars waiting on sidings, one or two grain elevators, and a cluster of houses.

"Can you imagine living in a dump like that?"

"They don't even have a rink."

"Prairie kids skate on ponds, Stupid. They use magazines stuffed in their pants for shin pads. Wait till you see them on the ice in Regina."

"But they sure have classy women."

"She ain't from the prairies, Stupid."

All afternoon Harvey looks out the train window and

thinks about Sybil Chalmers, and the words of the song keep going through his head *"...without a dream in my heart/ Without a love of my own..."* in time to the rhythm of the wheels of the train on the track. He wonders whether she recognized him. Of course she did. Then why didn't she say something? Because he didn't give her a chance. Was that all? No. Maybe she was embarrassed too? Not if she was the Sybil Chalmers from grade seven. Nothing seemed to embarrass her. Was that true? He remembers how he avoided her at school. Everyone avoided her. Did she have any friends? Harvey remembers seeing her once or twice on the street with her mother. He too referred to her as "Blue Moon", as everyone did, even when she could overhear it. Sometimes they called her "Blue Moon" to her face. That must have hurt. What finally happened to her? Harvey remembers that she did not return to school in grade eight. She and her mother must have left town.

These are the thoughts that are going through Harvey's mind as he sits quietly looking out the train window. When he thinks of grade seven he feels sad and ashamed, but when he thinks of Sybil Chalmers sitting one train car away from him he feels excited. Perhaps he will be able to somehow wipe away all that teasing and ridicule she had to endure. And Harvey begins to think that he should walk back there and apologize to her. Wouldn't his team-mates be amazed if they saw him sitting there chatting to her and her mother like old friends? But Harvey decides that it would be safer to do it when they are not around. He begins to rehearse the scene in his imagination.

"Excuse me, but didn't you go to Kootenay Junior Secondary one time?"

"Why yes, how did you know?"

"Well, I'm Harvey Santini, and I used to be in your class."

"Why you're not the Harvey Santini I used to know. I mean he was just a little fellow."

"Yes I am, and I want to apologize."

"Oh don't be silly, Harvey."

"We treated you very badly..." Harvey spends the rest of the day trying to get the dialogue to go right, and to generate enough courage to put his plan into effect. By late afternoon he has made up his mind. His plan is to stay behind when the rest of the team goes down to the diner for dinner.

"Not hungry right now," he says. "Maybe I'll go later."

So Harvey sits alone for twenty minutes, and then gets up and moves towards the door at the end of the train car. He is frightened. His heart beats fast and loud. He pushes open the first door and stands waiting in the noisy platform area between the cars. Then he draws in his breath and pulls open the second door. He begins to walk casually down the aisle, keeping his eyes unfocussed until he is close to them, to where he thinks they are sitting. But when he looks at the seat where Sybil and her mother were sitting, they are not there. The seat is now occupied by an old couple. Harvey is relieved, and begins to breath easier. Then he wonders if perhaps Sybil and her mother are in the diner. This thought troubles him. The diner, full of his own teammates, is not the place to carry out this plan.

"Leave it till later," he says to himself, turning around and going back through the train to his own seat, where he waits for his friends to return.

"Ed must have driven that chick and her mother off

the train," someone remarks after they get back.

"What, you mean she's gone?" asks Harvey. It is the first time he has mentioned her.

"Sure has, Harvey, and her mother too."

Some years later Harvey is blowing trombone in a local dance band. It's not a very good band, but it is the best one in the district, and so they play regularly every weekend. They play mostly tunes and arrangements out of the swing era; you know the kind of thing: *Tuxedo Junction, Pennies from Heaven,... Blue Moon.*

Of course that tune always makes Harvey think of Sybil Chalmers. He remembers how beautiful she looked on the train, and he regrets his cowardice in not speaking to her the first time he saw her. He wonders if he will ever see her again.

The band needs a female vocalist, and Harvey thinks of her singing *Blue Moon* whenever they play it, which is at least once a week. He has been thinking of her now for years. She grows more and more voluptuous and desirable in his imagination. And she is always connected with that song: *"Blue Moon/ You saw me standing alone/ Without a dream in my heart/ Without a love of my own/ Blue Moon..."* Sometimes he dreams of her spontaneously, without the aid of the musical cue.

Harvey wonders how he can track her down. He worries that if he does not find her soon they will both be so old that they will be repulsive to each other when they finally meet. Already he is approaching middle age. What should he do? He has tried to forget her, but whenever he thinks he has rid himself of that troublesome memory, he hears the tune *Blue Moon,* and there she is, back in his head again.

Somehow he expects her to turn up as a famous singer in a big name band in the States, or maybe to surface suddenly as a star in a Hollywood musical. But he never hears of her. Perhaps she is dead. This thought makes him very depressed. It is as though part of his own life has been suspended. The idea of tracing her becomes more and more obsessive.

In a final effort to locate Sybil Chalmers, Harvey Santini writes a story and sends it to *New: West Coast Fiction* that publishes it. That story is what you are reading at this moment. The third person hero is only a literary device. I am Harvey Santini. That is why I know so much about this situation. My goal is to reach Sybil Chalmers, wherever she may be. Surely she will notice the title of this story and be intrigued enough to read it and find out that I am writing about her. Or, even if she does not see it immediately, someone else will read it and tell her about it, and she will eventually contact me. Surely she will. That is why I have gone to the effort of writing this story.

But Reader, I beg your indulgence to let me return again to the ease of third person narration, so that I may tell you in a more detached manner what happens next. Shortly after the story is published, Sybil Chalmers discovers it. However, instead of making contact with Harvey directly, she chooses to send her lawyer, who lays libel charges against Harvey and the editors of the magazine that contains it.

Why has Sybil responded in this way? Harvey has written this story as a tribute to her magnificent voice and her beauty. He has written it as an apology for the way he treated her in grade seven. He has written it to confess his cowardice on the train. He wants to tell her that her song has touched him more deeply than any other song has touched him. Yet she is bringing libel charges against him. She does not deny that the first part of the story is essential correct. She is the same Sybil Chalmers who sang *Blue Moon* in the grade seven class of the Kootenay Junior Secondary School. She is the Sybil Chalmers who travelled with her mother on the train through the Prairies three years later. However, the second part of the story is completely false. It seems that it has somehow looped ahead of itself, for she has not yet brought charges against the writer of this story or the editors of this magazine. It is this strangeness in the story that constitutes the grounds for her libel action.

Harvey has a number of possible responses open to him. He can claim that all names in the story bear no relation to anyone living or dead. He can change the names of the principal characters and the name of the song. He can even change the offending ending of the story. He considers these various alternatives and decides that none of them is feasible. This story does not have the freedom of fiction. It is a true story that has meaning only as it relates to the actual events. To change any part of it would render the whole work meaningless. Falsification would commit these words and images back to the flux and swirl of unorganized and unintegrated experience. It would push the song and the girl and the part of Harvey Santini himself into the oblivion of never having actually occurred, where no one stands alone among strangers without a dream, without a love of his or her own, where this feeling, where feeling itself, is unconnected and so unbearable.

There is also the other problem. If Harvey changes the name of the song, or the name of the girl, or the school, or even his own name, Sybil will not read the story and recognize herself and him and their situation. The pattern will remain incomplete and so the story will not make sense.

In the end he cannot change the story or retract the truth. Sybil sues Harvey and the magazine, winning a devastating court settlement. Neither he nor the magazine can find the money to pay. The magazine folds and Harvey changes his name and goes underground. What else can he do? Years later he starts a small literary magazine devoted to enigmatic reminiscence. The name of the magazine is *Blue Moon*.

My Career with the Leafs
Brian Fawcett

I'll explain how I came to play hockey for the Toronto
Maple Leafs. It was surprisingly easy, and other people
with similar ambitions to play in the Big Leagues might
be able to pick up some valuable tips. I'm a poet, you
see, and one of the things we do as part of our job is an
occasional public reading. I had a reading to do in Toronto,
and one of the first things I did when I got there was to
drop down to Maple Leaf Gardens. The day I went, the
Leafs happened to be practicing.

As I sat in the stands watching the Leafs skate around
the rink I got an idea. I walked down to the equipment
room, and politely asked a man who turned out to be
the trainer if it would be okay if I joined the practice.

"Sure thing," he told me, just like that.

I asked if I could have a uniform to wear.

"Sure," he said. "What number would you like?"

"How about number 15?" I said innocently.

The number belonged to Pat Boutette at the time, but
he was injured and I knew he wouldn't be around. I felt
a surge of ambition—maybe I could beat him out of a
job! Minutes later I was out on the ice with the Toronto
Maple Leafs.

My Career With the Leafs

I skated around for a while, carefully declining any involvement in the passing and shooting drills while I tried to get my floppy ankles to co-operate. Instead of co-operating they were beginning to hurt, so I drifted in the direction of the coach, Red Kelly, who was yelling instructions at the players. I leaned casually on my stick the way I'd seen Ken Dryden do on television, and looked down at my skates. I watched the drills for two or three minutes until the ache in my ankles started to fade, then edged closer to Kelly.

"Mind if I take a turn?" I asked as evenly as I could.

"Not at all," he replied. "Let's see what you can do."

Somebody pushed a puck in front of me and as I reached for it I tripped on the tip of my left skate and fell flat on my face. What to that point had almost been a dream turned abruptly into a nightmare. I lay on the ice for a second, peering at the puck as if it had tripped me, and wondered why I couldn't wake up. I thought about quitting then and there.

I had nothing to lose, so I didn't quit. I got up, picked up my stick, and looked Red Kelly in the eye. He didn't move a muscle—didn't laugh or anything. I pushed the puck forward and skated after it in the direction of the goalie—it was Gord McRae I think—slowly gathering speed. About fifteen feet from the net I deked to my left without the customary deke to the right. The deke took McRae with it, and I cut to the right. The net was wide open and I shovelled the puck into it on my backhand.

All of this is incredibly difficult for a left-shooting skater to do. In fact, the whole manoeuvre is an impossible one, and everyone who saw it knew, including Kelly, who was staring at me with his mouth open. For my part, I had no idea how I'd done it, except that it had been awful easy.

"Not bad," Kelly shouted. "Not bad at all."

If scoring that first goal had been easy, the rest of the practice wasn't. I'm not a great skater at the best of times, and I wasn't in shape. I seemed able to score goals almost at will, but I had difficulty with the defensive drills, particularly the ones that involved things like skating backward. I fell several times, and one time I went into the boards so hard that Kelly skated over and told me to take it easy.

As the practice ended, he asked me if I could drop by his office after I showered. I told him I'd be pleased to, and after a shower I can't remember at all, I was sitting in a stuffed red naugahyde chair staring across a big desk at Red Kelly and Jim Gregory, the General Manager of the Leafs.

Kelly was writing something on a pad of yellow foolscap. Gregory did the talking.

"You've got some interesting moves out there," he said. "I caught the whole thing from up in the box. Where'd you learn your hockey?"

I decided to tell them the truth.

"Well," I replied, "I really haven't played organized hockey since I was about twelve. I watch Hockey Night in Canada, of course, and I guess I've learned a lot from that."

"Where do you come from?" he asked.

"That's kind of a hard question," I replied, trying to figure out what the truth was. "I'm from the West Coast. Well, not the coast, actually. I'm from up north."

"What brings you to Toronto?"

"I'm a poet," I said, "here on business, doing a public reading."

"No kidding," he said, looking reasonably satisfied with my answer.

"I guess you know Rota. He's from up there."

I was stumped. I didn't know any writer from up north named Rota. Kelly saw my confusion.

"New kid," he said. "Plays for Chicago."

"I've heard of him," I shrugged. "But I never played with him. He's a bit younger than I am."

There was a silence, as if the two of them were trying to decide which of them should speak. Finally, Gregory stood up and cleared his throat.

"How would you like to play hockey for the Toronto Maple Leafs?" he said.

"I'd really like that," I said quickly. "I'd prefer to play just the home games, though. I hate travelling."

Gregory seemed puzzled by my request, but he agreed to it, probably because I didn't ask for anything else.

"We play Boston Monday night," he said. "We'll see you at the rink at 6 p.m." He paused. "Make that 5:30, and you can get in an extra half hour of skating."

I stood up. "I can probably use it," I smiled.

Kelly grunted, and then grinned, and I followed him out of the office and down the long concrete corridors of Maple Leaf Gardens to the players' entrance. He shook my hand.

"Good to have you with us," he said, with a lot of sincerity.

"It's good to be part of an organization that takes chances," I said, with even more sincerity. "Toronto treats its visitors well."

Kelly smiled and waved goodbye as I stepped through the open door into a fine early winter blizzard.

The next thing I knew I was sitting in the Leafs' dressing room beside George Ferguson, suiting up for the game. Kelly came in and announced the player assignments.

"Fawcett here is going to be playing home games for us," he shouted, pointing vaguely in my direction. "He'll play on the wing with Ferguson and Hammerstrom for a while, and we'll see how things go. Any questions?"

To my surprise, a fair number of the players knew who I was, and it turned out that some of them had even read my work. Out of the corner of my eye I saw the two Swedes, Hammerstrom and Salming, exchange glances. Maybe they thought having a poet on the team might take some of the heat off them. They were still relatively new in the league, and they were taking a lot of physical and verbal abuse from the rednecks and goons who were worried about foreigners changing the game and taking their jobs. The rap on the Swedes was that they were chicken, particularly Hammerstrom, who the papers were saying was allergic to the boards. Personally I thought his skating more than made up for those faults.

I wondered a little at Kelly putting me on a line with him, but decided that he was trying to compensate for my poor skating. Every team in the league would stick their goons on our line, that was certain. Kelly probably figured Hammerstrom would skate his way out of trouble, and I would talk my way out.

We'd see soon enough. It was nice to be able to play with Ferguson, who I thought was one of the smarter centres to come into the league in a while. I planned to do what any rookie should — keep my head up and my mouth shut. It would be a new way of working, that was for sure.

The first period of that game was nothing to remember. My check, predictably, was Wayne Cashman, probably the dirtiest player in the league. I went up and down my wing without incident, partly because Cashman wasn't much of a skater either. He cut me with his stick several times, but I didn't bleed much, and I ignored it when he got me with the butt end just as the period ended. I waited until I could breathe again and skated off to the dressing room with the rest of the team.

Early in the second period Lanny McDonald and Don Marcotte were sent off for trying to remove one another's vital organs, and Kelly sent me out with Hammerstrom on a five on five. The Bruins sent out Greg Sheppard and Cashman. The face-off was in our end, and Hammerstrom won it, got the puck back to Ian Turnbull, and he banked it around on the boards to where I was waiting. I circled once, almost lost my balance, and headed up the ice. As I crossed the red line, I saw Cashman skating toward me with a gleam in his eye. I kept going toward Orr at the blue line, did the deke to my left as if to move between Orr and the boards, and then cut sharply right. Orr went for the first deke and so did Cashman, who by this time was right behind me prodding at my liver with his stick. When I deked to the right, Cashman ran into Orr and both of them went heavily to the ice. I had a two on one with Hammerstrom, and I slid the puck over to him. He drew Al Simms over, passed back, and I had only Cheevers to beat. I did it again; deked left, cut right, and plunked the puck over the bewildered netminder into the upper right corner of the net.

I stuck my stick up in the air the way I'd seen it done

on television, and was trying to honk my leg when I ran into Hammerstrom and we both fell down. Turnbull came over to congratulate me and Salming skated over to dig the puck out of the net. He handed it to me, grinned, and said something in Swedish I didn't understand. Hammerstrom grinned at me the same way and pointed to Cashman, who was skating in small circles at centre ice with his head down.

It was a tight-checking game, and the score was still 1-0 halfway through the third period. That was as far as I got that night. I skated into the corner for a Ferguson pass, Cashman went in behind me, and only Cashman came out.

Eventually I came *to*, but that was well after the game was over. The Leafs had won it 2-0. Cashman got a penalty for hammering me, and Sittler scored on the ensuing power play. That's what they told me, anyway.

I made it to the practice the next afternoon, none the worse for having spent the night in the hospital to make sure I didn't have concussion. I didn't get much sleep because the interns kept coming in every half hour to see if I was going to go into a coma.

"Are you there?" they asked, and lifted my eyelids with one finger to flash their penlights at my pupils. About 4 a.m. a very young intern came in. He was a hockey fan.

"You're the new guy with the Leafs, eh?" he asked.

"Yeah," I croaked.

"Nice move you made on that goal you scored," he said. "Where'd you learn that?"

"Watching television," I answered, telling the truth.

"I hear you write poetry too," he said.

My head hurt, so I just grimaced.

"Pretty strange," he said. "Watch out for Cashman."

He checked my eyes so carefully I thought he was looking for poems, but he said I'd probably be able to leave in the morning.

At the practice the next day, Ferguson told me to watch out for Cashman too.

"You were lucky," he said. "Cashman spent two periods setting you up. We all knew it was coming, but I guess you had to pass the test like anyone else."

"Some test," I complained. "All I can remember about it is my bell ringing when it was over."

I played the three games in that home stand, scoring again in the last one against the Rangers, and setting up a goal by Ferguson. The team was away for the next three games, and then back for three more. While they were away I worked on my skating, circling the rink again and again until my ankles were too sore for me to move anymore. I tried skating without a stick, but found, as I had when I was a kid, that skating that way was beyond me. I needed the stick for balance and without it I could barely stand.

When the team came back, I confided to Ferguson that I couldn't skate without a stick.

"You're kidding," he said.

"No," I told him. "It's true. I only got skates every three years, and the first year they were too big and the third year they were too small."

Ferguson had a good eye for details. "What about the second year?" he asked.

"I had weak ankles back then."

"You still have weak ankles," he said.

"I use the stick for balance," I said, as we went on circling the rink.

Ferguson was skating backward to tease me. "Skating is easy," he laughed. "For me it's like breathing."

"I feel that way about some other things," I replied, "but not about skating."

"You don't look as if breathing is very easy right now," he pointed out.

While we unlaced our skates after practice, he asked me cautiously what it was like to be a writer.

"It's my way of breathing," I said.

"How'd you get into it?" he asked with genuine curiosity.

"I guess I was about thirteen," I said. "Right after I quit playing minor league hockey."

Ferguson and I became friends. He taught me a lot of the basics of pro hockey and I gave him books to read in return. I was interested in Rilke and an American poet named Jack Spicer at the time, and he pored through everything I lent him. I always had books in my equipment bag, and he dug through it regularly to see what was there. He asked me if Canadian writers were as good as Americans.

"The old guys are pretty tame," I said, "but there's a few writers under forty who might turn out to be interesting."

"Jeez," he said, "how long does it take to get good at it?"

"Usually about fifteen years of hard work," I said. "A few get good earlier than that because they have special attentions or come from environments that encourage them," I went on. "But that's rare. Most of us have to learn pretty well everything about the culture twice, and that takes time. After that, there's the job of keeping on top of it as it changes. A lot of writers get one good review of their work and they have to please their public, or, worse, they decide that they're geniuses, and don't have to listen to anything. So they imitate themselves until they lose their ability to learn. After that they just get drunk, or academic, or spend all their time trying to please the reviewers and filling out grant applications."

He wanted to know about the grants, so I explained to him the economics of trying to be a serious artist in a country that wants to have serious art without having to put up with the inconvenience and cost of paying the artists.

He looked skeptical. "Except for that, hockey is pretty much the same," he said after a moment's thought. "Only hockey players get screwed up more easily and a lot faster."

"That's because there's more people paying attention," I said, "and there's more money involved."

That home stand was a good one. I scored my third goal, drew assists on one of Ferguson's, and another on the power play, passing from behind the net to Sittler in the slot. Only four goals had been scored while I was on the ice, and after seven games I was plus five. Then the Leafs were off again on a five-game road trip and I went back to my solitary skating, circling the ice over and over again until slowly, very slowly, my skating began to improve. I skated clockwise first, and then counter-clockwise. Going counter-clockwise was easier, maybe because on the corners my stick was closer to the ice. But I couldn't quite master skating backward, and stopping remained a problem unless I was close to the boards. But I developed reasonable speed skating straight ahead, and during games I combined my lack of stopping skill with my speed to provide the team with some excellent bodychecking.

Ferguson and I went out on the town the night after the team flew in from Los Angeles. He showed me the important sights of Toronto, like Rochdale and Don Mills, and later that night we walked down to Lake Ontario and threw rocks at all the empty milk cartons floating in the water. There had been a thaw, and it was like spring—dirty snow was piled up everywhere, abandoned cars were being towed off the streets, and the curious sensation I'd had of being in Middle Earth began to dissipate. There were lovers everywhere, discussing Parliament, and kissing and fist-fighting as the fog rolled in from the lake to meld with the darkness coming up from the East.

We played our only other home date of the season with the Bruins several weeks later. As the game approached, I got a lot of good-natured ribbing from the guys about what to do with Cashman.

"Check him into the boards with a powerful metaphor," advised Sittler.

"And then slash him with an internal rhyme," someone else chimed in.

I laughed at the gags, but deeper down I was worried. The press had picked it up and were amusing them-

selves, mostly at my expense. Alan Abel in *The Globe &
Mail* wrote something about it being a test of whether
the stick is mightier than the pen, and in an interview,
Cashman noised it around that he not only disliked my
style, he detested poetry. Anybody who wrote poetry,
he said, had to have something wrong with their hor-
mones. That wasn't all he said, either. He told the
interviewer he was going to show the fans that there was
something fishy about me, promising to make fillets out
of me *and* my poetry.

As I skated out for the pre-game warm-up, Cashman
gave me the evil eye, so I gave the fans a demonstration
of how fast I could skate through the centre ice zone.
Kelly, out of kindness I guess, kept our line away from
Cashman's as the game began, but on the second shift
I saw the Bruin right-winger head for the bench right
after the face-off, and Cashman came over the boards.
Somebody froze the puck, and as we lined up for the
face-off deep in Bruin territory, Cashman skated up to
the circle, and around me once with his stick about a
quarter of an inch from my nose.

"I hope you got a nice burial poem written for yourself," he sneered. "You skinned my behind and I'm
gonna carve yours off and throw it to the crowd."

I looked him right in the eye and mustered up all my
powers of language.

"Suck eggs," I said.

On the face-off Ferguson drew the puck back to
Salming and I skated to the corner to wait for a pass.
Cashman ignored the puck and followed me. I ducked
an elbow. It missed me, but the Ref didn't miss it,
because I slid down the boards as if I'd been pole-axed.
Cashman got whistled for an elbowing penalty, and then

got a misconduct penalty when he tried to chase me into the stands. I skated away from him, and three of my teammates stayed between us to make sure I stayed alive. Kelly kept me on for the power play and I banged Sittler's rebound past Gilles Gilbert to make it 1-0.

When I got to the bench, Kelly told me Howie Meeker wanted to interview me after the first period. It was Saturday, and the game was being televised nationally.

I'd forgotten it was Hockey Night in Canada. You get like that in the pro's — you forget everything that makes the world tick for real people. You also pay a price. The price I was going to have to pay for my forgetfulness was an awful one. I hadn't brought any poems in my equipment bag. I was being handed the largest audience any poet in this country ever dreamed of and I wouldn't have a thing to read.

A few minutes later I was sitting in front of several television cameras with the customary towel over my shoulder, watching Howie Meeker introduce me to the nation and thinking that the dream was going to turn into a nightmare if I couldn't think of something quickly. My mind was a blank.

"We've got Toronto left winger Brian Fawcett here in the Hockey Night in Canada studios at Maple Leaf Gardens," Meeker announced in a voice that sounded more nasal in real life than on television.

He was hunched toward the cameras and I noticed he sat closer to them than I did. I hadn't seen a brush cut for years or, for that matter, as much make-up as he had on his face, and I was sorting through all that novelty without listening to what he was saying. Luckily, he was babbling as inanely as usual at the camera and ignoring me completely:

"... nice to see a young player come up to the NHL with a good grasp of hockey fundamentals and play sound, heads-up positional hockey the way you've been doing. Gee whiz, but I just get thrilled when I see a young kid with his mind on the game skate away from a player like Wayne Cashman. And it pays off, don't you see? It must have been less than a minute before you scored that beautiful goal like you were born with a stick in your hand and skates on your feet."

He hadn't actually asked me a question, but he seemed to have finished.

"Actually, Howie," I said, too nervous to do anything but tell the truth, "I haven't played much hockey since I was twelve or thirteen years old, and I'm thirty, so I'm not much of a kid any more. I've been mainly concerned with language, and more specifically with disjunction in poetry, for the last few years. You might say I've been learning the tools of an extremely complex trade."

Meeker appeared not to have understood. Maybe he thought I was speaking French. He ignored everything I said, and went off on another rant.

"Well, Brian, how do you like being with a team like the Leafs, eh, with their tradition of ruggedness and hard work?"

"Well, Howie," I said, still not sure if he realized that I understood English, and pretty sure he didn't know I was a poet, "I find the ruggedness something of a problem. Northrop Frye and Margaret Atwood created a problem a few years ago by writing some books about the importance of Nature and the frontier, and a lot of similarly empty glamour nonsense about rugged Canadian pioneers, and as a result a lot of the writers in this country now go around wearing logging boots and punching people for no reason. I used to do it myself, actually."

Meeker was staring at me, his jaw somewhere down around his navel. I took this as a signal to continue.

"I mean, violence may be natural, but Nature isn't a very good model for behaviour. It's been really over-estimated."

I knew I was gesticulating too much, and starting to yap. I'd forgotten about the cameras—it was Howie Meeker I wanted to convince. I couldn't stop.

"Art is really about civilization," I said, "not about Nature. All Nature does is overproduce, then waste most of it, and then resort to violence when the garbage starts to stink. When human beings follow Nature, you get guys like Hitler."

I was really flying, so I went to Meeker's question about hard work next.

"Hard work, like you say, is really important, Howie. The more I know about this game, the more I begin to realize that the real secret is hard work. I guess that goes for hockey as well."

Meeker, for some reason, seemed to have lost his voice, so I went right on.

"If you'd given me a little more notice, I could have brought some work here to read, but I guess these interviews are a bit too short to give the folks at home any real idea of what's going on, let alone a sense of the breadth and skill and variety of good writing going on in this country today."

Meeker stuttered back to life.

"Ah, ahhh.... Yes, well.... Well, Brian, I wish you and

the Leafs the best of luck in the upcoming second period," he said, regaining a measure of control that didn't show in his face.

"Back to you, Dave Hodge!" he said hoarsely.

I smiled politely at the camera until fade-out. I'd seen a few guys start to pick their noses when they thought they were off-camera, and I wanted people to remember what I'd said.

Meeker turned on me. "What was that all about, you crazy sonofabitch?"

I began to explain, but he walked out of the studio without listening to my answer.

The dressing room was oddly silent when I returned. I sat down next to Ferguson and pulled the towel from around my neck. He was sitting with his head between his knees, as if he were air-sick.

"Didn't you know about Meeker?" he asked incredulously.

"Know what?" I said, stuffing the towel into my equipment bag as a souvenir. "He seemed kind of ticked off when I talked about writing, but then he did ask those dumb questions, and he didn't stop me from answering them the way I wanted to."

"Geez, man, that's the unwritten law of hockey," Ferguson said. "You're supposed to pretend you're really dumb."

It was my turn to be incredulous.

"Darryl thinks there's some kind of agreement between the owners about it," he said. "When you get out of Junior Hockey, you're given a sheet of things you can say to the press. You talk dumb, talk about teamwork, and all that crap."

My head was reeling. When I was a kid I believed that the world was full of secret rules and conspiracies, but this was real life — the Big Leagues. I couldn't believe what I was hearing.

"I mean, a few years ago," he continued, "when Kenny Dryden started getting interviewed, he used all kinds of literate words like 'tempo' and so on, pronounced all the words properly, and there was a terrific uproar. But he was in law school and they had to accept it. I dunno. They may get him yet — force him to retire."

Ferguson shrugged, and a note of hopelessness entered his voice. "Rumour is," he said, "that this whole business about us being stupid and inarticulate is an explicit policy of the Feds — right from the top."

I looked around me to see if he was kidding. A couple of guys just nodded and looked the other way, but most of them were glaring at me. Kelly looked really angry.

"Aw, come on, you guys," I said to no one in particular. "Why put up with this? I've seen what's really true. Look at the books lying around the dressing room."

Several players slipped large hardbound books into their equipment bags. Sittler, everyone knew, was a big Henry James fan — said it helped his passing game. And Tiger Williams had come up from Junior already heavily into Artaud. The league had its share of jerks, it was true, but unless you noised it around, you were left alone if you had intellectual interests. I guessed they were mad at me because they thought I might have let the cat out of the bag. Hockey, Kelly told me later, was in enough trouble.

There was a TV set in the dressing room, and we watched as Meeker came on the screen to do the highlights of the period. My goal wasn't one of them. A few of the guys exchanged significant looks, but everybody remained seated, as if they were watching something very sad.

When a commercial came on, I asked Ferguson who'd died.

"You did, dummy," he said.

"Aw, come on," I said. "Why? Is it that bad? All I did was to get Howie Meeker mad at me."

"It's a lot worse than you think. You'll be blacked out," he said, grimly. "No radio perks, no television interviews, and as little newspaper coverage as they can give you. What you *will* see will all be bad."

"That's okay," I said, philosophically. "I'm pretty used to that."

I scored the winning goal in the third period by going around the defence in the usual way, and I didn't even get third star. I went up and down my wing against Cashman, took his checks, many of which were flagrantly vicious and should have drawn penalties, and I threw a couple of my own in his direction. Cashman was given third star, actually, and Meeker said he was the one Bruin on the ice who had dominated his opponent.

Ferguson and I had a few beers after the game. I invited the rest of the guys, but nobody seemed interested.

"You're really a goof," Ferguson said cheerfully. "Do you know that?"

"How was I supposed to know?" I said, irritably. It seemed like everybody knew the rules but me.

"Look," I said, "I didn't go through the system like you guys did. For me it was all watching the tube, and thinking about it. How was I supposed to know—I mean, I've never believed much of what I've seen on television, but I did think Hockey Night in Canada at least was for real."

Ferguson grunted. "Rules are rules," he said. "Nobody but you believes they're supposed to be just."

"I'd settle for knowing what they are," I said bitterly.

"Would you really?"

"I'm not sure," I admitted. "I guess I really want to know who the big shots are who make them."

I didn't find out who the big shots were, that night or on any of the ensuing nights that season. I played my hockey as well as I could, and I played it in more or less the kind of obscurity I had been warned to expect. I scored nine goals and built twelve assists in twenty-seven games, and I was invited back for training camp the following season even though I played increasingly less often toward the close of the season.

As I was packing up to go home, the two Swedes came over and mentioned how much they'd enjoyed my presence during the home games, and asked if I'd be able to visit them in Sweden during the summer.

"I've got a lot of writing to catch up on," I told them. "My season's really just starting now."

Salming grinned that same grin I'd seen in my first game.

"I understand this," he said. "No fun to go to Sweden if you're interested in the Pros in English language."

"Something close to that," I admitted.

He and Hammerstrom left the dressing room laughing. They sure weren't like the Scandinavians I knew from watching Ingmar Bergman movies. I wandered over to where Ferguson was packing his equipment, and said goodbye. His bag was full of books, and he was having a hard time getting them all in. Finally, he had to give up, and he left with a pile of them under one arm. He turned at the door.

"I'm going to try to write some stuff myself this summer," he said. "Mind if I send you some of it?"

"Do," I replied. "You've got my address?"

"Sure have," he smiled. "Well, see you. Stay in shape."

"You too," I said. But I was talking to his shadow. He'd disappeared.

That summer passed in a flash, and by mid-September I was back skating and shooting again with the Leafs. The season started, and by December I had four goals and as many assists and, I thought, I was doing okay.

But the team wasn't doing well at all. We were fourth in our division, and Ballard could be heard snorting and snuffling all the way to Buffalo.

Then, before a practice right after a road trip that had gone badly, King Clancy walked into the dressing room, announced that Kelly had been fired, and that John McLellan was the new coach. Two days later Ferguson was traded to Pittsburgh. The day after that, McLellan called me into his office.

"Brian," he said, "I talked things over with Jim, and we, uhh...."

He seemed to be stumbling for the right words.

"We don't think your heart is really in this game. You're not skating...."

"I can't skate," I cut in, but he ignored that and went on.

"We want you to retire."

"I'm practically a rookie!" I sputtered.

"You're thirty-one," he said, "and you're not going to

get any better. Meeker is still after your behind, and you're a target for every goon in the league. Both Jim and I spent some time over the summer reading your work. You're a better poet than a hockey player. You've got to go for that."

I fussed and fumed, but I ended up agreeing with him. I had two, maybe three years of good hockey in me. With poetry I had maybe forty years, and I would only get better. I'd miss the crowds and the attentiveness of the critics, even though they'd done a good job of ignoring me. But I wouldn't miss Toronto and its bars, and I wouldn't miss the poetics, which, try as I did to ignore them, are as venal and profit-oriented at Maple Leaf Gardens as they are in the English departments of the nation's universities. If more poets were to play hockey instead of pretending flowers or vacant lots are really interesting, things might get better. But I wasn't going to hold my breath.

"You're right," I told McLellan. "I'll retire right now."

And I did. I walked out the way I had come in, gave back the blue on white and the number 15, and stepped out into the dull Toronto streets as if it were the next morning and not the next year I'd awakened to.

Three weeks later I got a letter from Ferguson, postmarked Atlanta. In it was this poem:

> It's cold in Pittsburgh, colder still
> in Philly. The north wind blows all night
> from Canada, and these raucous crowds
> that hoot and holler for our blood, Hey!
> They're the coldest thing of all.
> Skate and shoot, the coaches tell us

My Career With the Leafs

Skate and shoot. But masked men block the goals
and I am checked at every turn.

Each year more miles to go
More senseless contests of the will.
My heart is like the puck; often frozen
too often out of play, too often

stolen by the strangers
in the crowd.

Hockey Night in Canada
Diane Schoemperlen

We settled ourselves in our usual places, my father and I, while the singer made his way out onto the ice and the organist cranked up for "O Canada" and "The Star Spangled Banner." Saturday night and we were ready for anything, my father half-sitting, half-lying on the chesterfield with his first dark rum and Pepsi, and I in the swivel chair beside the picture window with a box of barbecue chips and a glass of 7Up.

My mother was ripping apart with relish a red and white polka dot dress she hadn't worn for years. There were matching red shoes, purse and a hat once too, but they'd already been packed or given away. Trying to interest someone in her project and her practicality, she said, "Why, this fabric is just as good as new," pulling first one sleeve, then the other, away from the body of the dress.

But the game was starting and we were already intent on the screen and each other.

"They don't stand a chance tonight," I said, shaking my head sadly but with confidence as the players skated out.

My father grinned calmly and took a drink of rum.

"Not a chance," I prodded.

"We'll see, we'll just see about that." Even when they played poorly for weeks on end, my father remained cheerfully loyal to the Chicago Black Hawks, for no particular reason I could see, except that he always had been. He must have suffered secret doubts about the team now and then—anyone would—but he never let on. I, having no similar special allegiance and wanting to keep the evening interesting, always hoped for the other team.

We were not violent fans, either one of us. We never hollered, leaped out of our chairs, or pounded ourselves in alternating fits of frustration and ecstasy. We did not jump up and down yelling, "Kill him, kill him!" Instead, we were teasing fans, pretend fans almost, feigning hostility and heartbreak, smirking and groaning gruesomely by turns, exaggerating our reactions mainly for the benefit of the other and sometimes just to get a rise out of my mother, who was by this time humming with pins in her mouth, smoothing pattern pieces onto the remains of the dress, and snipping merrily away with the pinking shears, while scraps of cloth and tissue paper drifted to the floor all around her.

The dress, I discovered, was to be reincarnated as a blouse for me, a blouse which, by the time it was finished (perfectly, seams all basted and bound, hem hand-done), I would probably hate. Between periods, she took me into the bathroom for a fitting session in front of the full-length mirror. I did not breathe, complain or look as she pinned the blouse together around me, a piece at a time, one sleeve, the other, half the front, the other half, back, collar, the cold silver pins scratching my bare skin just lightly.

By the time we got to the three-star selection after the game, my mother was off to the back bedroom with the blouse, whirring away on the Singer.

When her friend Rita was there, my mother at least played at watching the game. Whenever the crowd roared, my father groaned and Rita began to shriek, my mother would look up from her stamp collection, which she was endlessly sorting and sticking and spreading all over the card table, and smile encouragement at the TV.

"Who scored?" she asked innocently, as she put another page in her album and arranged another row of stamps across it. Russia was her favourite country for collecting, the best because their stamps were bigger and grander than any, especially ours, which looked stingy and common by comparison. The Russians had hockey players, cosmonauts, fruits and vegetables, wild animals, trucks and ballerinas, in red, blue, green, yellow, even shiny silver and gold. We had mainly the Queen in pastels. My mother's everyday fear and loathing of Communists did not enter into the matter.

"Just guess, Violet, just you guess who scored!" Rita crowed.

"Don't ask," my father muttered.

"Most goals, one team, one game," Rita recited. "Twenty-one, Montreal Canadiens, March 3, 1920, at Montreal, defeated the Quebec Bulldogs 16 to 3."

"Ancient history," said my father. "Besides, who ever heard of the Quebec Bulldogs anyway? You're making it all up, Rita. Tell me another one."

"Fewest points, one season," Rita chanted. "Thirty-one, Chicago Black Hawks, 1953/54, won 12, lost 36, tied 4."

"Not quite what I had in mind." My father rolled his

big eyes and went into the kitchen to fix more drinks, one for himself and one for Rita, who took her rum with orange juice, no ice. I said nothing, not being sure yet whether I wanted to stick up for my father or fall in love with the Canadiens too.

Rita had followed the Montreal team for years. Unlike my father and me, she was a *real* fan, a serious fan who shrieked and howled and paced around the living room, calling the players by their first names, begging them to score, willing them to win with clenched fists and teeth. She did not consider her everyday dislike of those Frenchmen (as in, "I've got no use for those Frenchmen, no use at all") to be contradictory. Hockey, like stamp collecting, it seemed, was a world apart, immune to the regular prejudices of race, province and country — although she did sometimes berate my father for siding with a Yankee team.

When the Black Hawks lost another one, Rita and I (for I'd been won over after all by her braying) took all the credit for knowing the better team right off the bat, and heaped all the blame upon my father who was now in disgrace along with his team — a position he took rather well. When they did win, as far as he was concerned, it was all or mainly because he'd never given up on them.

After the game my father and I usually played a few hands of poker, a penny a game, with the cards spread out on the chesterfield between us. My mother and Rita were in the kitchen having coffee and maybe a cream puff. The hum of their voices came to me just vaguely, like perfume. I wanted to hear what they were saying but my father was analyzing the last power play and dealing me another hand. I won more often than not, piling up my pennies. For years after this I would think of myself as lucky at cards. In certain difficult situations which showed a disturbing tendency to repeat themselves, I would often be reminded of Rita's teasing warning: "Lucky at cards, unlucky at love."

Later, after Rita had gone home, I would find the ashtray full of lipstick-tipped butts which I pored over, looking for clues.

My mother had met Rita that summer at Eaton's where Rita was working at the Cosmetics counter. Rita still worked at Eaton's, but she was in Ladies Dresses now, having passed briefly through Lingerie and Swimwear in between.

To hear Rita tell it, you'd think their whole friendship was rooted in my mother's hair.

"I just couldn't help myself," Rita said, telling me the story. "There I was trying to convince this fat lady that all she really needed was a bottle of Cover Girl and some Midnight Blue mascara and up walked your mother with her hair."

Patting her hair fondly, my mother said, "I couldn't figure out what she was staring at."

I already knew that before Rita had come to live in Hastings, she was a hairdresser in Toronto. She'd been to hairdressing school for two years and still took the occasional special course in cold waves or colouring. She was about to open her own beauty parlour just when her husband Geoffrey killed himself and everything was changed. It was not long after that that Rita gave up hairdressing and moved to Hastings to stay with her younger sister, Jeanette. Six months after that

Jeanette married a doctor and moved back to Toronto. But Rita stayed on in Hastings anyway, bought herself a second-hand car and rented an apartment downtown in the Barclay Block above an Italian bakery (which was the very same building my parents had lived in when they were first married, a fact that I found significant and somehow too good to be true).

My mother always did her own hair, putting it up in pincurls every Sunday night so that it lay in lustrous black waves all around her face and rolled thickly down past her shoulders in the back. But what Rita meant was the streak, a pure white streak in the front from the time she'd had ringworm when she was small. Even I had to admit it looked splendid and daring, although there were times when we were fighting and I wanted to hurt her and tell her she looked like a skunk. Rita's own hair was straggly and thin, half-dead from too many washings, a strange salmon colour, growing out blonde, from too many experiments. Her bangs hung down almost to her eyebrows. Sometimes she wore them swept back with coloured barrettes, revealing the delicate blue veins in her temples.

"Anyway," Rita said, pausing to light another cigarette with her Zippo, "I finally got rid of the fat lady and your mother and I got talking. Just seeing her hair gave me the itch again—I could just picture all the things I could do with that hair. We went up to the cafeteria for coffee—"

"And we've been friends ever since," my mother said in a pleased and final-sounding voice, the way you might say, And they all lived happily ever after.

My mother had never really had a friend of her own before. Oh, there was a neighbour lady, Mrs. Kent three doors down, who would come over once in a while to borrow things that she never returned—the angel food cake pan, the egg beater, the four-side cheese grater. And so my mother would go over to Mrs. Kent's house occasionally too, to get the things back. But it was never what you would call a friendship, so much as a case of proximity and Mrs. Kent's kitchen being sadly ill-equipped.

I had never seriously thought of my mother as wanting or needing a friend anyway. Friends, particularly best friends, I gathered, were something you grew out of soon after you got married and had children. After that, the husband and the children became your best friends, or were supposed to.

But then she met Rita and it was as though Rita were someone she had been just waiting for, saving herself up for all those years. They told each other old stories and secrets, made plans, remembered times before when they might have met, had just missed each other, almost met, but didn't. Rita was at least ten years younger than my mother. I suppose I thought of her as doing my mother a favour by being her friend. In the way of young girls, I just naturally imagined my mother to be the needy one of the two.

When Rita was in Cosmetics, she would bring my mother make-up samples that the salesmen had left: mascara, blusher, eyebrow pencils, and sometimes half-empty perfume testers for me. And her pale face was perfect. Once she moved to Ladies Dresses, she hardly ever wore slacks anymore, except when the weather turned cold. She was always trying out bold new accessories, big belts, coloured stockings, high-heeled boots. I could only imagine what she'd bought while she worked in Lingerie—the most elegant underwear,

I supposed, and coloured girdles (I didn't know if there were such things for sure, but if there were, Rita would have several), and marvellous gauzy nightgowns.

On her day off during the week Rita was usually there in the kitchen when I came home from school for lunch. While my mother fixed me a can of soup and a grilled cheese sandwich, Rita sipped black coffee and nibbled on fresh fruit and cottage cheese. This was the first I knew of dieting as a permanent condition, for although Rita was quite slim and long-legged, she was always watching her weight. My mother, who was much rounder than Rita anyway, had taken up dieting too, like a new hobby which required supplies of lettuce, pink grapefruit and detailed diet books listing menus, recipes and calories. She'd begun to compliment me on my extreme thinness, when not so many years before she'd made me wear two crinolines to school so the teachers wouldn't think she didn't feed me. How was it that, without changing size or shape, I had graduated from grotesque to slender?

"How's school going this week?" Rita would ask, offering me a tiny cube of pineapple, which I hated.

She listened patiently, nodding and frowning mildly, while I told her about Miss Morton, the gym teacher who hated me because I was no good at basketball; and about my best friend Mary Yurick who was madly in love with Lorne Puhalski, captain of the hockey team and unattainable; and about everybody's enemy, Bonnie Ettinger, who'd beat up Della White on Monday in the alley behind the school.

It was easy to get carried away with such confidences in the hope that Rita would reciprocate, and I almost told her that I was in love with Lorne Puhalski too, and that Bonnie Ettinger was going around saying she'd knock my block off if she ever got the chance. But I talked myself out of it at the last minute. I wanted so much to have Rita all to myself but somehow it never was arranged.

With Rita there, my mother could listen to my problems without worrying too much or wanting to do something about them. She and I probably learned more about each other from those kitchen conversations with Rita than we ever could have any other way.

Sometimes it was as though they'd forgotten all about me. One day when I came home for lunch my mother was sitting wrapped in a sheet on the high stool in the middle of the kitchen while Rita gave her a cold wave, something she'd been threatening to do for weeks. I made my own sandwich.

My mother was saying, "I was so young then, and everybody said I was pretty. We were in love but when they found out, they shipped him off to agricultural school in Winnipeg. I still think Sonny was my own true love."

"What about Ted?" Rita asked, wrapping pieces of hair in what looked like cigarette rolling papers and then winding them nimbly onto pink plastic rods.

"Oh, Ted."

Ted was my father of course, but it was strange to hear my mother call him by his name when usually she called him "Dad" or "your Dad."

"Yes, well, Ted. That was different. I was older. I'm even older now. I didn't tell Ted about Sonny until long after we were married."

I went back to school that afternoon with a picture of my mother as another person altogether, someone I had never met and never would now. This woman, mysterious, incomplete and broken-hearted, pestered me all day long. The stink of the cold wave chemicals lingered too, bitter but promising.

At other times it was as though my mother could tell me things through Rita that she could never have expressed if we were alone.

One Saturday night after the hockey game I left my father dozing on the chesterfield and went into the kitchen.

Rita was saying, "When Geoffrey hung himself, his whole family blamed me. They said I'd driven him to do it. They kept bringing up the baby who died and then Geoffrey too, as if I'd murdered them both with my bare hands. I had a nervous breakdown and they said it served me right. It was then that I realized I would have to leave town." She spoke calmly, looking down at her lap, not moving, and a sense of young tragic death wound around her like scented bandages, permanent and disfiguring, the way Japanese women used to bind their feet to keep them dainty. She was doomed somehow, I could see that now, even though I'd never noticed it before.

"You have to be strong, we all have to be strong," my mother said without looking at me. "We're the women, we have to be stronger than they think we are."

I could hear my father snoring lightly in the other room, no longer harmless. The kitchen was snug with yellow light. The window was patterned with frost like feathers or ferns and it was just starting to snow. My mother pulled the blind down so no one could see in. We could have been anywhere, just the three of us, bending in together around the kitchen table, knowing things, these sad things, that no one else knew yet.

That night Rita slept over. An odd thing for grown-ups to do, I thought, but I liked it.

After I'd gone to bed, it reminded me of Christmas: something special waiting all night long in the living room: the tree, the unopened presents, Rita in my mother's new nightie wrapped up in an old car blanket on the chesterfield.

Around the middle of December, Rita flew to Toronto to have Christmas with her sister Jeanette and her doctor husband. My mother had somehow not considered exchanging presents with Rita and was horrified when she appeared the morning she left with three gaily-wrapped boxes, one for each of us. Even more surprising was my father, who handed Rita a little package tied up with curly red ribbons. She opened it on the spot, still standing in the doorway, and produced a silver charm of the Montreal Canadiens' crest.

On Christmas morning we opened her presents first. She'd given my mother a white silk scarf handpainted with an ocean scene in vivid blues and greens. My father held up a red Chicago Black Hawks jersey with the Indian head on the front and the number 21 on the back. I got a leather-covered date book for the new year in which I immediately noted the birthdays of everyone I could think of. Rita's presents were the best ones that year.

After dinner, we called all our relatives in Manitoba and then my mother took some pictures of the tree, of my father in his new hockey sweater and of me eating my dessert behind the chicken carcass. My friend Mary

called and we told each other everything we got. I thought
Rita might call later but she didn't.

Between Christmas and New Year's my mother went
out and bought a braided gold necklace to give to Rita
when she got back. The silver charm was never discussed
in front of me.

Not long after Rita returned from her holidays, she
was moved from Ladies Dresses into Ladies Coats. Now
when she came over she wore a knee-length black coat
trimmed with grey Persian lamb at the collar and cuffs.
She always hesitated before taking it off, caressing the
curly lapels, picking invisible lint off the back, giving
my mother and I just enough time to notice and admire
it again. She knew a lot about mink and ermine now,
how the little things were bred and raised on special
farms, how vicious they were, how many tiny pelts it
took to make just one coat. She lusted uncontrollably,
as she put it, after one particular mink coat in her department but had resigned herself to never being able to
afford it and seemed both relieved and disappointed the
day it was bought by some doctor's wife.

"Just between you and I," my mother said right after
Rita phoned to say she'd sold the fabulous coat, "I think
mink is a waste of money. It's only for snobs. I wouldn't
wear one if you gave it to me." Ten years later, my
father bought her a mink jacket trimmed with ermine
and she said, hugging him, "Oh, Ted, I've always
wanted one."

It was an extravagant winter, with new records set for
both snow and all-time low temperatures. My father
seemed to be always outside shovelling snow in the
dark, piling up huge icy banks all around the house.
He would come in from the cold red-cheeked and

handsome, trying to put his icy hands around my neck. Rita came over less and less often. She said it was because her car wouldn't start half the time, even when she kept it plugged in.

On warmer days when Rita wasn't working, my mother often took the bus downtown to her apartment. When I came home from school at three-thirty, the house would be luxuriously empty. I curled up on the chesterfield with the record player on and wrote in the date book Rita had given me or worked on the optimistic list my friend Mary and I had started: "One Thousand Things We Like." Well into its second spiral notebook, the list had passed seven hundred and was coming up quickly on eight with

> cuckoo clocks
> Canada
> lace
> my mother's hair
> comfortable underwear   and
> having a bath without interruptions

being the most recent additions.

My mother returned just in time to start supper before my father got home from work. She was distracted in a pleasant sort of way, all jazzed up and jingling from too much coffee or something, gabbing away gaily as she peeled the potatoes. Rita had given her some old clothes which could be made over into any number of new outfits for me. There was a reversible plaid skirt I'd always admired and wanted to wear right away but my mother said it was too old for me.

One Saturday afternoon when we had been out

shopping together, my mother suggested we drop in on Rita before catching the bus home. I had never been to her apartment before and as we walked up Northern Avenue to the Barclay Block, I tried to imagine what it would be like. Small, I supposed, since Rita lived alone — and was, in fact, the only person I'd ever known who did. Such an arrangement was new to me then, a future possibility that became more and more attractive the more I thought about it. The apartment would be quite small, yes, and half-dark all the time, with huge exotic plants dangling in all the windows, shedding a humid green light everywhere. The rooms smelled of coffee and black earth. The furniture was probably old, cleverly draped with throws in vivid geometrics. The hardwood floors gleamed and in one room (which one?) the ceiling was painted a throbbing bloody red. I thought that Rita and I could have coffee there just the two of us (my mother having conveniently disappeared) and she would tell me everything I needed to know. Why did Geoffrey hang himself, what happened to the baby, do you go out with men sometimes, do you think I'm pretty, do you think I'm smart? She could tell my future like a fortune.

We climbed a steep flight of stairs up to the second floor. The smell of baking bread rose up cheesy and moist from the Italian bakery below. I'd forgotten that my parents had lived here once too, until my mother said, "I always hated that smell, we lived in 3B," and pointed to a door on the left. I could not imagine anything at all about their apartment.

My mother knocked loudly on Rita's door. Further down another door opened and a woman in her housecoat leaned out into the hall, expecting somebody, I guess, or maybe just spying. "Oh, it's you. Hi," she said and ducked back inside.

My mother knocked again, and then once more.

"Maybe she's working," I offered.

"No, she's not. She definitely told me she was off today."

"Where can she be then?" I was pretty sure I could hear a radio going inside.

"How would I know?" my mother said angrily and sailed back down the hall.

Only once did I find my father and Rita alone in the house. I came home from Mary's late one Saturday afternoon and they were drinking rum at the kitchen table, with the record player turned up loud in the living room. They seemed neither surprised nor sorry to see me. There was something funny about Rita's eyes when she looked up at me though, a lazy softness, a shining, which I just naturally assumed to be an effect of the rum. She poured me a glass of 7Up and we sat around laying bets on the playoffs which were just starting, Montreal and St. Louis, until my mother came home from shopping. As it turned out, the Canadiens took the series four games straight that year and skated back to Montreal with the Stanley Cup.

Rita stayed for supper and then for the game. I went back over to Mary's and then her father drove us downtown to the Junior A game at the arena. Rita was gone by the time I got home and I went straight to bed because I'd had one shot of rye in Lorne Puhalski's father's car in the arena parking lot and I was afraid my mother, who still liked to kiss me goodnight, would smell it.

They were arguing as they got ready for bed.

"She lost her son, Violet, and then her husband too," my father said, meaning Rita, making her sound innocent but careless, always losing things, people too. But he was defending her, and himself too, protecting her from some accusation, himself from some threat that I'd missed, something unfair.

"Well, I *know* that, Ted."

"Don't forget it then."

"That's no excuse for anything, you fool."

"I didn't say it was."

"Be quiet, she'll hear you," my mother said, meaning me.

an excerpt from the novel

The Saxophone Winter

Robert Harlow

The town had grown up so that it had two centres. Uptown there were the school grounds and the residential streets. Downtown clustered around the civic hall, which stood in a little park, and the streets—all named after British cities—connected downtown with uptown. The river came in from the west and curved south so that it held the whole community in the crook of its arm. At the southwest was a range of a half-dozen hills called the Castles because they stood as if separate from each other, although they weren't. The smaller five hills were good for downhill skiing; the central and tallest hill had a ninety-foot trestle on top of it, used by the men who jumped on Sundays for a ten dollar prize, winner take all. Halfway down the hill's left-hand side there was another jump built into the slope which was called the boy's jump, and at the bottom of the hill, was a meadow that ran all the way into town and stopped at the skating rink. Long River was very compact, miniature. Its population was maybe four thousand, and without the highway, railroad, cement plant, and the lumber mills further west along the river, where it seldom flooded, there would be no reason for its existence. The plant and the mills worked short shifts now, when they worked at all.

Christopher's father was General Foreman under Harrison Dodd, the Municipal Engineer, whose department looked after the powerhouse, the water system, the roads, the streetlights, and the sidewalks. It wasn't the job he should have had, but it was a good one in 1938. Fielder's father had a two-ton truck, only it was owned by the Royal Bank.

When he walked from his house on York Street to downtown, Christopher had to pass first the half-burned high school and the two-storey elementary school. When he and Fielder headed down from Fielder's place over on Sheffield to go skating, they often wanted to go into the school and look around, but they didn't dare. Evil-eye Grandison came by every hour, as if it were his duty to guard the place from vandals.

He and Fielder walked on past the school with their skates slung over their shoulders. The outdoor rink opened during the holidays at 2:30 and closed down at 5:30 and then opened again from 7:00 to 10:00. Howard Streeter, who was old enough to have grey hair, ran it with the help of some rink rats who got free skate time and sometimes a little money for scraping the ice and shovelling snow off it after a storm. Howard seldom left his ticket booth and candy shop, which was between the women's and the men's dressing rooms, except to kick someone out. He wore laced rubber hightop boots with his pants tucked down into them. He didn't just point the way when he told someone to leave, he kicked them and kept on kicking them until they were out the door. His rubber boots did double duty. They weren't so hard-toed that they did any real damage to those they came in contact with, and they kept his feet dry when he was out on the rink with the hose making ice.

Fielder never did anything unless he could do it well. He could shoot marbles, play basketball, play lacrosse, and skate. He didn't have skis and his mother sent him by bus to his grandparents at the coast in the summers, so Christopher had never seen him swim or dive. The rink was crowded. Fielder never just entered a room, he plunged in, especially into a room full of people bigger than he was. The rink was a place where those who had quit school and didn't have a job hung out. All of them were over sixteen; some were over twenty. It was a long day for them. They had to come early to sweep the ice, shovel snow, sweep the floors, build fires, and then reserve a place on the benches that were nailed to the walls on both sides of the dressing room.

It was important to follow Fielder's natural example at the rink. The rats sat around looking as if they were just going to go to sleep, but if someone came in hesitant and alone, one of them would ask, "What d'you think you're doing? Hey look what's here. Didn't you hear? No York Street snots allowed in today, especially you." Everything stopped then—no skates were laced or tightened, people heading out the door onto the rink turned to watch, everybody on the benches sat up, and Howard Streeter pretended not to notice.

The rat couldn't throw you out. Your nickel was already paid. But you didn't say that and spoil his fun. You sat down near the door and took your boots off and stuffed them under the bench where ten other pairs were. There was silence, which was part of it.

"Going to take a hint, kid?"

One word in reply was an excuse to get worse than you were already going to get. And there was no appeal.

Howard's reply was always, "Go tell your mommy." And there was no hurry; it kept on happening whether something was done or not. The worst thing they could do was shove you down the hole in the outhouse attached to the far end of the dressing room. Not all the way down, but close enough to make you think you were going to wind up in ten feet of shit at the bottom.

The idea was to take it. Say you did do something in retaliation and somehow won—only a fantasy, because no one ever did win—say you called the police or your parents, you'd be decked after that every time you came around a corner, or worse. Stories in *Chums Annual*, or *Triumph*, or *The American Boy* where the little guy stood up to the bully and won were stupid. In real life there wasn't an end to the story; it kept right on happening. There were two ways out: one was to put your head down and wait until they were through with you, and the other was to grow big enough to join them. Or not.

Fielder sat down and began to put on his skates. No one picked on him. It was a kind of class thing, or maybe it had to do with being powerful in a certain way. The Police Chief's kid got it the worst. The Magistrate had four boys and they travelled together.

Christopher sat beside Fielder and unlaced his boots. John Purvis was there on the bench down at the back of the room. He coughed and got up and came over. He was nearly eighteen now. He'd quit school when he was still fifteen, but not because he was dull. He never gave a reason.

"I got four from Paraguay." He reached into his jacket pocket. "I ordered a bunch on approval. Look. Twenty-five cents."

The stamps had yellows and purples and bright blues

and reds on them. "You gonna get them?"

"The old man's away again."

Christopher nodded. John's father's second wife looked like a hen with glasses on and didn't want to fix meals for him, let alone give him money for his stamp collection. She had married John's widowed father, who was a commercial traveller, and had her own children since. Sometimes she locked the doors on John, and Howard let him stay and keep the fire going all night so he could sleep on the bench nearest it.

Purvis had a face like a rising moon. It was big — big eyes, mouth, teeth — and its skin was yellow with a tinge of orange. Somewhere in the Purvis family there was Indian blood.

Now he said to Purvis, "I've never bought a Paraguay."

"Do you like these? Four for two-bits is a bargain."

"We could buy two each?"

"I'm broke."

"I could lend you. I've been saving."

Purvis got up. "No thanks. They don't have to go back until December 27th." He coughed and laughed at the same time. "Maybe I'll get a dollar out of the old man when he goes on his Christmas drunk."

"Hope so. Those are good ones. Are you skating?"

"No. I'm making ice for Howard at the supper break."

Fielder got up. "Going to skate or collect stamps?"

"Both."

"The joint closes at 5:30."

"Go then, go."

He stood up and looked out onto the ice. There were maybe a hundred people there, going around and around to the waltz music Howard played through a loudspeaker connected to his gramophone. Outside, a fence surrounded the rink. The boards were grey, weathered, twelve feet tall. Fielder was already warmed up and flying. Backward, forward, quick loops and on to full speed again, dodging between people and bouncing off the boards. It was good exercise for hockey, and it was a game: seeing how fast he could go before Flynn, Howard's rat on the ice, whistled him off.

Christopher left the gate and began to skate stiffly down the boards, and then out into the middle where the ice was nearly clear of people. He rode his skates hard and got them comfortable on his feet. Fielder went by. He chased him, caught him, gave him a hip and sent him into the boards. Fielder came back, grabbed him, and they tripped and fell. People swerved and skated around them. They lay dead on the ice. Callaghan jumped them, and then Christopher looked up and saw Emily swerve away, unsteady on her skates, and hold onto the boards. Flynn's whistle sounded. Christopher jumped up and stood beside Emily. Flynn ushered Fielder off the ice and signalled for Christopher to follow. He took Emily's arm and held her up. "Come on," he said. "Flynn won't touch me if I'm helping you."

She laughed. "I'm not very good at skating." Her face was red. He held her left hand in his left and put his arm around her, because that was the thing to do, and they moved off, not quite in time with the music. He hadn't skated with a girl before, let alone put his arm around one, except when Miss Garrett was invited by Blenkin to come to P.E. to teach them ballroom dancing. Last time, he'd got Monica Lewis to waltz with.

Every now and then she tripped, but he managed to hold her up until she was able to skate again. They were beginning to laugh, and Emily was more relaxed. Flynn appeared in front of them, skating backward. "I told you to get off."

"Come on, I'm not bothering anybody."

"I put Fielder off." He looked righteous. "Got to be fair." He was the oldest of the rats, and on the ice he sounded like a schoolteacher.

Emily pulled away and stopped at the gate to the women's dressing room. "Thanks," she said.

"I'll be back," he told her.

"Not until the next change," Flynn said.

Christopher went inside and saw that Fielder was pitching pennies with Smith. Obviously, he was winning, because Smith wanted to go double or nothing. Fielder nodded and pitched to within an inch of the wall. "Emily Gordon?" he said, while Smith was getting set to pitch.

"We're friends," Christopher said, not sure where the words or the easy tone of voice came from.

"Since when?"

He decided on the truth. "Since the fire."

"I was at the fire."

"Afterward."

Smith pitched. His one-cent piece hit the wall and then it spun in a circle and fell closer than Fielder's.

"Does that count?" Fielder said, too loud.

"Tricky," Smith said. "Come on, gimme."

Fielder gave him four cents and sat down on the bench.

The music stopped, the whistle sounded out on the ice, the people reversed and skated the other way to a new waltz. Christopher got up and went outside. The sun was far gone. In a few minutes the lights would be turned on. He looked up. The clouds over the river were thickening. It might snow. He hoped so. The hills out at the Castles needed another foot or two to make for really good jumping.

He wanted to see Emily again. Saying they were friends in front of Fielder and Smith had released a new feeling in him. He skated hard to hold the emotion down until he saw her in the crowd with Dody Wentworth. They were skating slow and easy. Emily's ankles were strong; her skates stood straight on the ice. He cut in front and faced them while he skated backwards. "You just never tried very hard before," he said to Emily. She looked pleased, and he watched her eyes watch him as she skated to the music.

"Were you skating with him?" Dody asked.

"Until he got kicked off."

"Kicked off?" She made it sound as if he'd won a prize. Emily wanted to skate with him. He could see it in her eyes. She glanced at Dody, and Dody's face grinned. "What is this, huh? Who do I get to skate with?"

"Be on the other side," Emily said.

He turned and skated forward again. Emily was on his right and Dody, laughing so hard she was sliding around instead of skating, held onto his left arm. It was hard going, awkward. Dody never got in step and kept giving him the hip as if they were playing hockey. Emily stood straight on her skates and went stiffly forward. In the middle, he was off balance. People were beginning to look. The lights came on and their shadows flickered around them as they moved along the ice. Dody got control of herself, and then she saw Trudy Olson skating alone. "Bye, you two," she said in a loud voice, pronouncing them gossip, and left to tell Trudy about it. He didn't mind. Fielder and Smith knew. Dody and now Trudy knew.

He looked at Emily, and she said, "Dody's a nut."

He skated with her, his gut-muscles tight and his breath short. It began to snow. The flakes were dry and powdery. By the time they'd gone around twice more the rink was white; there was snow in her hair and, when she looked up at him, he could see it sparkling on her eyelashes. He put his arm around her and said, "Let's see how fast you can skate."

She nodded. "And then I have to go."

He sped up gradually, and she skated with him until the first corner, then she coasted around it. On the next straightaway she couldn't keep up; she collapsed and hung on so that he stopped skating and they coasted until they came to a halt at the women's dressing room.

"Thanks," she said.

"This is the third time—" he stopped, awkward.

"For what?"

"Parting," he said, and had to laugh. "I mean, you never say goodbye. Just thanks."

She frowned.

"Are you going home alone?"

"With Dody."

He did a perfect circle on his skates and wound up in front of her again. "Well, see you."

"Walk with us," she said. Her voice had a low note that made it soft at the edges.

He did the circle again. People had to get out of his way and, as he went past her going into the loop, he told her Yes, and he didn't see her going into the dressing room because he was hit and knocked down by a pair who were waltzing. Flynn blew his whistle. "That's it for you. Off, get the hell off."

"Quit picking on me," he shouted.

Flynn looked at him, surprised. "Kid, do what I say or I'll break your damned arm." But there was a small smile on his face.

Christopher laughed, and ran on the points of his skates at Flynn, dodged him and headed for the gate. It felt as if suddenly everyone was saying Yes.

Half the rink was getting ready to leave. He got down on his knees and felt under the bench where he'd left his boots. Smith and Callaghan were sitting there. "Move," he said, and found them. "Where's Fielder?" Smith pointed. He looked around; Fielder was eating a chocolate bar. "You win?"

Fielder nodded, and Smith said, "There's something stupid about double or nothing. Ineluctably, aromatically stupid." His act was big words. He found them in his dictionary and used them any which way.

"It's okay when you win," Fielder told him.

"Punch him out," Callaghan said.

Fielder began to move. Callaghan and Smith stood up, and Smith grabbed at the chocolate bar before Fielder could get to the door.

Christopher wedged himself between them and put an elbow in Smith's chest. Fielder shoved Callaghan out of the way.

"Outside," Howard shouted from the candy counter. "And watch that hot stove." He sounded like everybody's parents.

They stopped shoving, and Fielder escaped through the door to the rink. Christopher went after him. When they were on the ice, he said, "I'm going with Emily."

Flynn was there. "What did I tell you, Waterton?"

"I'm going. I'm going." He still had his boots in his hands to show him. To Fielder, he said, "Want to come?

Dody Wentworth's with her."

Fielder looked at him. "What's going on?"

"Nothing. She invited me."

"Emily did?"

"And Dody's with her. Come on."

Fielder skated in a circle. "I can't figure you, Waterton. They're in grade eight, eh? Bloody cradle-snatcher."

"Are you coming?"

"No."

"All you have to do is walk with her."

Fielder skated away. It was snowing hard. Howard would close the rink soon. He had a cowbell he rang that meant time was up. Christopher skated back to the door and went in. Smith and Callaghan were gone. He knew what was going to happen now, and it made him wish he hadn't asked Fielder to come. He'd go with them all right, but it would be in his own time and they'd be kept waiting. He changed into his boots and dunked his skates in the tin tub of hot water on top of the stove to get them clean. The door opened a dozen times, and then finally Fielder came in.

"Too late," Christopher told him.

"Don't give me that, Waterton."

"Are you coming?"

"Maybe."

"They're waiting." He could see Dody standing near the entrance of the women's dressing room.

"Where's my boots?"

"How am I supposed to know?"

"We came in together."

"They're beside whcre mine were." Christopher pointed, then bent over and fished them out.

Fielder sat down and took his skates off. Now Emily

was at the women's entrance too.

"Dody Wentworth," Fielder said. "The things you do for a friend."

"Hurry up. They'll leave."

"Why don't I walk with Emily and you go with Dody?"

"Come on, Fielder."

"Keep you out of mischief."

Christopher tied the laces of his skates together and hung them over his shoulder.

He waved at Emily and held up one finger to show they'd be right there.

They moved together to the main exit door. Dody's eyes were big and she was quiet, as if that were protection — like a rabbit in the snow. Emily stood solid as she always did. "Fielder's coming too," he said. He opened the door, and Fielder went out first.

"You open doors real good," he said.

Dody laughed and caught up with him. She was no more than an inch taller than Emily, but she was loose at the hips and the shoulders. Gangly. She stood beside Fielder, looked up at him and then turned to Emily with her eyes wide open and her hand over her mouth. Emily didn't react. She looked away from her and up into Christopher's face. Then she smiled, confused a little by Dody and Fielder. It was a serious thing she'd done and the smile trusted that he wasn't just funny like Fielder was being. They began to walk, and her mitt, wedged between his elbow and his ribs, was a sensation he'd not felt before.

Signing Up:
The Larry Robinson Story
Jim Smith

I was near the back of the Air Canada jet to Vancouver, on the way to the Writers' Union annual convention/ booze-up. It's a position I don't like, too far from the cabin, and I was nervous as hell, sort of like I was in the last minute of that last game against Calgary—the last 1984 playoff game—and then, while still climbing out of Toronto International, I spot in row 26—way ahead of me, that's how far back I was—Larry Robinson.

Well, Larry is one of my very few hockey heroes, since I have never played, and also came late to watching the game. And I'm not sure when exactly I noticed him as a player who struck a chord, but what I do know is there were just about tears in my eyes last year when they rolled that red carpet out onto the ice and after a while Bob Gainey—the captain—gave Larry, the assistant captain—the battered old Stanley Cup, which had been stolen once and found at the side of a road which I've driven on—and a bit later he said (Larry said, that is)—he had waited seven years. Seven years for that moment.

I thought he would retire.

What I did was sort of stupid, but I got Jo-Anne to get

her camera, and I got our little imitation silver Stanley Cup from the bedroom—which I had got for her at the Forum itself, and which had not been stolen when our house was broken into during the semi-finals that same year—and I moved over and sat in front of the television screen and she snapped off two shots, which I still have, of me in my Canadiens sweatshirt, smiling like an idiot with the 3-inch Stanley Cup up in the air beside the colour screen with the ghostly image of Larry holding the 3-foot Stanley Cup and talking to someone out-of-frame just like I was.

And I was sitting back of the wing, which made me nervous but I said that before, and saw him and knew it was him, and I thought well maybe he is going to Expo in Vancouver with his family now that they've won the Cup. I wondered how I would get his autograph because Jo-Anne and I would treasure it quite a bit and I couldn't help but think how surprised Jo-Anne would be when I handed it to her as the gift I brought back to her from my trip to Vancouver. I closed my eyes for a while and thought about how I would give it to her. I would be really casual and say well, I didn't have time to get you much, but there was this little thing, and I would watch her closely when she read it.

I thought about my approach (I don't get autographs well), and figured I would check with the stewardess (that is, I'm sorry, the in-flight service manager), whose name I remembered was Anne. I thought, this is a good omen, since I was getting the autograph for Jo-*Anne*.

But Anne didn't have a passenger roster after all, so I said, well, I'll just go and ask him if he is Larry Robinson myself. Anne asked me to come back right away and tell them, and was excited that there was a celebrity who someone knew was on board. As I walked away, I heard her call the other two attendants over, and say, yes, Larry Robinson was on board.

By this time we were at a cruising speed of 500 mph plus something and we were, I think, seven miles up (one for every year Larry had waited to once again hold and touch the Stanley Cup, strangely enough), and we were over Montana or something with a mountain visible in it and no franchise team so Larry had never played there. I walked back, but he was not there in his seat, so I stood back a bit further, about row 30, just lounging and a little self-conscious since I knew that several passengers on the flight had seen me talking with their service manager and had probably seen her get excited and then talk to the others after I left, and now here I was doing something else that let them watch something.

He came back with his kid, and I waited for them to get settled and then I walked up the aisle slowly, heart thumping away like I was planning on hijacking the plane or shooting a winning goal. I remembered Jo-Anne's definitive warning not to, definitely not to, make any of my usual stupid remarks anywhere in the airport or plane about hijacking, or saying hi to a friend named Jack.

Or bombings or crashes or anything, and when I got to slightly just behind the seat and leaned over and asked him if he minded if I asked him if he was Larry Robinson — a curious construction of phrase when I think back on it — and he said, well, no, but told me that people ask me that quite a lot and I said, boy do you ever look like him and I knew very well how red my face was and he said, well, maybe I should do an imitation, and I said, sorry to have bothered you, and he said, that was okay.

I went back to my seat, which was smaller and more uncomfortable than when I had stood up over Montana, and I didn't seem to fit in it the same way after struggling over my seatmate and almost upsetting his drink and apologizing.

And, for heaven's sake, by that time we were about to begin our gradual descent over British Columbia to the city of Vancouver with its stupid Canucks. How the time had slipped by so fast, I didn't know, and I hadn't even got to the thin sports section of today's *Toronto Star* which I had bought in the tuck shop of Toronto International.

Yeah, sure, I was disappointed. I was humiliated. I was afraid, for some stupid reason, that every one in the plane thought I was gay and had been trying to come on to the tall, skinny red-haired guy, brazenly in front of his wife and happy little kid. The movie I had played and replayed for myself about how pleased Jo-Anne would be when I handed her a Boarding Pass that had "to Jo-Anne and Jim from Larry Robinson" would never happen, and despite this, Larry Robinson, Montreal Canadiens' defenceman, Stanley Cup winner, had saved me from a country's worth of nervousness and anxiety. I thought to myself what a strange thing the human consciousness is and what fascinating games it can play with itself. And others.

Two things came from this trip. The first was that I realized the ability to escape fear was in myself. I could fool myself into forgetting to be afraid. The second was my decision to write to Larry Robinson, and send him this story, about how he helped me fly from Toronto to Vancouver. This way, Jo-Anne and I might thus end up after all with an autograph that says "to Jo-Anne and Jim from Larry Robinson."

I'm a weak guy. In the meantime, I took my Boarding Pass and scrawled a few words across it. I'd have something to show Jo-Anne from this trip after all.

from a novel-in-progress, Salvage King Ya!

Iron Man

Mark Jarman

I skate into the corners and ugliness floats with me. 33 years of TV afterburn in my retinas; the team doctor talks of tests. Below my art deco condo are fountains, a Victorian funeral home. On the back steps of the Victorian funeral home a woman sprays roses blue, in the wind; some of it flecks my souped up car.

I recall: We drove down where big rivers come to pieces in the California breakers; fooled around and fell into murmuring sleep, waking with the great grey ocean spread in front of us, the horizon, the salt tide working in the doors, her boyfriend's new BMW sucking into luciferous sand. *Something pulls us down.* Amazing the room down there, car just starts sinking, to disappear helpless before demon gravity. What will I tell my boyfriend? Tell him, "I lost it." Houses on stilts grin above surf. Later, the boyfriend, big fist in the centre of a curve, a tilt of red atoms, music, nose broken again. Rats, I said. Light and land and sea and sand all run into each other after a bit and you can't see. I have no idea which side my bread is buttered on.

"Is that real blood?"

Iron Man

"As Seen on TV."

Young, I wanted to be hockey's ace, a flash center with a perfect face in the New York Times, with berserkers taking care of each wing, gorgeous brides of Jesus mouthing my name behind the plexiglass. But I ended up playing the point, no-name defence, staying at home with the old goalie, tying up the goon squads in front of the cage.

The beautiful waitress X is taller than me, taller still than the Intended. Such length in the wrist is unfamiliar. She has eyes (What colour is that?), elegant posture, ballet slippers. I imagine a forties apartment, plants into blinds, bookends of first edition hardcovers, terrifying Cape Dorset prints, African heads, borrowed furniture, also a beat baseball glove, a good arm in slow pitch, the restaurant league. Perhaps a thing for jocks.

You're not hockey players, she says to one of the other tables. A film noir dress, pale lipstick, laughing at them.
Yeah, Detroit.
You're not.
Yes! We are!
Show me your teeth, she says.
All three pull out their teeth.

I can't stop staring at her. She makes me shy. Her voice, damaged in childhood by bronchitis, is now husky and sexual; drives me bonkers. I pose moronic questions just to hear her talk. I drink in her section till I'm dumb. Later I'm under a tree somewhere, a river bottom. I have played out my option. I'll catch on somewhere. Or is it over?

Gravity my religion: *Stay up.*

I was with a farm team in upstate New York. A shot at playoff money, then a losing skid, Toledo winning. A forward lost an eye in the last game. We were bounced again. Banished. Exile.

I stood outside that Adirondack rink for the last time, with little but an equipment bag and the car trunk rattling with hacked-up sticks. I put the car in reverse, angling out to flee the sharpened roofs of New England villages, I put the car in reverse then did not use that gear again for 3000 miles.

I love skating in circles before the game; anything is possible coasting ice in that breeze. I'm a battery with two poles: I want to be cool and I want to jump! I'm fossil, an old bird moving my extinct cells through the middle of a mountain. I'm a brain suspended on skates, Mercury coming in for a clean hit.

When playing in upstate New York I noted trees, say a beech, marked by a green X, meaning chop it brother before it's gone hopeless with disease. Some vague malaise creepycrawling through the hardwood, the nations, trees giving up the ghost that shouldn't. Possibly wind damage, said a landscaper. Hardwoods have a great crash, rocking the earth for hundreds of yards, crumping down each side on the shaky upstate cottage where I lived between road trips.

What we have here: Small parts flung from me, pin-wheels and armored sputniks and ghosts of iron gas dust, no problem, I'm taking care of it, alright?

What we have here: is the dirge of traffic, a framebent Chrysler, a chamber driving west, is 30 games; 3 goals and 3 assists, a team strapped in, NO SMOKING lit up, turbulence Utah to Nashville, bleached stewardesses limping up and down the aisles like manic brides, is my heart bleeds. I tried subtlety; what is basic survives.

You don't look married, the beautiful waitress tells me. Her voice, lean face. I try to stop peering into the side of her skimpy undershirt. Dressing for the holocaust. Muscles come up off the ribs, knife cutting green onion, into pale stripes inside, 96 tears, ski goggles. I ate my weight in blue crab. How does one look married?

Alabama. Played with the Birmingham Bulls, Salt Lake City, K.C., Nebraska, both coasts, Billington, Billings, in Saskatchewan for $100 a game, under the table, no tax. I circle and I circle but at least I'm not a gofer, not a messenger wheedling in monoxide. I move and I hit and cause havoc. Swedes stay out of my way. I have garbage goals and shoulder ailments, but I'm no flunky on a bus strap or sweating into a hot dog grill. And most of all, and I can be reduced to my knees thanking whoever over this, I do not toil for the Canadian Imperial Bank of Commerce.

I never play well in L.A.

On the boulevard they're brawling, slashing each others' tires, gluing bits of razor to their boards, aim it at a stranger's face in the water. Aryan surfpunks flexing, defending their beach, their wave.

"Big boards or little boards in now?" I ask.

"Anything Mr Man, I can catch a wave on anything dude. Amateurs out there." He points. "Guys can't surf dick. One old hippie, snap, wave breaks his leg..."

I'm out in the surf like a seal, with They The People, and monster wave action. Woman wiping out bonks me upside head with her board. Her top rips half off, breast bare with California water foaming, nipples hard in the cool; OHMYGAWD! she yells, grabs me, nearly drowning in undertow. To stay up with air in our open mouths. The rich look on at our nakedness, the illegal aliens look on, fully dressed in the heat, the coyotes and chickens look on our nakedness. Firecrackers start up farther up the beach, blood and stitches and computer generated graphics dancing in my head. GET ME A T-SHIRT!!! she cries, hunched modestly in the waves. Pinwheels and rockets' glare, bombs bursting in air etc. I get her my Sid & Nancy t-shirt. Can I take you out for dinner? No, you cannot. Team fined me for a suntan. I never play well in L.A. Fireworks hang in sky like jellyfish tendrils, stars like pieces of light wearing away, a movie wearing out.

Low cloud, skinny birch ride the mist, sky haired with ravens. Can't see thirty feet. Logging trucks gear down in the hills; noisy at night in my cabin. I have retired in a sense to the lake, to the cabin's earthy smell, ska and bluebeat on a reel to reel, cattle skulls and sea-shells on the pine wall, retired to Salvage King Ya!, to the junkyard, to what is left me, to think. I will drive a schoolbus, put coal into trucks, do Joe jobs, anything. *I'll catch on with another team.*

Before the game I put vaseline on my face. Less cuts. A brace on my left knee, swearing when a lace breaks.

Give the grinders credit, says the coach, they're not up on the scoreboard.

True, mumbles the goalie, they're on waivers. Grinders of the world unite, you have nothing to lose but your teeth. Red light on so often the goalie got sunburnt, hawhaw old joke. Listen, dump the puck in—hit whoever the fuck touches it, alright? Got it? Hit. Finish the check. A beer a hit. The Kansas City forward was on fire and they put him out with an axe. The bus broke down in New Mexico and tequila was 60 cents a shot, bottles in Mexico when we slipped over were a buck. The KC forward had to stop, lost too many partial plates throwing up into the river. Bep was coaching. Better like beer, says Bep, cause no hard stuff from now on. After the fight the waitress watched my eye change colour; jade, rose, purple. I liked the attention.

The problems are mental: On the bench in Rochester, panting and peering at the stick's woodgrain, and I wonder what tree is this stick from? Quebec ash? B.C. fir? What feller touched a chainsaw to it? Did that shy woman from Vancouver cycle by it?, and then the coach yells at me to place a few elbows to noses and I fly from tree to bone and I do it pronto. Always a song in my head.

There are some so sensitive they can't go out to buy smokes without writing an epic poem about it. The implication always seems: I'm so much more feeling than you louts.

Pinching in from the blue line, bench shouting BE THERE! BE THERE!, and I catch a puck across the throat. Can't breathe. Cross check 27 in front of our net and somehow put him in perfect position to deflect the puck past our goalie. Everyone stares at me. Mea culpa. I stand up to their forward and he smashes his helmet into my cheekbone, cut; aches for days and I wonder if anything is broken, but at the same time any of it goes down I'm thinking (at the same time) of some woman who sat beside me in school reading about Iago, old King Lear, Mr. Big. They tell me I need to concentrate. I can't lose with the stuff I use. King Lear meets Maxwell Smart.

I drive. An old tractor turns the earth; white birds pivot, gulls gathering as if to mark a whale or school of fishes. Pesticides. Shirt Is Blue is off in the desert shooting arrows at weather balloons.

I drive to games. I loathe the Ohio Turnpike; lost among the big rigs, kilometers clicking, behemoths on a patina of black ice, storm off lake, I'm dwarfed by trucks all around my little car, a dinghy among ocean liners. Uranus spins on its side; I spin my '59 Volvo on the highway from Banff, looking over my shoulder to see where the car is going. Something keeps it on the highway, though I'm facing the wrong way after dizzying circles, stalled. The traffic I passed is catching up. I start it up and drive to Calgary contritely with the **pack.**

The coach gives a stirring speech on beating them in the alley. There is a forward in front of our net; the goalie chops his legs with a goalstick, an axe whacking a tree. They score at that exact moment. We're down 6-0. The coach went white that year, made ads for pizza. Kid, he said to me, you can't make gold out of straw, you can't make gold out of straw. I felt real soap opera remorse. I was cut and passed into the kingdom of invisible, of the inevitable.

I rolled snake eyes. In a mindless fury I tried to get
back to some otherworld midnight. The Czech player
was bald and on the ice, under the lights, his bare scalp
looked green. Women and their walking, unlacing,
snaps and pretty buttons, leaving partners, that pleasant
moment when you drive and both agree it is time to
stop, a quaint cabin near Glacier Park, in each other's
arms for the night.

In Peoria, in the I, the International League, the brawl
went on for half an hour. At the end the captain and
McSorley's brother met at center ice and McSorley
knocked him out with one punch. Happened to the
same guy before, knocked out twice by the same guy.

My waitress X is leaving to a college in the east. The
city will seem empty, just knowing.

In certain skeletal light, mountains leap forward, a
beauty of white thorns, and I think This is how it is on
the moon. From that high ice, trout spray down, rosaceous
graffiti on their flanks, lunkers in search of an absent
ocean. The river straightens and they are hooked by
Americans or their guides.

The coach says to the press, He's greasy but let's face
it, in the playoffs you need greasers. Overhead the
Americans cruise sharkfinned torpedoes through the
balloons, over my Dominion. Two floors below me
bodies are ferried back and forth in discreet station
wagons, grey with smoked glass. Across the avenue at

the daycare, youngsters learn to shrug. They come out at 10:30 on the dot and scream.

Police pass in iron cages. Blue and red lights leap from square to square in rooftop flashers. I-80 on the edge of Nebraska; a new town is a coal glowing at the rim of the universe. Where are we? Tongues of flame on a skull, Wurlitzer playing the country within, pigs roasting on Midwest spits, SAC missiles, riot guns. Where is the waitress? *Have I lost your long body so soon?* The bus pulls out.

The Puck Artist

Levi Dronyk

At the age of nine I discovered that I needed more than food and shelter. Yet I knew nothing of purpose, of what was important to me. There were friends, but they meant very little. Then I saw television. *Hockey Night in Canada.*

It was at my uncle's, during the regular whiskey ritual he performed with the Oldman, while my aunt and mother sat apart from the men, knitting, chatting and shaking their heads over each drink poured.

Over the noise of the women's gossip and my cousins' shrieking, I saw the first goal, scored by Jean Beliveau. Or was it 'the Rocket'? It was beautiful, and at that moment, not knowing that all I wanted was a sense of originality, I found something inside my uncle's TV set.

My imagination surpassed television technology in that I had slow-motion instant replay. For the record, I invented it that Saturday night:

the Canadien split two checks at center ice, left an embarrassed defenceman at the blue line, held the other away with a strong arm as he cut for the net, keeping the puck on his backhand, leaning forward, already manipulating the goalie, a head fake, a dipped shoulder. Clear of the second

*defenceman, the Canadien convinced the goalie the shot was
coming from the forehand; he flopped in that direction just
as the Canadien whistled a backhander.*

The puck was swallowed by the roar. The Canadien
raised his arms, and I looked at my own, skinny, covered
with goosebumps. I heard one of my cousins scream, and
mistakenly thought she was also thrilled over the goal.
But she was only in a panic about her date arriving in
twenty minutes. Apparently, it was a big deal to be going
out with Billy Semeniuk.

Back home that night from my uncle's, while listening
to the Oldlady bitch at the Oldman for drinking too
much, I drew the number 4 on the back of my pyjamas,
and replayed the telecast yet again. Then Sunday, listening to Danny Gallivan call the play-by-play, I scored a
thousand times. Beliveau got two. 'Rocket' Richard, one.
I dreamt of stickhandling across Montreal Forum ice. A
puck was all I had. I needed a stick, and a pair of skates.

The stick came from the lumber yard and hardware
store where the Oldman worked. I hounded him relent-
lessly. He threw in a roll of tape just to get rid of me; all
he wanted was to get back to 'the boys' in the back room,
sitting on nail kegs, sipping whiskey, 'shooting the shit'.
A puck and a stick, but still no skates. There was no
money for skates. The priorities were bread, meat and
whiskey, then poker and used cars. I remember the cars,
as many as five lined up outside the house. The Oldman
turned them over regularly, for little or no profit.

I stickhandled on the icy roads of Blackwater, to
school and back, at noon, at recess, always stickhandling,
head up, hands up high on the shaft of the stick. Down
the road, sometimes having to dodge traffic. Once, Billy
Semeniuk almost ran me over. He swerved to avoid me

and the truck went into a 'doughnut', a complete 360. I was scared when he got out of the truck. He just laughed and told me to keep my head up. But the Oldlady, who saw everything through the kitchen window, said it was 'too much goddamn sticks all the time'. She wanted me to go to church on Sunday, and catechism classes on Saturday. No way. She threatened to 'throw those sons a bitchin hockey cards into the stove'. Fortunately the stove was natural gas, not wood burning.

I didn't blame her. It was the school principal. At a Home and School meeting, he'd told her that if I spent as much time on my spelling and arithmetic as I did memorizing the backs of hockey cards, I'd be an honours student. I stuck with the cards—goals, assists, total points and penalty minutes. The principal was an asshole. He took our class to the Rink once, and I remember watching him skate, arms flailing, legs jerking, the ass of his pants all wet from falling so much and I lost all respect for him. I was the only kid there without skates, and he couldn't have cared less.

At night, when I should've been doing homework, I was out in the back yard packing down the snow with my boots and a snow shovel. I'd line up three pucks and rattle shots off the garage wall. The Oldlady would flick the porch light off and on when she wanted me in. Sometimes I'd ignore her, and she'd scream, 'break that goddamn stick across your back'. I'd send her to the penalty box. A five minute penalty for intent to injure. Then I'd go inside and complain I was the only kid in the world without skates and a back yard skating rink.

I couldn't believe it. The middle of December, and the Oldlady was outside clearing snow, down to the frozen earth so she could flood me a rink. And me with no skates telling her that wasn't the way to do it. She called me an 'ungrateful little bastard' and said I'd be happier when she was 'dead and buried in a grave'. My point was that a successful back yard rink had to be started in October. After the garden was harvested, it had to be dug up, raked and packed down with a roller. Then the boards could be placed, and the flooding would start around Hallowe'en, and with any luck there'd be skating by Remembrance Sunday. I figured the Oldlady was flooding me a rink of bumps and hills in December because I was getting skates for Christmas.

I was wrong. The Canadiens sweater, toque and leggings helped soften the disappointment. The Oldlady cut the number 4 out of an old white rag and showed me how to sew it on the back of my new sweater. I didn't spend much time sulking over the skates situation; talked the Oldman out of some 2-by-4 scraps, and stole some nails while he visited the back room.

I built a goal. The 2-by-4 frame wasn't quite regulation size, and for netting I used old burlap potato sacks, but to me it was the opponent's goal at the Forum. Toe Blake tapped my shoulder. I hopped the boards. I was a rookie, and in the Canadien tradition, I saw little ice time, except for the powerplay. I waited in the slot, gun loaded. Trigger impatient. *Bang*. Red light flashing behind the potato sacks.

My break came when one of my fat friends, Larry Vietch, showed me his new skates. I was jealous, but showed him nothing but nonchalance. He said Santa brought them. 'Yeah, sure.' It was mid-January and I was only sorry I hadn't known sooner. Larry hated the skates. His preferences were food and television, particularly doughnuts, potato chips, the Lone Ranger,

Wild Bill Hickok, the Cisco Kid and all those sidekicks like Pancho, Jingles, and Tonto. We used to play 'guns' in the summer, first thing in the morning, having something to do with 'cowboys' and 'sunrise'. By breakfast time, the fat boy was pooped and sweaty. I'd killed him forty or fifty times, while remaining unscathed.

How he hated those skates. His obese mother withheld doughnuts to get him on the ice. She scared me: it was the fear of being fallen on. I usually waited outside for him, shoveling or sweeping his ice to kill time, waiting for his mother to throw him out. Then he'd skate on his thick ankles for twenty minutes, go back inside and whine that his feet hurt, that he was tired and hungry. She would shout that he wasn't trying. But in the end, he got his doughnuts. I'd tiptoe in, watching from a safe distance, and once Larry was lost in sugar and Roy Rogers, I'd ask Mrs. Vietch if I could try out the skates. More goosebumps the first time she said yes. Soon I was skating like a beloved Canadien, head up, puck attached to the stick blade like it was in love.

The back door slammed. Virgin Mary shook in her frame above my bed. But she was safe. I had her surrounded with hockey stars cut out of *Weekend Magazine*. Memorizing hockey cards and listening to the radio. The deejay mourned Buddy Holly, playing "That'll Be The Day" yet again. It was Saturday, February 7th, 1959.

The Oldman, on his way to the lumber yard to finish the books before opening at eight-thirty, left without lighting the heater. I got up. Remember, 'light the match first, then turn up the gas'. I also lit the stove, put milk on, then got dressed: long underwear with trapdoor; les

Canadiens leggings over jeans, with old 'sale' catalogues between them, all secured with rubber rings; the sweater over a parka; and of course, the ridiculous red, white and blue toque.

My back yard rink, more like the Company's really because Imperial Lumber owned the property, was covered with fresh snow, which I cleared before running down the alley to Veitch's. I shoveled their ice, and the sidewalks too. The shovel scraping against cement woke Larry's older brother. He stuck his head out the door. I wanted to throw something at him. He looked meaner than usual—his eyes narrowed, and fat, liver lips hooked in a sneer.

"Goddamnit Krapko, it's seven fuckin' thirty!"

"Oh."

"Whata ya want?"

"Nothing."

I could see he was looking for something to throw, so I ran around to the back of the house. He thought I was gone. I tried the back door. It opened. The skates. I pulled them out, slowly. It took me thirty seconds to close the door. Larry said it was okay to take the skates, as long as I didn't keep them overnight. A dumb rule, but I respected it.

Back on home ice, I glided through some figure eights, first without, then with the puck. I practised skating backwards, head up, ass out. After firing a hundred wristshots at my makeshift net, I was ready for a game.

Sammy Martinyuk was a drinking buddy of the Old-man's. He built a classy back yard rink every winter for his kids, Kenneth, a sickly boy who kept skipping grades in school, and Sharon, a tough girl who was built like a linebacker and hit twice as hard. She actually played middle linebacker on our Southside, under-twelve football team. All three were out on the ice. Sammy was painting a faded blue line while the kids skated around and over him, jumping as close to his brush as they could without hitting it. Sammy laughed when he saw me.

"Baniak, yak tam kolo vas?"

I answered in English. I'd lost my first language. To compete with 'the English' was to learn their language. According to the Oldlady, 'the English' included everyone who didn't speak Ukrainian. She was also big on 'modern education', whatever that was, and constantly reminded me that if I talked like a 'd.p.', I'd end up with a 'd.p. job shoveling shit for some English bastard with two cadillacs'.

Baniak, eh?

Literally, a *baniak* is a pot; in the vernacular, it becomes a 'dummy'. Among Ukrainians, it's used in a self-deprecating context, or, as with Sammy, an endearment. If 'the English' used the word, or the malicious 'bohunk', which amounted to calling a Ukrainian 'nigger', to address us, a fistfight usually resulted. Two weeks earlier, I'd popped Doug Atwood in the mouth for calling me 'bohunk'. He'd thought to yell and run. He wasn't fast enough.

"Gonna have a game?"

I hit the ice, did a quick turn and stopped hard. The ice spray messed with Sammy's paint job.

"Tchikaj, tchikaj, the paint's not dry," Sammy shouted.

Sharon, never impressed by anything I did, skated by, dipped her shoulder and knocked me over the boards. A *baniak* in the snowbank is how Sammy described me. Sharon laughed. Kenny had a coughing fit and Sammy yelled at him to get in the house. Sharon waited for me to retaliate, but I didn't.

"Hey Sharon, wanna get a game going at Lambert's?" I said, "We could get Fatty and Raymond and Dash."

Fatty Johnson lived next door, so I yelled for him.

"Hey FATTY!"

He was probably listening to his sister's 45s. Once, he played "Splish Splash" fifteen times in a row.

"Hey, Fateee."

"Baniak, quiet, sshh," Sammy frowned. "Why you have to be so noisy? How come?"

"I dunno."

"You old man, he don't teach you like that."

Raymond Krasnik's father glared at me. He was the neighbour on the other side. Old Krasnik never said anything. Sammy said he wouldn't say shit if he had a mouthful. Colonel Nick, Sammy called him. 'Colonel Nick the D.P.' 'Colonel Nick, that dumb prick' was how Sammy began stories about him in the back room at the lumber yard. Colonel Nick was wearing his military overcoat and fur hat. Apparently, he'd been an officer in the Polish army during the war. 'Probably the first one to surrender to that *baniak* Hitler.'

"Is Raymond home?" I asked.

He only glared at me.

"The bugger don't speak English," Sammy said.

Sharon and I left for the Lambert rink, one of the truly great back yard rinks. It was approximately two-thirds regulation size. There were boards all around it, and behind the goals chicken wire had been installed to the height of eight feet. Talk about classy, the goals were of welded steel with nylon cord for the net. There were three strings of lights across the ice and floods at either end for night hockey. Blackjack Lambert, who played defence for the Blackwater Pontiacs, built it all. That winter he'd added a shack, complete with benches and a potbelly stove. It was a courtesy to visitors like me, but I usually walked over in Larry's skates. Besides, Blackjack never lit the stove, and the shack was always full of snow. It just drifted in.

Wayne Dashenko, 'Dash' because he was a fast skater in the winter and runner in the summer, and the Dwerninsky brothers, Donnie and Pinka, were warming up. Pinka had the pads on. A cigarette hung out of his mouth. At twelve, he was already a chainsmoker. I picked up a stray puck and snapped it high. It screamed past Pinka's ear and tested the chicken wire.

"Fuckin' Crapper," he mumbled, "Keep 'em down, ya punk."

Crapper. I hated that nickname, but when your name's Metro Krapko, it's a natural. Fully, it was 'Meatball Crapper', and first used by Blackjack's nephew Robby. I hated 'Crapper'. Robby was okay.

We were honoured that day. Blackjack himself came out to play. I'll never forget it, because he tossed me an old pair of gloves, the palms worn thin from stickhandling, and said I could keep them. Better still, I was on his team. Me, Sharon and Blackjack against Dash and the Dwerninsky brothers.

"Stick to Dash," Blackjack told me. "Smack him into the boards, knock him on his ass."

I took it all very seriously. Blackjack asked me if I was constipated. Then he laughed and slapped me on the ass with his stick. I played my heart out. Dash got his goals, but none came easy. I was on him like ugly on ape. I hit him, slashed him, bumped, hooked and tripped him. I suckered him, out-hustled, elbowed and muscled him in the corners. We had a great time. Blackjack egged us on. We never stopped skating. Like the oil wells across the road, we kept pumping, and like them, believed we'd go on forever.

And old Pinka was sprawling and cursing. I deked him so sweetly, he almost swallowed his butt. He whacked me with his goalie stick and called me a 'fuckin' punk bohunk', which was okay, I said, because he was one too. Blackjack fed me breakaway passes. Sharon hit Dash so hard against the boards that he had to sit out for a while. Coming back, he was feeling just a little mean, and gave me a two-hander across the neck that made me forget it was Saturday. Sharon hit Pinka in the head with a backhander. We all laughed, even Pinka. It was a soft shot. The only harm done was Pinka lost his cigarette, one he'd just lit. Blackjack told him to get his greasy head off the ice. Pinka grinned and dug another smoke out of the pack before getting up.

"Here, smoke this," Blackjack ripped a shot into the upper corner. PING, it sang, grazing the post on the way.

By noon, my fun was over, stolen from me by the arrival of five of Blackjack's friends. Then Robby showed up. There was a game in the works. They were short of four a side. One short. Me. I wished. Then Billy the Kid Semeniuk showed up.

"Aha," he shouted, "it's that time again gentlemen, the great hockey challenge, where the puck artist rises above the scorn of the masses, men against men, boys will be boys, wot, where the weak shall merely fade and the one great puck artist shall inherit the frozen earth to skate upon as yet he dares to skate into the icedream heaven where cold arms embrace..."

"Fuck off Semeniuk," was the most popular reply.

"Blow it out your ass Kid."

"Fuckin' everyone wants to be a preacher!"

"Yeah, save it for Sunday school."

"Gentlemen," he answered, "I hope your blades are sharper than your wits."

"Ah come on, jam it Kid!"

The collective voice.

"You realize of course, that the wit and the blade are inseparable."

"So's yer head from yer ass," Pinka mumbled.

Only I heard him.

We were chased off the ice. Pinka said he knew where there was a bottle of beer. He left blowing smoke rings and whistling "Be Bop a Lula". His brother went the other way, uptown, to the pool hall. Donnie was an ace shooter, the best in town until Pinka learned the cue and became unbeatable. He became famous in Edmonton a few years later. His victoria over Benny the jockey is considered a classic.

'A magic pirouette' is what Billy the Kid called it, the two revolution spin he did after scoring a goal.

'Hey hotdog where's the mustard?' Blackjack invariably said.

'I am ze puck artiste, mmmm wah!'

Sharon and I watched them play. I believe she identified with Blackjack, with his bulk and physical strength. I was with Billy the Kid all the way. He was the greatest. The Oil Kings were interested in him, but Billy didn't care. He was fifteen, nearly sixteen. He called the Oil Kings 'sanctimonious puck busters'.

"Yeah you got a problem, Kid."

Blackjack had dubbed him the Kid, after seeing the Audie Murphy movie, the one with Fats Domino singing

"I found my thrill on Blueberry Hill'.

Billy the Kid scored again, fashioned another whirl.

"Yeah, you still got a problem, Kid."

Billy blew Blackjack a kiss.

"That punk mouth is going to be your downfall."

"This mouth is going to suck the tits of angels."

Yeah. Billy the Kid was something. He walked around Blackjack again, and the puck being quicker than the eye, it was in the net before I'd finished marveling at the first move.

"Child's play, for kids, like me. But what say you Blackjack? What, a man's game? Nay, not for the rough-necks or the toolpush, neither for the whiskey drinkers nor lusty fornicators, right Blackjack? Speak to me, my sage."

Blackjack laughed. One of his friends cursed. Then Blackjack caught Billy the Kid with his head down and knocked him ass over tea kettle. The Kid was dazed. Blackjack looked worried.

"Nice check Blackjack," Billy grinned.

"You okay Kid?"

"Blackjack, ass black, big and mean, biggest *putka* I ever seen."

I could've watched all afternoon, but the desire to play was greater. Sharon didn't feel like going to the Rink, so I went alone. I stopped at the lumber yard to bum some money. The Oldman was weighing nails for a customer. His pals were in the back room.

"Hello *baniak*."

Sammy Martinyuk was there. And Dash's old man. He had the Pacific Petroleum dealership and owned a yellow Bluebird bus to haul farmers' kids to school and back. Louis Lagrande was there. While his wife and children lived off welfare, he traveled from town to town looking for card games. He was the best dressed bum around. They were drinking coffee. No whiskey yet. They'd start later, or sooner, soon as one of them rose from his nail keg to go to the liquor store.

"Can I have two bits Dad?"

"What for?"

"I'm going to the Rink."

"That don't cost anything."

"Wanna get a hot dog."

"Where'd you get the skates?"

"Larry's."

"Where's your boots?"

"At home."

"You walking?"

"Yeah."

"In skates?"

"Sure."

He flipped me a quarter. I crossed the tracks to the Northside. Walked through town. I stopped at the theatre to check out the movies. Playing: *Pillow Talk*. I made a face. The road by the library wasn't sanded, so I stick-handled the length of it. I turned right after the school, stopped at the Curling Rink. I bought a hot dog and watched curling, the most boring game in the world, worse than bowling, or golf. I punished the dog in record time, and left. The Rink was a block away.

It was the facility for all Blackwater hockey teams, from pee wee to senior, that played teams from other small towns, like Gibbons, Thorhild, Newbrook, Fort Saskatchewan, Radway, Bon Accord, Half Moon Lake and Bruederheim. There was adjacent ice for figure skating, and public skating, where Sousa marches played

over the public address. Kids played crack-the-whip.
Adults drank coffee and whiskey from thermos bottles.
Teenagers skated hip to hip, stealing quick kisses.

There was lots of action on the hockey ice. A veritable
free-for-all. Twenty of us chasing one puck. The more
prominent stickhandlers included Moon Myroon, Jimmy
Donald, Bobby Walker, Nicky 'the Stick' Toronchuck,
Harvey Court, Randy Hnatiuk and Les Tarapatsky.
Among the others was my only enemy, Clark Bonk.
I don't know why, but he chose me as his rival. He was
at best, when playing over his head, an average athlete.
I was considered excellent in the big three—hockey,
football and baseball—and was routinely chosen first or
second in pickup games. Hockey was my newest sport,
but I was getting better every day.

Clark Bonk always covered me in the Northside/South-
side football games. I must've burned him for a million
touchdowns. Our quarterback, Raymond Krasnik, was
always looking at me in the huddle, telling me to go
deep. And in baseball, Bonk always had to pitch. He was
lousy. I hit more homeruns off him in one summer than
the Babe hit off American League pitching his whole
career. I should've felt sorry for Clark Bonk. I wanted to,
but my contempt always won.

That Saturday, he was more determined than usual.
Maybe the pirouette I'd adopted from Billy the Kid
rubbed him the wrong way. He kept hitting me with his
stick. I took it, and gave it back. He high-sticked me.
I gave him the butt end. He swung his stick, missed my
head, and I dropped my new gloves, and he dropped his,
just like we'd seen on *Hockey Night in Canada*. I smacked
him in the head three or four times, not one a serious
blow, pulled the sweater over his head, and gave him a

couple more. Bobby Walker pulled us apart. Moon Myroon escorted me to the penalty box. Everyone laughed over that, except Clark, who left the ice, after promising to kill me. I thought nothing of it. I should have.

When I came off the ice, the rink shack fell silent. I loosened my skates to give my feet some air before the walk home. I looked up. He was standing over me. Mike Bonk was a year older and maybe fifteen pounds heavier than me, but at that moment he looked like the giant from *Jack and the Beanstalk*. I thought I heard 'fe fi fo...'

"Bohunk son of a bitch," was all he said before beating the living shit out of me.

Someone pulled him away, or he would've beaten me unconscious. The room was a red blur. All I knew was how much it hurt. I managed to transfer the pain to Clark Bonk's impending death. Bobby Walker wiped my mouth with a wet paper towel. The pain returned. Tears burned. Randy Hnatiuk walked with me as far as the tracks. I remember being grateful that I hadn't lost any teeth. My chest burned, and I felt like throwing up.

"Lord Jesus Christ what in the hell happened."

The Oldlady was surprised, but far too solid for hysteria.

"Got beat up," I said, as best I could.

"Who did it?"

"Nobody."

"Who's nobody. You tell me."

I knew what she'd do. She'd phone, offering to go over and put Mike Bonk across her knee. She'd curse out the whole Bonk ancestry, and later, hound the Oldman. 'Those goddamn Bonks, not one of them worth a shit', and remind him, over and over, 'if one of those little sons a bitches lays a hand on him, I'll throw him in reform school by myself, you tell them that, if you don't I sure as hell will'. I also knew she'd find out. One or two phone calls and she'd know. I told her.

"Mike Bonk."

"Mike Bonk?"

"Yeah."

"Goddamn English bastards."

"Mom don't phone."

"Go lay down."

"Please don't phone."

"I said go."

"Don't phone." I started crying.

"Now go."

She cranked the phone.

"Julia? Give me the Bonks. No, not Bill Bonk! Frank Bonk! Yes, goddamnit, connect me, and get off the goddamn line!"

I fled to my room, hitting the bed hard. I turned the radio up to obscure her voice. It blared "Sea Cruise". While I sniffed and slobbered, Frankie Ford sang 'oo-wee, oo-wee baby', and the Oldlady shouted obscenities, promises and threats, the power of the words left to my imagination.

Asked to kill Clark Bonk, my imagination gave me a screenplay:

> On the football field, after school, with the entire student body circling us, Clark Bonk on his knees before me. Beaten body, he snivels for mercy. The circle closes. 'Death,' it shouts. I bow, sweeping my right arm before me. Three quick steps. I hoist my right leg, connecting perfectly under Bonk's chin. His head flies. Straight. True. Between the uprights, three points. And still it

flies, into the blue until lost in clouds. The cheering circle
tightens.

That was my movie. I saw it many times, frame by
frame, in slow motion and speeded up. Nothing could
distract me from it, not the hockey broadcast on the
radio, neither the music nor the arguing of my parents.
I fell asleep to Clark Bonk's head turning end over end,
floating through a nimbostratus cloud shaped like a rat,
disappearing into the mouth, whipped by the tail as it
came out the cloud'd ass.

My revenge came that spring, vicariously, through
Randy Hnatiuk. It was after Little League practice.
Randy was showing Clark how to throw a curveball,
one of those fat, roundhouse curves that need the
element of surprise to work. Clark couldn't snap his
wrist right, and Randy said that teaching him to throw
a curve was like teaching a steer to read. Bonk threw a
bat at him. Randy ducked. Then, in a most peculiar
move, Randy tore off one of his spikes and charged. He
swung the shoe, ripping Clark's cheek with the cleats.
He further kicked Bonk in the nuts. Seeing him on his
knees, doubled over, blood and tears mixed with insults,
I wanted to kick him in the head, to fulfil the fantasy,
but I couldn't. Randy screamed at him to get up, but
Clark Bonk wisely stayed down. Randy walked away,
to piss in the dugout. We pissed in the dugout all the
time, but only after the coach was gone, and only in the
visitors'. Two years later, when Randy and I were best
friends, we took Sonja Bankow and Cheryl Poderski
into the home dugout and kissed them.

It was the same every Sunday, the Oldlady screaming

that it was time for church. The Oldman, hungover, yelling for peace and quiet.

"Get your ass out of bed. Drive me to church."

"Shut up already, I'm up I'm up, Jesus..."

"Metro, get up, go to church for once."

As usual, I feigned sleep. She could shake me but not move me. 'Okay, you wanna go to hell, you'll go to hell.' But mine was a good fake, an honourable one. I could always wait her out. That Sunday, she was easier on my ears. I guess the beat-up face helped. The Oldman looked in on me.

"You okay?"

I stuck with the sleep act. They left. I got up. The Oldman wouldn't be back. He'd sit at Elsie's until church was over, drinking black coffee, smoking Export A and playing birdie-in-the-bush with his friends, all of them waiting to pick up wives after church. Then he'd go to the lumber yard, maybe to unload a trailer of cement, all by himself, with no help from his friends.

In the mirror, I saw a fat face with black rings, with gaps of yellow and purple, the left eye worse than the right. It hurt to open them. Nose hurt too. 'It's broken.' 'Nah, it's just crooked.' My mouth wasn't swollen enough to keep me from eating. I warmed up some leftovers, *perohy* fried in butter, then simmered in heavy cream, fresh from my uncle's farm. I cracked a quart of plums, and drank the juice straight from the jar. Setting the garbage pail in the middle of the kitchen, I spat plum pits into it. When I missed, it was Clark Bonk's fault.

Getting beat up was no excuse for not returning Larry's skates. All I needed was his fat brother wailing on me. But I had a plan, a doughnut bribe. Larry was the only one up when I got there. He was pouting over the skates, but brightened when I showed him the bag of home-made doughnuts, six of them, three sugared and three others jellied. He forgave me and said I could have the skates again, for the day. I'd been counting on it. So I left him scattering crumbs over a pile of *Archie* comics, soiling the escapades of Betty, Veronica and Jughead. I hated all of them. Bunch of dorks; Veronica the bitch, Reggie the asshole, Moose the dolt, Archie the freckled fag, and poor Betty who only wanted to get into Archie's pants. They were so much smaller than life, each the antithesis of what a comic book hero should be. I preferred the irony of 'Spy vs. Spy', the bullet holes in Fearless Fosdick's chest, Alfred E.'s stoned grin, and the mercurial grace of the Flash.

I arrived at the Lambert rink before any one else. The beauty of the ice, swept clean and flooded during the night, and the brightness of the day, overwhelmed me. I could see my reflection. Something caught in my throat. Then those stupid tears. I quickly turned whatever it was off. I cut the fresh ice with figure eights. I shot bullets at the net.

"Hey Crapper, who fell on your face?"

"She kissed him just once, but oh what a kiss!"

Robby and Billy the Kid. As they laced their skates and taped new sticks, I told them the story of my poor face. Robby laughed at first, then got serious.

"Want me to get him?"

"No, it's okay."

"Never liked him much anyway."

"Yeah," Billy the Kid said, "but he loves you, madly, the unspoken passion driving him to..."

"Fuck off Semeniuk. I don't like him cause the son of a bitch bit my leg in a pile up. If you want me to, Crapper,

I'll fuckin' kill him."

"I'm going to get Clark," I said, "all by myself."

"Thata boy Crapper," Robby approved. "You whip his ass real good."

"Forget it," Billy the Kid said.

Robby gave him a nasty look.

"Really, forget it. It's no great tragedy. Leave it alone. You get him. His brother gets you. Robby gets him. Somebody gets Robby. Blackjack mangles that somebody and so on and so on. Forget it."

"That's chickenshit Semeniuk, that's bullshit." Robby was almost angry.

"Listen numbnuts, there's enough trouble in a lifetime without looking for extra. Skip the grief. All I'm saying is 'be cool, don't get all shook up'."

Billy the Kid whipped his arm across his hockey stick like it was a guitar and he was Elvis. He dropped to his knees.

"I'm in love," he sang, "I'm all shook up."

Robby fired a puck at Billy the Kid, who, after ducking, transformed his stick into a machinegun. Robby hit the ice laughing.

"So Mr. Krapko." Billy the Kid looked at me. "Leave it alone. Let him come to you. Don't ever go looking for it. If he comes after you, it no longer has anything to do with his big brother, right?"

His logic was lost on me, but not his eyes, or his voice, or the way he carried the puck as he spoke. I believed what he said but I also had to believe in revenge for a while yet, at least until my face healed.

"Wanna put on the pads?" Robby asked. "You're ugly enough to be a goalie."

"Nope."

Before he could insist, Pinka arrived. I was off the hook, but had to explain my face again. Pinka figured all the Bonks were 'a bunch of peckers'. I was getting nothing but sympathy. Pinka even offered me a cigarette, a wonderful gesture, considering they were like gold coins in his pocket. He looked relieved when I said no.

We passed the puck around. Picked the corners. Thumped Pinka's pads. We needed more bodies for a game. Billy the Kid Semeniuk directed the conversation. No one pretended to understand what he was talking about. No one cared, but we all listened.

"So you see," he completed the first dissertation, "any kid without an instinctive understanding of the game is genetically un-Canadian."

"Eat my shorts, professor," Pinka mumbled.

"Hockey's in our blood," Billy the Kid added.

"So how come all of us ain't in the NHL," Robby wanted to know.

"What I said, butternuts, is that we all have an understanding. Not everyone has the skills."

"Big fuckin' deal." Pinka wasn't impressed.

"But the game's losing its purity."

"What!" Robby demanded.

"Too much money. It's taking over."

"Fuck off Semeniuk, it's a job, they gotta get paid."

"I know. So it's no longer a game. And all of us have to grow up." Billy the Kid laughed, but it wasn't a real laugh.

"You're nuts, Semeniuk."

"Sure," Billy the Kid agreed, then changed the subject. "Howe got three last night."

"Frogs win?" Pinka asked.

"Yeah."

"Nobody'll touch 'em," Pinka said.

"You're right."

"Fuckin' French punks!"

"Not punk; puck," Billy the Kid said. "Puck artists, those Canadiens, like yours truly," and took a bow.

Pinka did the splits, kicking out Billy the Kid's low shot. Billy picked up the rebound, and without looking put the puck on my stick. I was amazed.

"Did ya hear about Zenny?" Robby said.

"What?"

"Got new seat covers, white ones."

"Everybody knows that," Billy the Kid said.

"Yeah? What about Friday night?"

"What about it?"

"Carol's on the rag, right? All over his new seat covers."

Robby and Pinka howled over that. Billy the Kid only smiled.

"Hope he got plugged in," Pinka choked.

"That's terrible." Robby stuck his finger down his throat. "On the rag? ugh! blah!"

"Actually," Billy the Kid was looking studious again, "they get very hot during that time, particularly at the end of the period."

"Yeah," Pinka chortled, "'specially if they're on the power play."

That broke Robby up all over again.

"You're nuts Semeniuk," he spat.

"I know, I know." Billy the Kid was getting touchy. "So I'm nuts, but what I say is t.r.u.e."

"They're different, man, they really are. We get a hard on, bang! let's go. It takes them more time. You wanna know something? They get a kind of hard on too. They do."

"Fuck off."

"You're nuts."

I'd followed the conversation through 'the rag' and 'getting plugged in'. I understood all that, but this new angle confused me. Again, I wanted to believe Billy the Kid; Pinka and Robby insisted he was making it all up. I thought of mean old Sharon Martinyuk with a hard on, and it seemed possible.

"No, listen you guys." Billy the Kid appeared very serious, his voice edgy. "There's this thing they have, a little organ, right! sort of a bud, and it's like a miniature cock. Like a magic button. Rub it, drives them crazy!"

That was too much. Pinka and Robby cracked up. Billy the Kid split a gut; holding his sides, he swore what he said was the truth, and nothing but. The laughter, of course, was contagious. I caught it. Dash arrived, and fell into it.

"Better than a punch in the face, huh Kid?" Billy the Kid winked at me.

I believed it was. Billy the Kid continued, giving us terms for the exotic things he described. I believed everything the puck artist said. His words inspired my bedtime movie that night. I lined up the girls at school, my cousins, and even more bold, I pictured grown women and tried to find their hidden little organs. I forgot about hockey. The songs on the radio seemed closer, blending easier with what I was thinking, fitting better now than they had with the Forum fantasies. For the first time, the songs became the soundtrack. The hockey passion was suddenly tempered. I had to know about Buddy Holly. I had to know about the wetness Billy the Kid so eloquently described. The new ideal, to be like him, required three things: skates, more sweet music, and the warmth of a strange new escape.

an excerpt from the book

The Hockey Fan Came Riding

Birk Sproxton

THE BEGINNING IS LANGUAGE

1.   The word fan is short for fanatic.

2.   My mother quit going to the rink when she learned that hockey can be heard as well as seen.

3.   The work puck is not in the Bible.

RIDING THE PINE

Riding the pine means collecting slivers in your ass while you sit on the bench. We had a guy on our team who got drunk because he was riding the pine and who rode the pine because he was always drunk. We dressed him for every game though, like a turkey for thanksgiving, just because he was so ugly. I forget what position he played on the ice, but we called him our tight end.

BLOOD AND GUTS

The hockey fan likes blood and guts, especially the enemy's guts and blood. But you can't always tell who the enemy is. One time I got highsticked in the chops and fell to the ice in a heap. Our trainer came running out and when he saw I wasn't bleeding, he gave me a little shot in the nose trying to draw some blood so the other guy would get five minutes.

Once I crashed into the boards with another guy and we started slugging at each other. A woman behind the screen said, Beat the snot outa that creep and I could tell she liked my style. I guess we would have killed each other, but the referee got in the way — stuck his finger in my eye and his thumb up my nose, which wasn't too bad considering it was supposed to be a fight, except that he was the brother-in-law of the guy that I was trying to kill and was trying to kill me.

SONG OF THE STAY-AT-HOME DEFENCEMAN

The last time I tried to score I got knocked ass over tea kettle at the blue line and they broke in on a two on one and tied the game. The coach yelled at me, screamed so hard he got a hernia. I got sent down for two weeks.

Those guys don't send you to the minors, they send you to the mines. You have to work, underground, in the miner leagues. You come out looking like a mole, you get squinty eyes and dirty pores and dirty gauchies, your eyes grow about two inches wider from squinting in the shadows. And hot. You get closer to hell and it heats up. Yup it heats up as you go down.

You have to be there, you can't hot dog around, streak with the wingers, deke everybody out of their underwear, scoring all the time. You just have to suck it up and hang in. Protect things. Stay home and look after the crease. Take the banging and whacking, lay a few good whacks yourself.

Other guys get the fun. You've got responsibilities.

Birk Sproxton

Keep them out of the slot, out of the crease. That's what you're there for. Keep it clean in front.

THE HOCKEY FAN MAKES A POINT ABOUT STYLE

He begins in the third person and then shifts into second: "The Oilers are piling up in front of the net to set up a screen or make a deflection and you have to be tough in there. Why not talk a little to the goalie and try to throw him off his game, maybe cause a breakdown in concentration?"

You are the second person of course, and I am the first, and those guys over there are third, but when you stand here beside me and we point to those guys we can sight along the same finger and see sort of the same thing, so why stick you in the middle of our sights, still within spearing range? That's how people get hurt.

FIRST BLOOD, 1950

Unused to the new zippered style, the hockey fan catches himself, up, short, draws blood, seeks help howling from his giggling sister (two hands are not enough). He maketh a storm; he prayeth devoutly for buttons; he contemplateth religious conversion.

THE HOCKEY FAN HITS MIDDLE AGE

I was right pissed off when I found she had put my skates in a garage sale. We don't even have a garage. Those skates had no blade left so I suppose they got thrown out, like garbage, as if they were worthless. I liked those skates. Pro's and Tacks, the best you could buy in Bell's Hardware in 1960. The boots were short — you had to sew on your own tendon guards — and made of leather, not that rubber and plastic crap they try to pass off for skate boots now. And the blades were steel, too. Just steel—not clear plastic, or blue plastic, or white plastic. All steel. And none of them wimpy rubber nibs on the tip of the heel. Made good weapons those skates. I got one in the head once but I've never seen the scar since I quit wearing a brush cut. Have long thick hair now and long slender eyelashes. And a pair of skates made of nylon, each with a little rubber tip on the heel of the blade.

THE PASTORAL TRADITION

Do you remember when the kids on defence stood back close to the goalie, lifting their sticks into the air and tilting heads back to catch snowflakes on their tongues?

At the other end kids flock around the puck.

HOCKEY IS A TRANSITION GAME

My father used to tell stories about how poor he was. "So poor," he said, "we were so poor we didn't have hockey sticks. Used bent willow branches and horse apples for a puck and snot string for laces. We were so poor we ate turnips all the time. At Christmas we got **cranberry sauce with our turnips and Mother** cut off the bottoms of our pockets so we'd have something to play with."

Now, for my sons, things have changed. They travel everywhere. Now they don't go to the pond; they go across the pond. Last year they played in Finland, Sweden, and the Soviet Union.

Birk Sproxton

THE HOCKEY FAN TAKES SHELTER

One of our games was in a bomb shelter, ten storeys down into Finnish bedrock. A cavern big enough for two ice surfaces, Olympic size, but no bleachers for the fans. Spooky, the ceiling coated with some kind of waterproof stuff, a sparkley white colour: ghost sheets woven with tinsel.

Vending machines guard the stairs and you can see the closed circuit television trained on the stairwell. The coffee has run out. Our opponents are from Rockford, Illinois, west of Chicago. They don't like us and we don't like them. Mark borrows my mitts; he has left his in the hotel. Where I stand, the ice sneaks out under the boards but I stay there anyway, like a dummy until the chill works its way up and down from brain to cock to toe. My feet are cold. My hands are cold. Whoever said the centre of the earth was hot? (Warmest place in the shelter is the men's room, but you can stand around only so long, hands like parentheses cuddling your jewels, before someone thinks you're weird.)

THE HOCKEY FAN GOES CRUISING

The cruise ship (Stockholm to Helsinki) snuggled into the pier at the bottom of a long runway. Down and down and down the chute we slumped, sheep-like, lugging huge wool coats and bags and bags and bags, each lugging three bags full of hockey sweaters and skates, toques and shirts (plastic bread bags), Canadian Club and V.O. (not to mention Johnny Walker Black Label) down and down the chute we carried the bags, dancing to our rooms, we danced through dinner, the ship shivering and shifting its way through pack ice, we dance, light on our feet, side-step the heavy check of tables and posts, we dance through dinner, humming the old tunes, dance on the floor, laughing I put my hand on her bottom (we're dancing), and she lifts her knee just inside my thighs and nuzzles up, gently, and whispers, do you like male sopranos, she did, she said it, just like that and a mean thing it was too considering I had risked a ripping good hernia hauling those bags on board. And she said that to me. Look at her, she's still smiling.

HOCKEY NIGHT IN LENINGRAD

Tonight the boys play outdoors. We bundle up and hustle past the grinning snowman in the foyer, line up for the buses, trying to remember which one smells of diesel fumes and which one is okay. I wear my Leningrad overshoes: one sock, one bread bag, another sock, another bread bag. Warmest my feet have been since we landed in Helsinki two weeks ago. The night is frosty and festive; steamed-up windows filter city lights.

This game is the hockey highlight of the tour (tomorrow we go to the ballet, Friday to the circus). We know they will pull all sorts of crooked tricks to beat us. **The favourite scenario has it that each period they** will ice a different and more experienced team than the last, saving their national team for the third. This is serious. In Finland the home crowd had a special chant especially for our fans. "Go Canada Go," the Canucks shouted. "Go Canada Go Home," the Finns shouted, as if we were Americans or something. And if the Finns didn't like us, and they're supposed to be on our side, imagine what these guys will do. Shave off whiskers, hunch down into their boots to look like thirteen year old kids, stick Tretiak into goal, anything to wipe out the rotten capitalist Canadians.

At the sports centre the flags are straight out, the temperature is minus 20 Celsius. A crowd has gathered and they gawk politely as we are directed into the hall to get warm. We are eighteen hockey players, and thirty mothers and fathers and sisters and grandmothers and friends. We share the warm hall with a few hockey officials, trade some pins and buttons.

Outside in the wind people are packed four or five deep around the rink. There must be three hundred here, shifting, stomping, breaths fogging the soft fluffy snow. This is a community sports centre, sponsored by Aeroflot, big letters painted on the boards. Red and white and orange, we weave into a dark field of fur hats and warm coats. I stamp my feet.

"Fred."

A tug at my sleeve. I have to turn my whole body, my hood is up and I can't see past the fur.

"Fred. You want a drink?" A young man in his twenties. He's talking to me.

"Yes," I say, "Vodka?"

"No," he says, "'vino."

We walk to his two companions, one of whom has a bottle tucked under his coat. He hands me a tumbler, pours it full. We lift glasses in salute. The wine is warm and good.

The second man lights a cigarette. I offer my pack.

"American, Salem Menthol," says the first man and takes one, proud of his English.

"My sons," I say pointing to Mark and Denis, who stand together behind the screen. Denis still wears the top half of his goal equipment; he has just finished his turn in goal (we're now leading 8 to nothing) and he has been quick to get off his skates and back out into the cold. He looks incredibly puff-bellied and skinny-legged, his orange hockey sweater trimmed with blue, a Canadian flag on his sleeve. He looks like a strange exotic bird who landed here by mistake. Mark too an odd creature in red jacket with white sleeves, huge leather mitts, a purple-coloured camera bag on his belly, and a grey Russian fur hat, a coup made earlier on the street near the Winter Palace. Together the boys define motley.

As we light cigarettes, a hand pokes in front of me. I am being offered coins. I shake my head. My friend Fred say, "Nyet, nyet, no beesiness here." We smoke and thank each other as the crowd noise picks up. The Russians attack our goal, but leave themselves open on defence and we break away only to be foiled by their goaltender. An exciting moment. I turn to my comrades but they have disappeared and my feet are getting cold.

In the hall a man gives us postcard pictures of the city. He explains by gesturing with his palms down that the gifts are from the boys on the hockey team. In return he accepts bubble gum. We are invited into our team's dressing room. Two tables standing end to end are spread with pastries and rolls. A giant silver urn of tea shines buddha-like in the corner.

Outside in the wind the goals add up. The Russian boys finally score. The crowd cheers. The wine bottle is gone.

My belly is warm.

Teeth

Fred Stenson

Sixteen minutes and seven seconds are gone in the third period of this hockey game. We are behind four to three. The score might suggest to some that we have had a titanic struggle here, but we have not. Of the seven goals scored, five went in accidentally off skates and legs. Our goalie slipped and fell on one of the other two.

If the technicians who are steadily creeping into this game ever equip players with a device for clocking average speed (an innovation I suspect and dread), this would show up as a far slower than average game. It's a Tuesday night, not long after Christmas, and all a-round me I see that fatigued, glassy look that tells me that the rest of the players, like myself, are lapsing into a low energy coma. At the end of the game, they might have to move all this meat off the bench with a stock prod.

They say that some people play this game for fun. I personally can't imagine it and suspect this of being something cooked up by the owners and the press. I do have a foggy recollection of thirteen-year-old kids flailing away on corner lots in the freezing cold for reasons other than money or coercion, but I also know that I was never one of them.

My parents gave me no choice in the matter. They drove me to the rink late at night or at dawn and counted themselves the finest parents in the land for doing so. The fact that I didn't like hockey was unimportant. I was taught to believe that it was something you did whether you liked it not—like school and community clean-up. For some parents, it's religion or music lessons; but my parents wanted neither Christian nor concert musician. They wanted a big, mean pro hockey player who would wish them toothless Happy Birthdays during the Hockey Night In Canada intermissions of their autumn years.

"Burns! Go on! Com'mon, get the hell out there!"

Amazing. For a moment, I totally forgot where I was. All the hockey rinks and benches of my life merged into one and I didn't know whether I was twelve, eighteen or twenty-five—a bantam, a junior or an NHLer.

I am an NHLer of course. And I am on our toasty warm home bench. The man yelling at me is Chip, our manager, all crimson with rage. And, he is yelling because my line didn't go on when the other line came off. For many seconds, there has been no one on the ice but our goalie and six members of the other team.

One of them shoots. Carrasco, our goalie, gets a leg on it. Another one shoots. He stops that too. We are all cheering now, like mad; but, still, NOT ONE OF OUR PLAYERS CLIMBS OVER THE BOARDS TO PLAY!

"Goddamn you, Burns! Get out there before I break your leg!"

There is a blood vessel on Chip's forehead big and beating like an exposed heart. I climb over the boards and my linemates follow. Just in time to see the third rebound come off our goalie, Carrasco's pad right onto the stick of one of the five players buzzing around his net. The stick flicks, Carrasco dives; but the puck pops over him and into the net. The red light goes on just as we, the cavalry, arrive.

Fishing the puck out of the net, I look through the eye aperture of Carrasco's mask. He has drawn stitch marks on the plastic each time it saved him from a killing blast to the face. The mask looks like a railway map of Southern Britain. From a distance this motif is ghoulish, but from this close, I can see Ronnie's eyes behind. They are red, watery and scared.

"Where were you guys?" he croaks, a dribble of water running out the bottom of the mask onto his padded chest.

I hand him the puck. "A souvenir, Ronnie. You were terrific." I whack him on the pads and skate to centre ice.

Later, after losing the game 5-3, we sit in the dressing room. We grunt orchestrally. A few tubas, a bassoon; I am more of a French Horn. There is no mood to this music, happy or sad; it is just there. Heavy, heartless breathing in a thought vacuum.

Again I slip quietly off to the ice-bound years of my adolescence. I was on the verge of rebelling, of telling my parents to varnish my hockey stick because it was my last. I was thinking about joining a tribe of travelling potters. I was about to do all that when a scout appeared after one of our play-off games. He took me to the best restaurant in town and told me to order as much of whatever I liked. While I ate, he mentioned several multi-digit money figures and I felt a sudden urge to take my hockey a little more seriously.

But, lately, something has gone wrong. I can't con-

centrate, not even on money. I just drift off. I start seeing the fifteen-year-old girls who hung around our
hockey practices. I can see their faces and my memory
has edited out every zit. The shy way they used to lurk
in the shadows when we came out of the locker room
with our hockey bags over our shoulders. I can hear
them giggling, but I can't hear my own manager when
he's screaming, "Go on, Burns! For the sake of sweet
Jesus, go on!"

Chip enters and slams the door. His hair is sticking up
valiantly from its sea of grease. His cheeks are flaming
and he brings the smell of whiskey in to do battle with
the robust aroma of sweat. He stomps up and down
between us, his every movement ferocious.

"You guys stunk out there, tonight!" he shouts at
last, relieving the tension.

Smitty Smith, the cornerman on my line, wrinkles up
his smashed nose and gives an attempt at a loud sniff
which winds up being a thunderous snort. "Still do," he
says, laughing and snorting. "Smell," he adds for the
slow ones.

Chip whirls, his coattails winding up like a propeller.

"Who said that?"

"I did, coach," says Smitty.

Poor Smitty, or should I say lucky Smitty, because,
surely, hockey is keeping him out of an institution for
the criminally stupid. He is regular cannon fodder for
Chip's postgame rages. Chip walks up to him and levels
a finger at the still snorting nose.

"Remember when I told this team that the next time
we got scored on because of a slow line change, some
lard asses were going to find themselves in the minor
leagues?"

"No."

(Chip chooses to ignore this.) "Your line, Smith, was scored on tonight when you weren't even on the goddamn ice!"

"But, Burnsy..."

"Screw Burnsy!" I can't say I care for the sound of this. "It was your line and I might just decide to put all three of you idiots down for a while. Maybe down there you could remember how to play hockey!"

This is a fairly idle threat. Obviously Chip would love to send most of us to the minor leagues and would except for the total lack of better players there to bring up.

"I'm telling you guys this team's on the verge of shake-up! Nobody's job is secure as long as we keep losing. There's three things wrong with you: No hustle! No brains! No speed! and NO GUTS!!"

"That's four," Smitty grins with happy idiocy, not a tooth in his giant head. He is so proud of his deduction.

The effect on Chip is quite fascinating. He begins to sag slowly like a pin-punctured inflatable couch. Frowning at the floor, he mutters in a vague monotone; something about the plane we have to catch to Montreal in the morning. He finishes by saying, "If we play like this against Montreal..." but his voice tails off into silence before he can entirely tell us what we're in for. He shuffles to the door, still sagging. Smitty really can't help himself; he has to give the old coach just one more helping hand.

"They'll kill us," he offers cheerfully.

Chip is at the door by now, with his hand draped on the knob, a rag. Hearing Smitty, he finds one last nerve of fury, yet unexploded. He swings around. His eyes travel the bench on which we sit. His eyes meeting ours. I wouldn't be surprised if there are tiny cross hairs in the middle of his vision. When his eyes reach mine, they stop. His mind pushes the button marked Torpedo.

"Burns. In my office after you shower."

When I step into Chip's office a half hour later, he is gnawing on one of his hands. A lonely cannibal. I feel something for him close akin to sympathy: disgust, I think. If Chip's stomach was a garbage bag, you wouldn't want to carry anything wet or heavy in it.

"You took your sweet time."

"Heavy dirt and grime."

I move a dog-eared scouting file off a chair and sit. Chip waits deliberately hoping the suspense will fill me with regret for my many wrongdoings.

"You're not putting out, Burns."

"I'm the team's highest scorer."

"Look, Burnsy," 'Burnsy' means an appeal to my sporting side. Chip is still under the impression that I have one. "You could do a hell of a lot more for this team. You're a great little hockey player when you want to be. You were a first-round draft pick."

"Fire the scout."

"But, cripes, just sitting there during a line change."

"I think it was my inner ear acting up again."

"Okay, alright. Water under the bridge." Such is Chip's obsession with this game, I'm sure he sees ice on the water and kids with great potential playing shinny on the ice.

He looks up, past my head, at a yellowing photograph of his last winning team; juniors he coached to a national final.

"You could lead this team out of the doldrums." His

voice has taken on that misty monotone again, as if he was talking from the cockpit of a time machine. "We wouldn't have to be in the cellar if you played your best game. Take charge. Like Bobby Clarke. The players look up to you." He pauses, frowns, takes a bite out of his hand and glares at me crazily. "They look up to you and you infect the whole bunch of them with a lack of desire!"

I feel this is a bit strong. I try to instill in them a sensible lack of hope.

"Don't you ever want to be on the all-star team, Burns?"

The answer to this question is no, but I won't break Chip's heart by telling him. The all-star game is sixty minutes of hockey I presently have the luxury of taking or leaving.

"The point is this, Burns, if you don't start putting out, I'm going to trade you."

I shrug.

Chip looks heavenward and grasps the air. Maybe God is lowering him a ladder.

"This rotten damn game! I can remember juniors I coached; big kids, tough as nails, crying their eyes out because they didn't get drafted. And you. Big fat contract. Commercials. Endorsements. And you couldn't care less if we trade you."

Chip rips open the bottom drawer of his desk and pulls out a whisky bottle. He spins off the top and it bounds across the carpet. He drains off a couple of inches from the neck of the bottle and scrapes his hand viciously across his mouth. His eyes are those of a cornered pig.

"What about me? What the hell do I do when I get fired off this tail-end team?"

Teeth

Perhaps Chip could sell endorsements for ulcer milk:
It was the third period of the game. We were behind and stinking the place out. It would be our sixth loss in a row and I could already hear the management baying for my blood. I can tell you, my ulcers were giving me hell. I reached for the mickey of rye in the inside pocket of my sports jacket; but my wife had taken it out and replaced it with a bottle of Abdomal the Ulcer Milk. My first thought was, I'll break that bitch's face; but when that Abdomal got down there and started to soothe...
"Get out of my sight, Burns! You make me sick."

A speedy jaunt in my Porsche and I am home to my luxurious two-bedroom condo by the river. The kitchen faucet exudes a thin stream of boiling-hot water which in former times was a simple drip. The dirty socks, the Kentucky Fried Chicken bones, the cones of cigar ash on the carpet, the beer bottles lying on their sides...

I had a cleaning lady once. She clucked her tongue and said how disgusting. A monkey wouldn't live like this and you a big-shot hockey player too. As a helping hand to a better life, she stole my liquor.

In the midst of all this filth, I sit in almost abject misery. If I was someone else looking in I would sneer. How dare you be abjectly miserable with a salary the size of yours, I'd say. And all I could say back at me would be a lot of whining about too many practices and road trips, about our grueling schedule. I would also plead my peculiar belief about the women of this world.

According to the popular myth, there are a million women in this land who are dying to take care of and slip between the satin sheets with me, a national sporting hero. I believe in this ghostly batallion of beauties with a kind of desperate fervour. I do my best to keep myself attractive for them. For instance, all thirty-two of my teeth are still straight and solid in their gums — a rarity if not a total exception among hockey players.

My secret is regular brushing, flossing and a total avoidance of anything resembling a fight, an elbow or a high stick. It was once said of me by a smart-ass reporter that I could go into the corners with fresh eggs in my hockey pants and never break a one. So what? It's true.

But where are these women? This is the greatest mystery of my life. Maybe they are in bed with my toothless teammates but I doubt it. I have a feeling that they are already married to lawyers and carpenters and accountants and that they limit their goings-on with pro athletes to a sly lusting after our brutishness in front of the colour TV Saturday night. Oh, please. Just one of you. Come to me!

But really, as I sit here in my bathrobe, sipping an orange juice past my perfect, mint-flavoured teeth — my jock strap drying on a chair between me and the national news — I look at my purple shins, the scars on my knees and ask, who in their right mind *would* be interested in this body?

Less than twenty hours later, the gate swings open and the Montreal Forum ice gleams ahead of me under the TV lights. Yes, for the first time all year, we are going to be displaying our talents on national TV. At last, our Moms and Dads across the land will have the opportunity of watching their favourite sons being thrashed by one of the nation's most powerful hockey machines.

We emerge to a chorus of jeers and boos from the rabid Forum fans. Our team name is the Bisons. That name always seemed like a prophetic and fitting title for our team. I devised my own little cheer from it to motivate me across dull spots in the play. It goes like this:

> *Go Bisons go!*
> *Big, stupid and slow;*
> *Onward to'rd extinction,*
> *Go Bisons go!*

The game begins and before it is a minute old, the Canadiens star right-winger has picked the puck from Steve Burke's skates, gone in alone on our goalie Carrasco and popped the puck past his internationally famous weak spot: low, to the stick side.

Soon after, we take a penalty and the Canadiens have us all hemmed in our own end again. It looks like just a matter of time until they bang another one in. I'm staying out of trouble by the blue line. It's safe and quiet there and a nice, short skate to centre ice after the goal.

All of a sudden one of our defencemen takes a wild swipe at the puck, connects and knocks it rolling up the ice. The Montreal defencemen have all closed in on our net for the kill and, as a result, I am the closest person to the puck by about twenty yards. I skate for it and have perhaps the cleanest breakaway of my life.

I try hard to concentrate. I haven't scored a goal in six games and Chip may just be getting serious about trading me. A new team might mean pressure, extra practices, or, God forbid, the playoffs.

The goalie is coming out to meet me. I should really deke and go around him, but I might screw up and lose the puck if I did. Better to shoot now. I pick a spot in the right corner and fire. Somehow I fan. I get practically no wood on the shot at all, but the goalie, seeing what I was planning to do, moved to cover the right hand corner. This opens up a little hole between his legs and, through that hole, my meagre shot trickles. It has just enough momentum to get over the goal line into the net. The period ends 1-1.

During the intermission, Chip tries to tell us that the Canadiens aren't that tough. We'll take 'em boys, he says. This is such a good one that several of us cannot stifle laughter.

Halfway through the second period, pucks start streaming past Carrasco's stick side. Every time we make a big effort to stop this shelling, we take a penalty and they pot another one. After the fifth goal, Carrasco comes skating over to the bench like a man possessed. He tries to open the door into the bench but Chip holds it shut from the other side.

"What's wrong with you? You're not hurt."

"Lemme in," Carrasco whimpers. "I saw it again."

He jerks his mask off. His face is white. A drop of sweat jiggles crazily on the point of his chin. "I saw the ghost again. He had on a white uniform. He skated in on me laughing. His teeth were all black. He slapped the puck and it went right through me! Right in one side and out the other!"

"You stop talking like a nut and get the hell back out there!"

Bond, our captain, leans over. "Jeez, coach, let him come out. He won't stop nothing like this. It's a mental problem."

"You're damn right he's got a mental problem. He can't stop a G.D. thing on his stick side. That's the problem!"

Carrasco stops yanking on the door. He throws

his goalie stick up into the crowd and climbs over the boards. He beats his way past Chip and runs on his skates down the alley to the dressing room.

"Fart!" screams Chip. "No one else in this league has half the crazy bastards I do. Bordeaux, get in there."

Bordeaux is our back-up goalie, a fuzz-faced kid from Montreal. His hometown is the very last place on earth he ever wanted to appear — on TV yet — playing behind a cheesecloth outfit like the Bisons. But fear drives him to brilliance and the second period ends without further scoring. 5-1 Canadiens.

In the third period, I score again. If the TV colour man was to discuss my goal after the game, he might describe it this way:

Burns was parked out in front of the net jostling with a defenceman and keeping up a constant stream of chatter. 'Watch it, you bastard, you almost got me in the eye. Hey, ref, this guy's trying to hack my head off here!' All of a sudden a defenceman on Burns' team winds up for a slapper from the point. It comes in like a bullet and, well, nobody could jump higher on skates than Burns when he thought he was going to get hit by the puck. So, there it was, the puck doing about a hundred and Burns up in the air this high; the puck hits his skate blade, whango! and it's right in the net. Heck, I must have seen Burns score five goals that way over the years.

But, the colour man won't be discussing my goal as it only serves to make the Habs mad. They come storming back scoring on poor Bordeaux almost at will. Soon, the Montreal crowd are cheering wildly every time the kid stops a dribbler.

Then, it happens. Steve Burke, who has been on the ice for every Montreal goal, goes nuts. He boards the

Canadiens' superstar right-winger so hard a pane of plexi-glass falls out into the crowd. The super-star drops as if shot and does not move.

The rest is axiomatic. Two of the Montreal players go for Burke with sticks up and threatening. One of our boys goes in to even up the odds. The referees race over to try and prevent total war. Fat chance. The super-star still isn't moving. His eyes are closed. He may be dead. All the Montreal players come storming off the bench which means that all our players must storm off the bench too.

I am on the bench and would love to stay here. But it just isn't done. All these things are as pre-ordained as the order of events at a Vatican high mass. I file dutifully onto the ice with my gloves held by the gauntlets and skate around the perimeter of the six fights now in progress, trying to look as unmenacing as possible.

The super-star is up now. Unhurt, and forgotten. The crowd that was gasping in fear for his career seconds ago is now too busy watching the fight to notice him up and skating off the ice. Right now, he's unimportant. One fight is busy spawning another. Oaths wing hither and thither in need of bilingual translation. Fans are up on their feet, clinging to the plexi-glass and crying for blood.

In the midst of all this bloody hubbub, it happens again. I begin to drift. I drift down the thousand or so benches I have sat on and pick up not a sliver. I drift right back to Buffalo Flats, the Alberta small town where I was allowed to live for a few years before I had to move on to bigger centres and better coaches. I am with a girl I had forgotten existed. Her name is Paulette. We're thirteen and we're in the dark beside the rink. She is letting me put my hand up under her heavy woolen sweater. It is the first time I have ever done this. It is freezing cold out. One of my ears is totally numb, but I don't own a hat. Hats are sissy. It's so cold that Paulette is afraid we might freeze solid. I think one part of me is already afflicted, but I don't tell her this. She may be able to feel the evidence anyway. She is most worried about freezing solid because it would mean that we would be found as we are; with my hand up her sweater.

I am so far gone, so absorbed in these philosophical matters, with Paulette and her sweater, that I hardly notice the kid who races over to me, screeches to a halt in a spray of ice and grabs hold of my sweater. I hardly see his pimply, writhing face, his madman eyes. I hardly hear the stream of abuse from his toothless mouth. While I am in Paulette's sweater, he is trying to pull mine over my head. Unable to do this and frustrated to total insanity by the faraway, seraphic smile on my face, he lowers his head and drives the top of his helmet into my mouth.

This, I feel.

Suddenly, Paulette is gone. Her sweater. Buffalo Flats. All banished back to the foreign past. The crazy kid is gone somewhere too. Dragged off by a referee or maybe by one of my teammates. I am back in the Forum. Standing at centre ice. I look down at the red dot and it is getting redder by the second, dyed by a stream from my mouth. A quick lick tells me that one of my two perfect, well-flossed and brushed front teeth is no longer occupying its traditional place in my healthy gum. I don't remember swallowing it. Slowly, I skate around the ice looking. It's got to be here somewhere. Teeth don't just vanish.

Then, I am corralled by our trainer and two of our players. I keep telling them I must find my tooth, but they are pushing me along toward the gate.

On the narrow bench in the dressing room. Mouth wadded full of cotton batting. The muffled roar of the crowd as the game peters out to its lopsided conclusion.

The game ends. The team trudges in. Chip follows, raving about a shake-up. I am not around to be raved at, however. I am off in the near future this time, rather than the distant past that I so often visit. In this near future, there are sticks but they are all embedded in weinies or the soft belly of an ice-cream bar. There are pucks too, of bacon. Body checks come annually at the doctor's office and he always announces that you are in great physical condition. Afterwards you go home to your pad, an old fashioned but modest and clean apartment. Meeker is someone more meek than someone else.

Somehow, every time I lick up under my swollen lip, I am reminded of this near future and the many sources from which money can come. Money, unlike teeth, can be replenished. A missing tooth is a hole in your head for life.

The Hockey Game
Wes Fineday

The knocking at my door woke me up. It was a Saturday
morning, which meant that there was no school. I got out
of bed, got dressed, then walked out of my bedroom and
across the hallway to the bathroom. The door was closed.
Someone was in there. I went back to the bedroom,
made my bed, picked up my books and put them on the
dresser. I had been doing my homework just before I
fell asleep. There was still quite a bit to do.

Grade nine sure wasn't easy, at least not as easy as
grade eight. I had finished my grade eight at boarding
school last year, had done quite well in fact. This year
was different. The Department of Indian Affairs had
sent me to live in Moose Jaw to do my grade nine. They
had explained to me that they had found me a "good
Christian boarding home" to live in. They also told me
I should consider myself lucky to have this opportunity.
At the time I wondered if it would be anything like the
school I had left.

I went back to the bathroom. It was vacant. I had a
good wash and went back to the bedroom.

They had driven me to Moose Jaw from the boarding
school and with that move everything had changed.

The Hockey Game

Now I was in a bedroom by myself instead of a dormitory with thirty other kids. The food eaten by these Christians was unlike anything I ever got at boarding school or at home. For breakfast they would eat dry cereal and pour milk over it to make it soggy. With this they ate toast that was also soggy with butter. For lunch and supper we would have meat and potatoes or rice. I'd eaten these before but not the way this woman cooked it. She used tomatoes and stuff that looked like powder that she kept in small jars over the stove. She must have had twenty different kinds of powder. It was awful. My stomach would hurt for hours after and sometime I would get ill and bring it all up.

When I tried to tell her that I couldn't eat the food she called me ungrateful and told me my parents would be glad to have something like this to eat. I doubted that. My parents liked eating rabbit and bannock, berries and potatoes just fine. But I didn't tell her that. Arguing would just get me into more trouble.

Another knock at the door. "Come and eat your breakfast," called a voice from the other side of the door. I got up and followed my landlady to the kitchen. There on the table was my breakfast — cereal, toast and milk.

While I was eating breakfast, the woman who was my landlady explained to me that they were going on a family outing. "Not too many more nice weekends before the snow comes," she said. "We're going to take advantage of this one." I could hear their two little boys playing downstairs in the basement. They were playing with the electric train set their father had set up down there. I was not allowed to go near it. I was also not allowed to play with their two boys without permission. I wondered about that sometime. I did not understand why they treated me so differently from the way they treated everyone else. I suspected they did not like me. The landlady's voice intruded on my thoughts.

"Drink up your milk now, and don't bother coming back until nine o'clock this evening. The house will be locked." These Christians sure don't trust Indians, I thought as I got up and took my dishes to the sink.

After breakfast, I wandered outside to the back yard. The landlord was already out there washing his car. I sat on the back steps and watched him. "Come over here and give me a hand with this," he called. So I did. When we were finished washing and waxing the car, he went back inside and soon they all came out. They seemed to be in a good mood, laughing and talking about the wild animal park. I got up and headed for the sidewalk and started walking down the street. I had nowhere to go, but I thought they would get mad if it looked like I was going to hang around the house all day. I was barely half a block from the house when they drove by. The parents were in front, looking straight ahead, the kids were sitting in the back, looking around. They waved as they went by. I waved back and smiled, trying to look happy.

I watched until the car turned the corner two blocks down the street, then I turned around and walked back to the house. I went into the back yard and stood on the backstep for awhile and finally sat down.

The back yard was separated by a tall picket fence from the yards on either side of it. There was also a garden at the back.

The neighbour's back door opened. A man and a woman followed by a little boy stepped outside. They did not see me. The man was dressed in shorts and a tee shirt, the woman in a bathing suit. They sat down on a couple of lawn chairs, which were placed around a small table. The little boy ran to the end of the yard, where there was a swing and slide and a sand box full of toys. I looked back at the parents. They had been joined by a small black dog with short curly hair. He was sprawled on the ground between the two people, soaking up the sun. I got up from the steps and went a little closer to the fence so I would be out of sight. They might get mad at me. From where I now sat, I could hear them talking about the new car they were planning to buy. The man talked about a contract for playing hockey. This meant they could get a new car. He also had another job. This would take care of their other bills.

I thought about my parents and family at home. My dad had more than two jobs. He had to catch horses before he could do anything. This was a job in itself. Our horses could run very fast and jump fences. Then he had to drive them out to the bush so he could chop wood and haul it home, where he sawed it into small pieces so it would fit into our cook-stove. He also had to haul water. And hunt. He usually did this when he was out in the bush chopping wood. I could see him standing on top of a load of wood on the sleigh, or maybe walking beside it if it was really cold. It was better to keep moving on very cold days. There would usually be a rabbit or two and sometimes even three if he was lucky. We used to run outside to meet him and fight about who would carry the rabbits into the house to give to my mom. She was very good at cleaning and skinning rabbits. She had been doing it for years.

Too bad my dad couldn't get a job playing hockey, I thought. I was sure the folks back home who played hockey didn't get paid to do it. They just did it to be together and have fun. I had heard my dad telling a story to some people about a hockey game. They had cleared the ice on a section of the creek that runs through our reserve. A group of young fellows had got together to have a game. There were just about enough of them for two teams, but one of the teams was minus a goaltender. They managed to talk Leo, who didn't know how to skate, into putting on a pair of skates and being their goalie. Leo shoved some newspapers up each pantleg and wrapped them around his ankles and tied them up with twine. Two of his teammates supported him on either side and pulled him out to his goal. He managed, barely, to stay on his feet by propping himself up with the crude goalie stick someone had hastily nailed together for him. For a puck, they were using a freshly frozen piece of horse dropping they had picked up in someone's barn. Dad said these really smarted if they hit an unprotected spot. The other boys had chopped down suitably curved willow trees for hockey sticks.

Leo's team won the game. Ecstatic over their victory, they all rushed off to the fire, which was roaring beside the creek. They didn't notice Leo until someone started laughing and pointing at the rink. There was Leo, crawling across the ice on his hands and knees toward the fire, dragging his stick behind him.

I smiled remembering the story. Suddenly, I heard a car starting. I had forgotten about the people next door. While I had been thinking, or daydreaming as my teachers called it, the neighbours had moved back inside. Now they had come back out and were about to drive off in their car. I looked up at the sun and realized I had been sitting there daydreaming all morning. And now I was hungry.

Back home if you were hungry you just went somewhere to visit at mealtime and you would be sure to get fed. I decided to give it a try. I tried to think of someone I could go and visit. There was Allen, who lived across the street and was in my class at school. But he hadn't been very friendly to me. I decided not to go over there. A few houses down lived another kid who was in my class. His name was Robert. He had asked me if I wanted to come to the field beside their place and play football. I had wanted to but I didn't know how to play football, so I had declined the invitation.

I got up and walked down the street. When I reached their house I almost turned around but I was hungry. I thought it was a funny thing no one ever used their front door since it was closer to the street. They all used the back door. Our house at home only had one door so we had no choice.

I stood there trying to muster the courage to knock on the door. The screen door was the only obstacle between me and the food I could smell cooking inside. That spurred me on. I knocked and waited. I could hear voices and finally a very tall lady came to the door.

"Is Robert home?" I asked, hoping she would invite me in.

"Yes, he's in," she replied. "But he's having his dinner. Why don't you come back in half an hour or so? He should be finished by then." With that she closed the door and walked away. I felt embarrassed, thinking she must have known why I was there. Well I wouldn't try that again. I turned around and retraced my steps to the back yard of the house where I lived. It was then I noticed the carrots in the garden. Too dangerous, I decided, my landlady would notice if I took even one. I sat down by the fence and immediately fell asleep. I must have slept most of the afternoon, because when I awoke the neighbours were back. I could hear them talking on the other side of the fence. I got up and went over to the fence. There was an outside tap sticking out of the wall of the house. The landlady ran a hose from it to the garden to water those carrots. I thought of them again. My hunger had returned. It was more urgent now. I turned on the tap and let the water run over my arms and hands. It felt cool and refreshing. I cupped my hands and filled them up, stuck my face in the water and felt a tingle go all the way down to my toes. I was awake again. I dried myself off with my shirt sleeves. Then I went and sat back down in my spot. There I felt safe.

"Make mine kind of rare, I like it like that," said the woman. Suddenly I was blasted by the aroma of meat cooking over a fire. I knew the smell, having often eaten meat cooked over a fire. I was just drifting off on memories of home when the man next door yelled, "That damn dog!" Just then the dog came bounding around the corner of the fence and into the yard I was in. It was carrying a steak in its mouth. The man was not far behind. He came running around the fence, still carrying the huge fork he must have been using to turn the meat. So preoccupied with what was behind it that it totally ignored anything in front of it, the dog ran right into me. The dog and the man came to a dead stop.

"Well, hello there. I didn't think there was anyone home here," the man said to me.

"There isn't," I answered. "They went somewhere for the day. They're not going to be home until around nine o'clock."

"Do you live here?" he asked, seeming to have forgotten about the steak.

"Yes," I answered.

"Have you eaten yet?"

"No," I replied, not daring to look at the man.

"We were just going to eat. You could join us if you wanted to. Come on," he urged. I did not need much urging. He speared the steak the dog had dropped, turned around and started to walk back into his yard, his dog and me close behind.

I did not leave any of the huge steak they served me. I could barely move, but I somehow managed to put away a large helping of ice cream for dessert. It was the best meal I had eaten in a long time.

The man's name was Jake. It turned out that he played hockey for the Moose Jaw Canucks. He gave me a couple of tickets to the next game against the Regina Pats. I didn't go to the game but I hope they won.

Wives

Peter Behrens

My friend Pierce Harkin lived with his wife on City
Councillors Street in Montreal. I'd played hockey with
Harkin at McGill, but I hadn't seen him in ten years.
After graduating, I'd gone to Toronto and gotten a job on
a newspaper. I married, was sent to Europe and then to
Indonesia as a correspondent for the Canadian Broad-
casting Corporation. My wife died in Indonesia and I
came home.

I met Harkin on a Sunday afternoon while I was walking in Mount Royal Park. He was a good-looking man
with sandy hair that was thinning on top, and a hard
middleweight's build. When I recognized him on the
carriage road beneath the Cross, he was wearing an old
tweed jacket and a pair of English corduroys. It was the
last Sunday in September and the carriage road was
littered with red and yellow leaves.

I hadn't had close friends at McGill but I'd always
liked Pierce Harkin. He had a cleanliness about him and
he never lied. We used to sit in the locker-room after
practice and talk of books we'd read. He spoke French
perfectly and was aiming for a political career. He had
good manners and behaved the same way to everyone,

with easy, unconscious grace.

We walked along the road to the Chalet and he told me
he and Luc Fortier, who'd also played for McGill, had
started their own law firm. I told him I'd quit the CBC
and was working as a correspondent for a group of British
newspapers. Pierce wanted to go downtown and have a
drink, but I told him I had other plans.

"We're having a party at Thanksgiving," he said.
"Why don't you come?"

"I'd like to, but I might be working in Ottawa."

He was already scribbling his address on a piece of
paper. "Not on Thanksgiving! Look, come if you get the
chance. It's good to see you!"

We shook hands and I watched him walk away through
the Sunday-afternoon crowds, with his soft, well-fitted
jacket and his comfortable stride.

I was in Ottawa the week before Thanksgiving and
almost forgot Harkin's invitation. I only thought of it
Saturday night as the train was coming into Montreal.
I wondered whether or not I would go, as I walked out
through Windsor Station. The station always affects my
mood, particularly in the autumn, when the floor is
strewn with leaves blown in from Lagauchetiere Street.

The next morning I spent a couple of hours reading the
papers, then had lunch at a cafe on St-Denis street. I had
a beer with lunch and a coffee afterwards, and sat until
the shadows fell across my table and the air got cool.
I went for a long walk on the Mountain and came down
the carriage road as the light was fading. The dusk
smelled of leaves and cold earth, and I made my way
through the still streets to Pierce Harkin's.

He lived in the middle flat in a three-storey building.
I climbed up an iron staircase and rang the bell. I could

hear the sounds of a party, and when Pierce opened the door the hallway behind him was crowded with guests. We shook hands and he pulled me inside and introduced me to Katherine, his wife. She was wearing a red wollen dress.

"You're Jack McDermot," she said, placing her hand on my wrist. "I met you in once in Toronto, at a woman called Betty Wilder's, do you remember?"

"No, but I'm pleased to meet you."

She reminded me of women in Rome, with her wide shoulders and black hair.

"Do you live in Montreal now?" she said. "Didn't you use to work for the CBC?"

"I used to, I don't any more. I work for some papers in England. I live in Carre St-Louis."

"Good for you," she said. "I like it down there." She sipped some wine. "Pierce said you'd know these people."

I looked at the guests crowded in the hall. "I might know some of them, but I've been away from Montreal for quite a while."

"You met Pierce at McGill, didn't you?"

"We played hockey the same year. What do you do?"

"I'm a photographer. I knew your wife, you know."

"Did you?"

"Yes, I just wanted to tell you. Not well, but I knew her, we went to school together. In Toronto, you know. I think the last time I saw her was when I was seventeen. She was a year ahead of me. I always liked her."

"What do you take pictures of?" I said.

She took another sip of wine. "This week I was taking pictures of Haitian cab drivers downtown."

"Good for you," I said. "I'm glad to have met you. I like your dress."

She laughed. She had a soft, clear laugh that reminded me again of women you see in Rome, walking through the Borghese Gardens with their elegant boyfriends.

I recognized only one of the guests, a woman from the Ottawa press gallery who seemed surprised to see me. Most of the others were lawyers. Pierce offered me a bottle of Danish beer. "Got any skates?" he said. His face was flushed. The room was warm and smelled of nutmeg and furniture polish.

"What?"

"Skates. Do you still own any?"

"I haven't skated since college."

"There's a bunch of us playing Thursday nights at the Winter Stadium. We could use another player if you're interested."

"Thanks. I'm not in town very much. I don't have any equipment."

"We can always dig you up some gear. It's a terrific way to keep in shape, more fun than running or squash. That stuff's for masochists. You don't have to be a regular, either. I'll give you a call some time. Nobody gets hurt. We keep the sticks low and go easy on the checking."

Later in the evening while the party was still going on, Pierce led me to his study in the back of the house. The walls were lined with books and with photographs Katherine had taken. He took a bottle of cognac from a drawer in his desk and poured us each a glass. I began looking through his library and he pointed out a couple of books he thought I should borrow. My books were all in storage somewhere, I couldn't even be sure which continent. He leaned against the desk, sipping cognac. His eyes were triangular-shaped and colored the bright, hard blue that makes you think of the Atlantic in July.

When I left some time after midnight they were out on the sidewalk, saying goodbye to their guests. Katherine kissed me on the cheek and Pierce said he'd phone about the hockey games. While I was walking away, carrying the books I'd been lent, I heard Katherine's clear, careless laughter, and looked back to see her and Pierce waving goodbye to a carload of guests. In the streetlight I saw how his arm held her around the waist and how she wore his tweed jacket gathered at her shoulders.

Pierce phoned two weeks later and asked me to play hockey at the Winter Stadium. Young lawyers are good at making arrangements and I found myself suiting up in borrowed equipment the next night and pulling on skates for the first time in ten years. Afterwards I bought skates and started playing once or twice a week. I was in poor shape but began doing conditioning exercises Pierce showed me. Pierce and Luc Fortier were the best players. When we'd played for McGill the League had been very rough—Fortier still wore a bridge in place of the teeth he'd lost at a championship game in Trois-Rivieres. At the Winter Stadium, however, it was a gentleman's game. There were no set teams, we improvised by sorting through whoever turned up on a particular evening. Everyone got his share of ice time. The players reminded me of boys I'd known at private school. They played for diversion and for comradeship. All were married, and most had one or two young children. In the locker room they told jokes about their wives.

Pierce was hurt in December. By that time the ground on Mount Royal was hard as iron, the trees stripped of leaves. He was a good player, a fast, tough wing who wasn't afraid to chase the puck into the corners and usually came out with it on his stick. We were digging for the puck when the blade of my stick came up and caught him in the eye. The game stopped and all the players rushed over the boards.

There was no blood but the eyeball, milky-colored, was bulging in the socket. Pierce kept cupping his hands as if he were trying to press the swelling down. It took two of us to hold him still while Fortier brought his BMW to the front door of the rink. We carried Pierce out to the car. Two men got in the back with him and I sat in front with Fortier.

We brought Pierce in to Emergency at the Royal Victoria. After he was wheeled away, Fortier went to phone Katherine. The other players began arriving with our street clothes. Fortier got hold of a staff doctor who knew Pierce, and who promised to find out what he could. A few minutes later the doctor returned to say Pierce wouldn't be released and there was no point in any of us waiting. Fortier said he'd stay until Katherine arrived.

I walked out to the hospital parking lot and watched the other players get into their cars. It was dark and had started to rain. I watched the cars drive away, then went back inside and sat in one of the chairs in the corridor.

A few minutes later Katherine came in at the other end. She stood by the nurses' desk talking with Fortier and the doctor who knew Pierce. She was wearing a navy blue overcoat and a scarf tied loosely at her neck. As I walked over, she was telling Fortier to go home, there was no reason for him to stay. He picked up his equipment bag and kissed her on the cheek. He brushed past me and walked away down the corridor.

Katherine asked the doctor when she could see her husband. She reached for my hand and squeezed it. The doctor said he'd find out where they had taken Pierce. When he had gone off, Katherine and I sat down on a pair of hard plastic chairs.

I had often thought of her that fall because she was the only person I still knew who had known my wife. We'd never spoken of my wife again, though. I described Pierce's injury. "You mustn't blame yourself," she said. An East Indian family sat facing us across the corridor. The mother was cradling a sick infant and the father and grandmother seemed to be arguing, quietly and bitterly.

The young doctor returned and took Katherine to see Pierce. She came back a few minutes later. "He's all doped up. He looks terrible. They're going to cut out his eye."

A nurse suggested we go to a waiting room in the surgical wing and we followed her down pale green corridors. The room where she left us was empty and smelled of floor polish. Katherine removed her coat and we sat in leather armchairs. There was music playing over invisible speakers. We sat without speaking and Katherine lit a cigarette. When the music stopped, I could hear the whirr of the electric clock above the door.

"You can go if you want to, Jack. There's really no reason why you have to stay."

I got out of my chair and went to the window that looked out over the mountainside. The rain smashed against the glass in big, angry pellets.

"Pierce is awfully lucky," Katherine said. "He'll pull through this all right. Hospitals are really funny places, aren't they? It would be a good place to spend a week with a camera, roaming the corridors. You'd have to be careful not to bother anyone, but you could get lots of powerful stuff. I hate these waiting rooms, though."

"The last time I was in a hospital was when my wife died," I said.

"I knew your wife, she was a very lovely girl."

"You went to school with her. You probably even knew her before I did."

"Probably. She was the year ahead of me, so I didn't know her well, but she was one of those girls I looked up to. When did you get married? Was she ill for a long time?"

"It happened suddenly. She died in Indonesia, you know."

"There was a notice in one of the alumnae letters."

I moved away from the window. She'd taken off her scarf and her neck was very white. "Hospitals in Indonesia aren't anything like this," I told her. "And it wasn't in one of the cities or the big towns—it was in a place you've never heard of. I'd never heard of it before. Maybe Pierce has heard of it, he reads a lot, he knows things like that. The hospitals are very dirty. No one speaks English."

Katherine glanced at the clock. "I'm so tired," she said. "I was up at six this morning, there was stuff in the darkroom I had to do. Then I was shooting all day."

"Don't worry," I said. "Pierce will be all right."

"Yes, he will."

She was being very brave, I thought. "Of course he will," I told her. "It'll take more than that to hurt him. More than a stick in his damned eye. You know what they did to my wife?"

"Excuse me," she said, "what did you say?"

"Do you know what they did to my wife?"

"No, I don't. I'm very sorry."

"She was run over by a bus," I said. "Doesn't that sound funny?"

"No," she said. "It sounds very sad."

"After she was hit they lifted her in the back of a truck. Her legs were broken, her pelvis, there were some bad cuts. She was in shock. When we got to the hospital, they just laid her down on the grass outside and went away. She wasn't talking but she was breathing, and she knew what was going on."

Katherine's face was very pale and beautiful.

"There were sick people on the grass—dozens. It wasn't even a real hospital, just a clinic sponsored by one of the political parties. I wanted to get her inside, out of the sun, but I couldn't find anyone in the compound who looked like a doctor or understood what I was saying. They have about a dozen major languages and God knows how many dialects. I didn't speak the right one. When I came back to her stretcher, there was an old woman squatting there pouring water on her lips. I suppose it was some gesture of mercy, but I knew she had injuries inside and shouldn't drink anything, so I knocked the ladle away and screamed at the old woman."

Katherine started to cry.

"What she actually died from was drowning—the lungs were full of water. I have all this in a report from the Canadian Embassy in Djakarta. They arranged an autopsy for some reason, autopsies aren't done in that part of the world, you know. Anyway, I watched some men carry her away."

Katherine was bent over and I saw the neat part in her hair, black as a raven's wing. She whispered, "They all keep their sticks low, those are the rules, those are the *rules!*"

I looked at her, thinking what a lovely wife she was.

"Don't worry," I told her, "it'll take much more than that to hurt him."

Goalie

Rudy Thauberger

Nothing pleases him. Win or lose, he comes home angry, dragging his equipment bag up the driveway, sullen eyes staring down, seeing nothing, refusing to see. He throws the bag against the door. You hear him, fumbling with his keys, his hands sore, swollen and cold. He drops the keys. He kicks the door. You open it and he enters, glaring, not at you, not at the keys, but at everything, the bag, the walls, the house, the air, the sky.

His clothes are heavy with sweat. There are spots of blood on his jersey and on his pads. He moves past you, wordless, pulling his equipment inside, into the laundry room and then into the garage. You listen to him, tearing the equipment from the bag, throwing it. You hear the thump of heavy leather, the clatter of plastic, the heavy whisper of damp cloth. He leaves and you enter. The equipment is everywhere, scattered, draped over chairs, hung on hooks, thrown on the floor.

You imagine him on the ice: compact, alert, impossibly agile and quick. Then you stare at the equipment: helmet and throat protector, hockey pants, jersey, chest and arm protectors, athletic supporter, knee pads and leg pads, blocker, catching glove and skates. In the centre of the floor are three sticks, scattered, their broad blades chipped and worn. The clutter is deliberate, perhaps even necessary. His room is the same, pure chaos, clothes and magazines everywhere, spilling out of dresser drawers, into the closet. He says he knows where everything is. You imagine him on the ice, focused, intense, single-minded. You understand the need for clutter.

When he isn't playing, he hates the equipment. It's heavy and awkward and bulky. It smells. He avoids it, scorns it. It disgusts him. Before a game, he gathers it together on the floor and stares at it. He lays each piece out carefully, obsessively, growling and snarling at anyone who comes too close. His mother calls him a gladiator, a bullfighter. But you know the truth, that gathering the equipment is a ritual of hatred, that every piece represents, to him, a particular variety of pain.

There are black marks scattered on the white plastic of his skates. He treats them like scars, reminders of pain. His glove hand is always swollen. His chest, his knees and his biceps are always bruised. After a hard game, he can barely move. "Do you enjoy it?" you ask, "Do you enjoy the game at least? Do you like playing?" He shrugs. "I love it," he says.

Without the game, he's miserable. He spends his summers restless and morose, skating every morning, lifting weights at night. He juggles absentmindedly; tennis balls, coins, apples, tossing them behind his back and under his leg, see-sawing two in one hand as he talks on the phone, bouncing them off walls and knees and feet. He plays golf and tennis with great fervor, but you suspect, underneath, he is indifferent to these games.

As fall approaches, you begin to find him in the basement, cleaning his skates, oiling his glove, taping his sticks. His hands move with precision and care. You sit with him and talk. He tells you stories. This save. That goal. Funny stories. He laughs. The funniest stories are about failure: the goal scored from centre ice, the goal scored on him by his own defenceman, the goal scored through a shattered stick. There is always a moral, the same moral every time. "You try your best and you lose."

He starts wearing the leg pads in September. Every evening, he wanders the house in them, wearing them with shorts and a T-shirt. He hops in them, does leg lifts and jumping jacks. He takes them off and sits on them, folding them into a squat pile to limber them up. He starts to shoot a tennis ball against the fence with his stick.

As practices begin, he comes home overwhelmed by despair. His skill is an illusion, a lie, a magic trick. Nothing you say reassures him. You're his father. Your praise is empty, invalid.

The injuries begin. Bruises. Sprains. His body betrays him. Too slow. Too clumsy. His ankles are weak, buckling under him. His muscles cramp. His nose bleeds. A nerve in his chest begins to knot and fray. No-one understands. They believe he's invulnerable, the fans, his teammates. They stare at him blankly while he lies on the ice, white-blind, paralyzed, as his knee or his toe or his hand or his chest or his throat burns.

To be a goalie, you realize, is to be an adult too soon, to have too soon an intimate understanding of the inevitability of pain and failure. In the backyard, next to the garage, is an old garbage can filled with broken hockey sticks. The blades have shattered. The shafts are cracked. He keeps them all, adding a new one every two weeks. You imagine him, at the end of the season, burning them, purging his failure with a bonfire. But that doesn't happen. At the end of the season, he forgets them and you throw them away.

You watch him play. You sit in the stands with his mother, freezing, in an arena filled with echoes. He comes out without his helmet and stick, skating slowly around the rink. Others move around him deftly. He stares past them, disconnected, barely awake. They talk to him, call his name, hit his pads lightly with their sticks. He nods, smiles. You know he's had at least four cups of coffee. You've seen him, drinking, prowling the house frantically.

As the warm-up drills begin, he gets into the goal casually. Pucks fly over the ice, crashing into the boards, cluttering the net. He skates into the goal, pulling on his glove and blocker. He raps the posts with his stick. No-one seems to notice, even when he starts deflecting shots. They come around to him slowly, firing easy shots at his pads. He scoops the pucks out of the net with his stick. He seems bored.

You shiver as you sit, watching him. You hardly speak. He ignores you. You think of the cost of his equipment. Sticks, forty dollars. Glove, one hundred and twenty. Leg pads, thirteen hundred dollars. The pads have patches. The glove is soft, the leather eaten away by his sweat.

The game begins, casually, without ceremony. The scoreboard lights up. The ice is cleared of pucks. Whistles blow. After the stillness of the face-off, you hardly notice the change, until you see him in goal, crouched over, staring.

You remember him in the back yard, six years old, standing in a ragged net, wearing a parka and a baseball glove, holding an ordinary hockey stick, sawed off at the top. The puck is a tennis ball. The ice is cement. He falls down every time you shoot, ignoring the ball, trying to look like the goalies on TV. You score, even when you don't want to. He's too busy play-acting. He smiles, laughs, shouts.

You buy him a mask. He paints it. Yellow and black. Blue and white. Red and blue. It changes every month, as his heroes change. You make him a blocker out of cardboard and leg pads out of foam rubber. His mother makes him a chest protector. You play in the backyard, every evening, taking shot after shot, all winter.

It's hard to recall when you realize he's good. You come to a point where he starts to surprise you, snatching the ball out of the air with his glove, kicking it away with his shoe. You watch him one Saturday, playing with his friends. He humiliates them, stopping everything. They shout and curse. He comes in, frozen, tired and spellbound. "Did you see?" he says.

He learns to skate, moving off of the street and onto the ice. The pain begins. A shot to the shoulder paralyzes his arm for ten minutes. You buy him pads, protectors, thinking it will stop the pain. He begins to lose. Game after game. Fast reflexes are no longer enough. He is suddenly alone, separate from you, miserable. Nothing you say helps. Keep trying. Stop. Concentrate. Hold your stick blade flat on the ice.

He begins to practice. He begins to realize that he is alone. You can't help him. His mother can't help him. That part of his life detaches from you, becoming independent, free. You fool yourself, going to his games, cheering, believing you're being supportive, refusing to understand that here, in the rink, you're irrelevant. When you're happy for him, he's angry. When you're sad for him, he's indifferent. He begins to collect trophies.

You watch the game, fascinated. You try to see it through his eyes. You watch him. His head moves rhythmically. His stick sweeps the ice and chops at it. When the shots come, he stands frozen in a crouch. Position is everything, he tells you. He moves, the movement so swift it seems to strike you physically. How does he do it? How? You don't see the puck, only his movement. Save or goal, it's all the same.

You try to see the game through his eyes, aware of everything, constantly alert. It's not enough to follow the puck. The position of the puck is old news. The game. You try to understand the game. You fail.

He seems unearthly, moving to cut down the angle, chopping the puck with his stick. Nothing is wasted. You can almost feel his mind at work, watching, calculating. Where does it come from, you wonder, this strange mind? You try to move with him, watching his eyes through his cage, and his hands. You remember the way he watches games on television, cross-legged, hands fluttering, eyes seeing everything.

Suddenly you succeed, or you think you do. Suddenly, you see the game, not as a series of events, but as a state, with every moment in time potentially a goal. Potentiality. Probability. These are words you think of afterwards. As you watch, there is only the game, pressing against you, soft now, then sharp, then rough, biting, shocking, burning, dull, cold. No players. Only forces, feelings, the white ice, the cold, the echo, all joined. A shot crashes into his helmet. He falls to his knees. You cry out.

He stands slowly, shaking his head, hacking at the ice furiously with his stick. They scored. You never noticed. Seeing the game is not enough. Feeling it is not enough. He wants more, to understand completely, to control. You look out at the ice. The game is chaos again.

He comes home, angry, limping up the driveway, victorious. You watch him, dragging his bag, sticks in his hand, leg pads over his shoulder. You wonder when it happened, when he became this sullen, driven young man. You hear whispers about scouts, rumours. Everyone adores him, adores his skill. But when you see his stiff, swollen hands, when he walks slowly into the kitchen in the mornings, every movement agony, you want to ask him why. Why does he do it? Why does he go on?

But you don't ask. Because you think you know the answer. You imagine him, looking at you and saying quietly, "What choice do I have? What else have I ever wanted to do?"

Competition

Barbara Novak

The sun felt like a warm hand on his back. Spring; and the sight of the snow melting into dark stains in the concrete made him impatient.

First the bass clef, then the treble bounced up and down as Lin Ho skipped up the steps to the library. This year Mrs. Ho embroidered the bright yellow clefs on the knees of his pants. Last year she'd stitched them on his back pockets. Lin didn't have the heart, or the courage, to refuse to wear them.

Under one arm he carried a book of Chopin mazurkas. He opened the heavy glass door with his free hand and waited for his mother to enter. Mr. Ho couldn't come today. He was short-staffed at the restaurant.

Inside the foyer they found Sister Noella studying the Competition Program. Lin liked Sister Noella. Her protruding teeth made her look like she was smiling even when she wasn't. She'd been his teacher now for four years, since he was five. At six she had him playing Bartok and Mozart. At seven he'd entered his first competition and won a scholarship. At eight he'd won an even bigger scholarship. Yesterday he won first prize with his Bach Partita for candidates 16 years and under, and tied for another first with a Dohnanyi Rhapsody for 17 years and under though he wasn't yet ten.

Lin loved music. But what he wanted more than anything in the world was to play right-wing for the Edmonton Oilers.

"Guess what I'm doing today!"

"What?" Sister Noella bent down so that he caught her familiar scent of Ivory soap and mothballs.

"I'm going to Brantford to play in an out-of-town exhibition game."

The nun looked pleased. "And what piece are you going to play?"

"No, Sister. I'm going to play hockey!"

"Hockey!" She straightened up. Sister Noella was very tall—much taller than Lin's father. Maybe six feet tall. Lin would have liked to know exactly how tall Sister Noella was but he was afraid it would be rude to ask. He wished he were that tall.

"Isn't that exciting," she added.

Lin didn't think she sounded excited at all. He started to explain that Brantford was where Wayne Gretzky grew up, but didn't have time to finish because the bell sounded and they had to hurry into the auditorium.

The first competition of the morning was for students playing sonatinas. Since Lin was already playing sonatas, which were harder, he wasn't entered in the sonatina class. He would compete in the Chopin competition, which was next. Ordinarily he liked listening to the other candidates. Sometimes everyone chose the same piece. Last year he'd heard a set of Kabalevsky variations so many times that when he got home he could play it by ear. But today he wasn't thinking about music.

For nearly a year he'd begged his father to let him

join the team. "Who ever heard of a Chinese hockey player?" Mr. Ho had muttered, even as he drove him to the arena to sign up. And now the team was going to play in Brantford! Lin had never been to Brantford before. He'd never been out of Woodstock. He was glad the competition was in the morning. It would be terrible to have to miss the game. As it was he'd be missing hockey practice, but he'd given the coach a note from his father so he'd been excused. The team bus would pick him up at noon in front of his house.

Turning around, he cast a glance at the clock. Fifteen minutes past nine. Quickly, Lin counted the heads in the front row where the sonatina candidates waited their turns. Each sonatina might take ten minutes, he figured, since they had to play all three movements. That meant it would take more than an hour before his class even began. And if his class didn't begin until 10:30 he might not get out until 11:30 or even later and he'd still have to get home and change into his hockey uniform before the bus arrived.

At the end of each sonatina he stole another peek at the clock until his mother placed a restraining hand on his shoulder. The pieces were shorter than he'd figured, averaging only six minutes. He calculated how much longer before the Chopin class would begin, and started to fidget again as he thought about the hockey practice he was missing, right before the most exciting game of the whole season. He wished he could play hockey just half as well as he could play Chopin. But he was as clumsy on the ice as he was nimble on the keyboard. He'd never scored a single goal. Sometimes the coach didn't even call him off the bench. But at the last game he'd made an assist. That had been more wonderful than any prize he'd ever won in music. He couldn't understand why everyone made such a fuss about playing the piano. It was like being praised for eating or sleeping.

Shortly after ten o'clock the winners of the sonatina class were announced. Then, to Lin's dismay, the judges filed out of the hall to take a break. The candidates for the Chopin class were called to take their places in the front row. Mrs. Ho squeezed Lin's hand as he jumped up. Sister Noella gave him a whispered reminder to play the mazurka the way Chopin, who was thin and small like Lin, would have played it.

The girl beside him in the front row asked if he were nervous. Lin was never nervous before playing in public, though Sister had warned him he might be when he got older. She wasn't nervous either, she said, carelessly flipping back one braid with a mittened hand.

Mittens! It wasn't cold in the auditorium. Nobody was wearing their coats. Why was she wearing mittens?

''To keep my muscles warm,'' she explained.

Her mother must have made her wear those mittens, Lin thought. He slid his music book lower on his lap to conceal the clefs on his knees. Then he peered around to count heads. Seven players ahead of him and five after, plus himself made thirteen. With any luck they'd be finished and out of there by eleven-thirty.

The judges returned and rang the bell. A girl with a pony tail and red glasses mounted the steps to the stage and sat down at the piano. Lin tried to concentrate. He knew the piece—a Chopin Waltz in B minor. It was supposed to glide along but this girl pumped her elbows up and down so it sounded jerky, and she was going too fast, losing control of the rhythm. That's what happened to him when he played hockey, he thought. He'd over-skate the puck and lose control—when he could get the puck in the first place.

He was picturing the moment when the coach would send him into the game when he suddenly became aware of an uncomfortable silence. His first impulse was to leap to his feet, certain that it was his turn, that everyone was waiting for him and he hadn't heard the bell. But no, the problem was at the piano. The sixth candidate's fingers hesitated over the keyboard. Lin heard nervous coughs and the rustling of programs in the audience behind him. Finally the boy's right hand plunked out a smattering of notes; his left bobbed help-lessly. Lin recognized a passage from the *Minute Waltz,* something he'd never wanted to learn. Lowering his head, he traced the clefs on his knees, unable to watch. He heard the boy start back at the beginning only to break down again in the fifth bar when his left hand came crashing in on the wrong chord.

One of the judges cleared his throat. "Perhaps you'd better use your music," he said.

Lin raised one eye. To his amazement, the boy grinned at the audience, shook his head and loped off the stage without a trace of embarrassment.

The girl beside Lin had taken off her mittens and was twisting them into tight blue balls. The bell sounded and she made her way quickly to the platform. Lin sighed when she too began to play the *Minute Waltz.* At least it was short, he thought. Longer than a minute but not by much. His hands, when he rubbed them together, felt surprisingly cold and a little bit damp. He slid his music book onto the floor and turned around to check the clock.

The girl finished to a spontaneous burst of applause and returned to her seat. Lin heard the scratching of pens as the judges wrote their comments. When the bell rang he stood up and edged along the row, brushing past the legs of the girl who had just played and those of the other candidates. His own legs felt rubbery which caused him to wonder whether he might be sick. Trying to ignore the ripple of laughter that greeted his knees as he crossed the stage, he sat down at the piano and adjusted the bench.

Later he couldn't remember having started to play the mazurka at all. Somehow, his fingers had been playing the music while he was crossing the blue-line with only forty seconds left in the game. He had perfect control of the puck. The goalie, his face hidden behind the mask, was ready for him. A defenceman swung around from the left, but Lin managed to check him and deke the goalie at the same time. With an amazing backhand shot he scored! His third goal! A hat-trick for Lin Ho!

The repeats. Had he played his repeats? With a jolt, Lin realized that he didn't even know what piece his fingers were playing. And that's when they stopped. There was no hope of picking it up anywhere, not even at the beginning. All he knew was that he was registered in the Chopin section for fourteen years and under. Taking a deep breath, he launched into a bridge of Chopin-like chords with runs in his right hand. Then he played the only music that was in his head—*The Minute Waltz*. He sensed he was playing it in the wrong key—it sounded too high—but he was afraid to shift now. Afraid even to look at his fingers, he shut his eyes.

It seemed to Lin that he'd been playing for much, much longer than a minute. In fact, he was sure he'd repeated this passage before. With a sinking feeling, he realized what had happened. Instead of coming to the end of the waltz, he was back in the middle again. Unless he could figure out how to end it, he could be trapped in the *Minute Waltz* forever. The third time through he improvised a suitable approximation of the cascade of notes that led to the final cadence.

The applause startled him. There were even some cheers. Didn't people know what a terrible mess he'd made up there? The judges must have known, and Sister Noella, and his mother. There she was, smiling at him as though it didn't matter. Lin bowed again, more in apology than in acknowledgement, and hurried off the stage.

The girl with the mittens stared at him as he took his seat. "What edition were you using?"

"My own."

Weeks of practice had worn certain pages of his music book so that now, when he picked it up off the floor, it opened automatically to the mazurka he was supposed to have played. He half expected the notes to have vanished from the page, so completely had they disappeared from his memory. The sight of them in the book, familiar and orderly, seemed impossible.

For the first time that morning Lin lost track of the clock. Oblivious to the remaining performances, he didn't even notice the judges coming to the front to announce the winners, not until one of them began to talk about how to play Chopin.

"The most important thing," he was saying, "is not the notes but the music."

Competition

Wrong notes were bad enough, thought Lin. But to play the wrong piece. And to play it in the wrong key and then have to make up the ending. That was a disgrace.

"...and that's why we were unanimous in our decision to award first prize to candidate number eight, Lin Ho."

Lin opened his mouth to protest but no sound came out. The judge looked down at him, a benign smile flattening his chin. Lin slipped the certificate between the pages of his music book quickly, as though he were ashamed of it. Then he joined his mother at the back of the auditorium, stiffening against the touch of her fingers resting proudly on the back of his neck. Sister Noella shook his hand and congratulated him. He stared mutely at the bits of white enamel poking out from under her top lip, unable to decide whether or not she was really smiling.

Outside, his nostrils filled with the first sweet scents of spring. It occurred to him that hockey season would soon be over.

The Drubbing of Nesterenko

Hanford Woods

Anyone who saw the fight between John Ferguson and
Eric Nesterenko in the 1964-65 Stanley Cup finals will
never forget it. I was not at the game but watched it alone
on television. Ferguson was always a great fighter, a
crude hockey player to whom it was most important not
to lose a fight. He took his fighting role seriously, he
sincerely believed it was a basic ingredient in the Montreal
Canadiens' winning formula. Canadiens' fans, players,
coaches agreed with his conviction, forgetting that before
his time and without similar brawling talents the team
won five consecutive Stanley Cups. Ferguson undoubt-
edly did contribute something to a number of the winning
years; he was also a guilty party to a few of the losing
seasons. He was hardness itself, a face of rock-solid
bone, a body of ungainly, awkward muscle. He had no
style: he remains to this day the one hockey player who
could lose a puck when no-one had challenged him for
it. He would pick up a free puck, lose it in his skates,
and, like a dog chasing its tail, whirl furiously, vainly
seeking it. A craftsman would approach the outer limits
of this berserk creature and deftly retrieve the puck
from its wildly thrashing parts. His disastrous encounters

with the game's technical side never embarrassed Fergy.
He laboured on, mounting rushes, firing aimless passes
to the four corners of the rink. He was often exasperated
by his linemates' inability to adapt to the rhythm of his
game. But his frustration never lasted long. He knew
that soon a fight would beckon. He need not go to any
subtle provocative lengths: any minor clash or incursion
upon whatever he considered to be his territory provided
ample pretext. With stick and arms raised he barged
into an opponent and thus the battle was on. Nonetheless
he was somewhat indirect. He never looked his opponent
in the eye to see whether or not he wanted to fight.
Which was to Fergy's advantage: it assured him of a
head start. He dropped his stick and was punching with
a quickness incredible in one so clumsy. He hit automatically, as though working out on a speed bag. With
his left hand holding the enemy jersey he threw over-
hand rights into the captive face. The psychological
victory was a consequence of the headbashing. He
entered each fight with an absolute confidence in his
ability to win it, though he rarely mixed with the other
good fighters in the league—Howe, Kurtenbach, Horton.
He seemed a completely mindless brute, though after
the fight, something like a vain exultation rose to his
sturdy, coarse face. Then he became almost self-conscious.
He continued to disregard his opponent, but he was
always a little embarrassed while skating to the penalty
box, his head bowed under the storm of adulation and
abuse his bouts occasioned. Before he entered the
penalty box he would straighten his sweater, adjust his
elbow and shoulder pads and look up at the clock. They
were nervous rituals: his sweater did not need straight-
ening, the clock had nothing to tell him. The wide berth

his fights created made him uncomfortable.

I thought I hated him more than any other Canadien player. I swore it would give me pleasure to see him injured. On one of his typically headstrong rushes, he tried to leap through the Toronto defencemen Bobby Baun and Carl Brewer, was stopped cold, and thrown on his back. He rose slowly and skated off the ice, stunned. He was really hurt, so it could not have been his head that struck the ice (the sports fan's idea of a joke). His spine had taken the knock. The mere thought of injury, let alone the sight of it, will usually cause empathetic tremors to vibrate through my frame. But it gave me pleasure to watch Ferguson's spasmodic, dazed efforts to leave the ice. I was not alarmed at this nor did I feel remorse. I was disappointed when he returned to the game.

My desire to see him injured was the reflex of my physical fear. Standing behind the second-level blue seats, Fergy within earshot, I bounced clever insults off his impenetrable skull during lulls in the game. My words never gave me the pleasure I hoped for: my voice cracked, uncertain in its delivery. I feared lest he should hear me, imagined him climbing into the stands and beating me to a pulp. I understood that wit was not his strong suit, could only rile him and lead to a painful physical assault.

Eric Nesterenko was my favourite hockey player, an eccentric choice. He still plays with the same weaknesses in his game, but none of his old peculiar effectiveness. It is not that he is no longer my favourite player: as I grow older I make less of such things. Nesterenko is very much a shadow of his former self, a memory of a player, so I tend not to think of him, or when I do, think of him as he was. It even embarrasses me that I used always to have a favourite player and that at one time Nesterenko wore this mantle. I want him to retire, to spare us the humiliation that comes of an over-the-hill veteran's unwillingness to recognize his decline. With Nesterenko I have given up hope.

At one time, though, he was the apple of my eye. He could never shoot well, skated aimlessly, had the unready habit of trailing his stick behind him in one hand and without exception never played well with any other individual or as a member of a line. The flaws in his game were always more apparent than the virtues but the flaws were merely apparent, the virtues solid and true. He had some beautiful moves, long parabolic skating strides, smooth and lazy shifts that were deceptive. He was a strong penalty killer, his roaming style adapted to breaking up rushes before they started. He was an especially great penalty killer when his team was two men short. Swooping in upon the puck carrier, harassing him with his long, gangling reach, retreating to intercept passes, ragging the puck for a few seconds before shovelling it deep into the opposition zone, he was able to reduce the most disciplined power-play to a rabble. He had a way of turning a game around. While the rest of the players on the ice became feverish, ineffective, Nesterenko alone would remain calm, surging between attack and defence, creating the chances for his heavy-shooting teammates. His is a minor legend of uncelebrated works, at a shy remove from the boys reeling off their vainglorious bar-room tales. Unfortunately, this is not the time to dwell upon his legend, its pale, delicate flowers: they are of the past. The blows with which Ferguson hammered Nesterenko to his knees are not of the past. Although only Nesterenko can awaken in the dark to the nightmare they rain down, in my own way I, too, can summon them. They taught me an unheeded lesson: to observe the most timid limits, they are a fate to be avoided at all costs. Ferguson's fists, immune from the Law, brutally smash me (swoon), the image of me as a beautiful creature belonging to a world of play and therefore a world lawlessly divine. It was as though, on that occasion, a fear that I should be violated had materialized, when my deepest instinct was always to remain untouched, to use the world but to produce a perfect narcissistic liberty.

A hockey player is an innocent who believes that it is important to win, who will risk a lot of himself in many different ways to reach that end. People who find hockey brutal are unnecessarily squeamish; like the players, for the purpose of argument, they forget that hockey is only a game, a stylized activity, a grossly distorted, incomplete miniature of life with all sorts of illusory goals and rewards attached to it. Hockey fights, even the worst of them, are burlesques. A player has to lose his head before anything real takes place, and what then happens has nothing to do with hockey. A man gets up each day and drives to work, in the evening he drives home. This is a pleasant charade, more or less like a hockey game. Reality is only admitted into this world when, crossing an intersection, his car is rammed by the reckless fool who has run a red light. Even then, it's rare if anything serious happens. The principals climb from their cars, the one angry at the other, the other angry with himself, they exchange insurance cards, wait for the police to arrive, worry over their cars. Two players clash for the puck in hockey, one tries to gain an advantage by holding the other's stick, the latter retaliates with an elbow in the neck, the former drops his stick and gloves, the latter follows suit, they begin a foolish bout of punching, shoving and grabbing. The object is to pull your opponent's sweater over his head and administer a good drubbing and publicly humiliate the resultant mummy. The linesmen intervene, generally before the end has accomplished itself in its full glory. The fight becomes a clownish wrestling match. The players, finally separated, menace and growl, unable to get at one another. They don't really want to, the thing has blown over, but they must blindly follow rituals. By performing in this tedious denouement they console themselves that their pride is intact. So in this world turned vain and idle, is honour maintained.

The Nesterenko-Ferguson fight violates these patterns. No contact preceded Ferguson's machine-gun punching, at least I saw none. Of course, the fight on these pages is not the fight as it was, but is the one that, implanted within me, has long lain buried in the sacred soil that nourishes all repressed events. And the original event is not so much the seed as the manure to some yet more ancient, timeless seed. I breathe this rich odour of decay.

I can still hear the voice of Danny Gallivan...*now Jarrett with the puck in the Chicago end, plays it along the boards toward the centre. Ferguson and Nesterenko race after it, they contest it along the boards...now Ferguson has dropped his gloves, Ferguson is going after Nesterenko, they're going at it...Ferguson pummels Nesterenko with a series of right hooks, Nesterenko is on his knees, he's not fighting back, he's cut, he's bleeding badly...linesman Pavlitch is struggling to pull Ferguson off Nesterenko, they can't get him off...*

I was mesmerized, my heart swollen with outrage, im-
potence, terror. Nesterenko had a reputation for sharp
elbows, a tendency to clutch and grab: he was the type
of player likely to irritate Ferguson. But Ferguson's
attack was not in response to any real or imagined ag-
gression, it was entirely primitive and brutal. Ferguson
was always impatient, could not bide his time or hold
himself back, could never envision victory as something
to be wooed and tempted through time. Instead, with
his every bullish move, he crashed headlong toward the
goal, a beast in its fury. His opponents were at a dis-
advantage: they had long since mastered this fury and
could not counter it with one, equally murderous, of
their own. So Nesterenko, a player who often dreamed
of other things as he played, who might infringe the
rules in the same absent-minded way he might obey
them, hardly thought to engage in this battle for the
puck. Despite his indifference, the engagement was
bound to be settled in his favour because of its open
nature. And Ferguson was either cursed or blessed with
the bestial stupidity that forced him to see his incipient
defeat and nothing else. He was unable to contrive a
solution either to the immediate problem, loss of the
puck, or any future problems, all of which took on the
character of this one. He was enraged at Nesterenko,
his abstraction, his unconcern at winning or losing.
Ferguson had to win, now and always. Winning was
life and losing death, and winning sanctified whatever
means used. It seemed that Nesterenko was almost
absent from the fight. Ferguson's fists hammered at
him and continued to hammer at him after he was little
more than butchered meat. Nesterenko slumped to his

knees, his arms dangled at his sides, he was unconscious
before he hit the ice. On the televison his blood was the
deepest black.

The outcome of the series was determined by the
fight. Nesterenko, his head wrapped in a towel, was
helped from the ice although he returned to the game
later on. He skated from the clinic at the south end of
the Forum to the Chicago players' bench, skated through
the swaggering contempt of the Canadiens on the ice.
Ferguson was one of them, impatiently circling, his
anger unappeasable, and those on the bench were ma-
levolently alert to the signal defeat of his broken posture.
He skated through the resignation of his teammates
who, with eyes lowered, were already fixing him as the
scapegoat of the defeat inevitably settling upon them
and then he dragged himself listlessly through the gate
and took his seat on the bench. He knew of no way to
explain to Ferguson his feelings, to clarify his fear. In
the eyes of the world he was guilty and must bear the
marks of his guilt: a swollen lip, an ugly cut over his left
eye that would soon discolour hideously. I could not
turn off the set. The score mounted in Montreal's favour,
6-0, a total wipe-out. I was drained of all strength, did
not care to defend myself from the din of the celebrating
Montreal crowd. I didn't sleep at all that night, tossing
from side to side, struggling to banish the dim image,
the ugly line of Nesterenko's blood, not red but dark
like the plague. I read the Montreal papers the next day
with an avid loathing and my shame dogged me. I imagined the newsprint smearing my fingers was Nesterenko's blood, dirty and reviled, ignobly displayed. The
columnists probed the wound mercilessly and brought
down their verdict: Nersterenko had been guilty of some

indefeasible incursion into Fergy's domain, he should never have been there, Fergy had acted within his rights. The writers drew strength for the pronouncement from the act's utter inexplicability. Talk on the streets was only of the fight, the fans vaunted Fergy's prowess as their own. The entire city revelled in their mean, stupid triumph but to denounce them would have been to confess my own inability to defend myself. Let all weak men die and abuse be heaped on their bones.

A couple of games later, when Montreal had won the series and the two teams were shaking hands, I knew that Ferguson extended his hand to Nesterenko as though no-one were there, as though the man he had beaten up had ceased to exist. Nesterenko must have ventured a timid glance at Ferguson, pondering momentarily whether to smash his stick over his head. He would have smiled slightly, weakly possessed of a desire to take Ferguson aside, hoping to entice him from his brutal purposes so that he (Nesterenko) might feel safe again. Nesterenko probably wondered if he were permanently embittered, if he could ever shake off his feelings of cowardice. For his part, as time passed, Ferguson grew more solid and stupid, especially after the Montreal team captain, Jean Beliveau, paid specific tribute to the work of his hammering fists. But Ferguson was merely the blind instrument of destruction. He reaped no rewards from his outburst other than a share in the winning team's glory and the knowledge that his anger continued to rule. Rather it was Beliveau, smooth, gilded idol of all Montreal, who was looked upon as the heart of the team, the architect of victory: his the glory. But Beliveau was no longer the gifted player he had once been and, in acknowledging Ferguson, was deferring deceitfully to the true, crude sources of victory. He spoke the truth that it might be void. Beliveau's words were law, they stamped Ferguson's act with the legitimate seal of power and success. And it was Beliveau whom I detested, Beliveau, the unholy marriage of French toadying to English condescension. Ferguson could never be the torchbearer for the myth of the flying Frenchmen, the myth of the unvanquishable blood-red Habitant jersey. And this lie perpetuated that myth: that the win was the consequence of superior skills rather than of an aberrant rush into brute force. While the entire city fortified itself on the team's win, smugly eating their poisoned fruit, I silently drank my cup of gall, unconsoled for being the solitary guardian of these bitter truths. I would have gladly traded places with the winners, would have preferred any ill-gotten victory to this defeat. I must suffer Nesterenko's fate in my imagination, would willingly have rewound that reel from my history. I had failed to learn anything. I was still floating listlessly through an undefined haze of antagonisms toward the city of Montreal.

So it was, some four years later, that the Boston Bruins skated out against the Montreal Canadiens in the opening game of their series. I wanted to forget I had my day in court to face. I cursed my stupidity, hung on, vainly regretted my action. I could neither forgive myself nor accept the ever so slight change I seemed to have willed into my life. I was angry. The city, its streets and buildings, and my father with his slightly fumbling prepossession, fed my anger. I made no attempt to purge myself. Instead, I focused my fires on the Canadiens. Through the Bruins I was sure to have my revenge

and my anger would expel itself in a vindictive, tri-
umphant outburst.

I do not know how my father and I wound up standing
at the game together. We had never done so before.
Since my arrest I had been nursing my grievances
secretly. All was outward calm. I had reformed, was
modest and deferential, had stepped humbly back into
the family portrait, servant to its fragile harmonies. I
must have suggested we go to the game together, urging
that we learn to live with our conflicting loyalties and
tolerate, no, appreciate even, each other's point of view.
The game would strengthen our resolve to live at peace.
I was, supposedly, going to the game in a fresh spirit but
really my heart was seething and I was anticipating the
Canadiens' and my father's fall.

We had tickets for standing behind the grey seats at
the north end, North Circle standing. In order to get a
good place you had to arrive early. Usually I stand a
level lower, behind the blue, but it's more crowded, the
jockeying for places next to the rail more fierce. No
need to expose my father to the inevitable squabbling
and pushing of blue standing. Besides, the blue has
places only along the sides and with grey standing we
could stand at the end and command the back and forth
streaming, which is the game's primary attraction to
my way of thinking. Still, my father would have to
undergo initiation into the basic ritual of standing at
a hockey game.

The game was scheduled for eight o'clock, the turnstiles would open at seven sharp. We arrived at the
Forum about 6:30 and hurried into the nearly vacant
lobby. I was preoccupied with the prospect of not finding a place next to the rail. Anyone who arrived later

than ourselves and took up a position near the entrance, indifferent to the lines already formed, I regarded as a thief after our merited rations, one capable of stealing the last crumbs from starving mouths. Until seven we must wait. Meanwhile the lobby filled, the shouts of the vendors bounced off the walls, the noise from the throng rose in anticipation. Each time the glass doors to the street opened, we were hit by a blast of cold air: a crowd becomes a bigger crowd by accretions.

About quarter to seven, the girls came out to sell programs: "Programme de la Soiree, Hockey Line-up Program": flute-like voices sing their wares. The girls are beautiful, their flimsy red jackets and bell-bottom black slacks a bold challenge to the Montreal winter, fashion's poor response to the slashing cold. The girls' accents are one in their French sing-song; they exist specifically for the consumption of the wealthy season-ticket holders: on the one hand the English wishing to forget the army of proletarians at their backs flinging about their incomprehensible joual, on the other a certain middle-class segment of the French uneasy over their origins, pleased to have these artfully fashioned melodious instruments to titillate their ears.

I bought a program, flipped through it, digesting its meagre information, one eye on the articles, the other on the hordes of line jumpers bent on keeping us from a spot next the rail. Players arrived periodically, some self-conscious in their street clothes, others swaggering through the crowd, others already intent on the game ahead. None acknowledged the remarks tossed their way, but all the same we knew they were public property. About five to seven the ticket takers began lugging the turnstiles into place, removing the iron grilles separating the crowd from the stairway to the upper levels. The ticket takers leaned against the turnstiles, chatted among themselves. Their position on the inside invested their predictions with an utterly unmerited authority. The excitement was building. Prior to the actual opening of the turnstiles, the ticket takers always tear the tickets of the first three or four people in line who can then be let through the moment the signal is given to lessen just that little bit of the initial crush. At seven o'clock, as on every other Saturday night for the last six months—save one, the week the ice show was in town and the Canadiens banished to a foreign arena—the head usher came to the stairway landing, calmly took in the nervous milling throng and called out, "Okay, open 'em up!" Then the crowd's reflexive forward surge, no lines, a dozen or so abreast, the fans had somehow to funnel their way into three entrances. Despite the aggravating slowness of the ticket takers (old men whose hands trembled as they tore the tickets), despite the alarming efficiency of everyone else at slithering, pushing, sliding his way beyond us (though I did manage to cut off that small monkey-like greaseball: I was damned if I was going to let him past), despite the unbearable pressure of the frantic mob behind us, despite the heart-sinking moment when I believed I'd lost my ticket, so tightly was I clutching it, despite all the risks to life and limb undertaken in just this way every Saturday evening, I was finally pressed into the turnstile, my ticket torn in half, the stub returned, as simultaneously my thigh drove the turnstile arm forward and down. Miraculously I found myself on the inside of the Montreal Forum.

But the race had only begun. I had all those stairs to climb. I never thought to take the escalator where I might be trapped behind people content with its sluggardly pace. I raced past the souvenir vendors and the lame and the old climbing as best they could, rose ever higher, no less than four turnings in the course of my ascension, arrived at the mouth of the circle standing, flashed my stub at the indifferent usher, the one behind him moved to block my path, insisted on verifying the ticket, satisfied himself, moved aside and then at last I was free to see where I was, to notice for the first time that I was once again ludicrously early and had the choice of every standing place in the building. Yet I ran on, from the south end to the north, laid claim to the spot directly behind the net, tore off my jacket and threw it over the rail, thereby claiming the spot beside me for my father who, slower than I, bewildered by my mad flight and disappearance, was just now emerging at the south end. Slowly he turned through a half circle, seemed to catch sight of me, and began to walk, half run in my direction.

My father slowed down, then quickened his stride again, covering the last few steps in a characteristic shambling trot. All those stairs must have been a strain but he managed a smile. What had induced him to participate in this rite? We now had an hour to kill before game time. He removed his coat and laid it on the rail next to mine. We took in the scene before us, the empty seats, the standing levels rapidly filling. He looked at his watch: 57 minutes to go. Our eyes met, we had nothing to say. We turned toward the rink. I wanted to tell him this was the moment I liked best, the ice surface smooth, clean and pure, the lines freshly painted, the goals a graphic illusion rising out of the ice. But before I could form these impressions into words, an ice cream vendor was upon us and my father wanted to know if I wanted an ice cream. I didn't but I jumped at the offer: if father and son were to go to the hockey game together, then it was the father's prerogative to cram the youngster full of the goodies he imagined him craving. I thanked him, thanked the vendor also. We ate our ice cream in silence and I dutifully licked the wrapper clean.

We did not broach the subject of the game, for neither of us could be trusted not to use it as a weapon against the other. It was a blank, joyless wait interrupted for me only by brief internal attacks of anxiety: my impending trial. And yet I had nothing to fear. The result was a foregone conclusion and that result could leave me neither more nor less free than I already was.

At 7:27 the Bruins skated out for the warmup, followed some two minutes later by the Canadiens. My father watched the Canadiens directly below us. They were already super-charged, flying as they would fly once the game began. My gaze drifted to the far end where the Bruins circled lazily, taking it easy in these last minutes before the storm. My father's heart was set on Ralph Backstrom, his favourite player, admired for his pinwheel motions, his tireless skating. And I had Orr. I smiled at the comparison.

I suggested we try to guess which Canadien would be the last to leave the ice when the warmup ended. I knew that Terry Harper, possessed of some superstition in this matter, made a ritual of staying out longer than all his teammates. My father was decisive: "J. C. Tremblay." Should I astonish him? I pretended to deliberate, then: "I'll take Ralph Backstrom." The siren sounded and the players flew around the rink for the last time. Almost as one J.C. Tremblay and Ralph Backstrom dropped from the pack, passed from the ice into the dressing-room.

We enjoyed our reversal. I bought us each a bag of peanuts which we consumed mechanically, mindlessly, even happily. The countdown continued.

By game time I was damp with sweat, my limbs were shaking, my teeth chattering. My father was stamping impatiently, first one foot then the other, grinding his teeth. A great current of sound swelled and swept through the building at the Canadiens' appearance. The Bruins were on the ice moments later, my wild savage shouts and pounding hands drowning out the boos. I heard nothing of the national anthem, saw nothing of my father. The red of the red line was the blood pumping through the veins behind my eyes. The ice sheet, with the players and officials standing at attention upon it, had taken its dazzling place inside my head, about to explode. The puck was dropped and the game was on.

Boston had conceived a brutal plan. While the Canadiens' fast skaters whirled through the opening shift, the Bruins patiently crouched, waited their chance to pounce upon them. First it was Cashman, a hatchet man who caught Cournoyer a hard check against the boards, then dropped his gloves and levelled the smaller man with a fast series of punches. As Cashman beat up Cournoyer, Derek Sanderson, a mod thug, waded into another small opponent, Dick Duff; victories for the Bruins. The crowd roared and screamed for justice and retribution, my father was silent, frowning, his pleasure spoiled by this resort to violence. I said nothing, my gloating not entirely free of shame.

The crude stratagem had worked. The Canadiens were intimidated, the Bruins had a free hand to go about their business like true professionals. As the game wore on the Canadiens contrived no serious attacking threats.

Hanford Woods

And when, midway through the third period, Derek Sanderson waltzed around the Canadiens' defence and scored a shorthanded goal, Boston led 2-0. The game was as good as won. But by then my pleasure was beginning to wane. Up to a point I had enjoyed my father's performance. I had been called upon to say nothing while his frustration, screwed-up ever tighter, expressed itself, at first in clickings of the tongue against the palate. Then it became suppressed cries of "Jesus Murphy!" and finally it errupted into shouts of bitterness toward his favourites. He tried, unsuccessfully, to temper his wrath, give it a speculative character: "Tremblay, you goat! What's wrong with that crowd anyway?" I explained to him in my mildest manner that they were not making the mistakes on purpose, that Boston was doing a good job of containing the Canadiens. And I pointed out, truthfully I thought, that the Bruins had Orr who had dominated the game as only he could and who in himself was the difference. My father would not listen to reason, only stammered more angrily. Another Tremblay pass went astray, my father turned to me, grabbed my arm. "Did you see that? Did you see that?" I could only shrug; he was becoming a wildman, creating a scene. My poor father turned away from me, snorted in disgust, convinced—of what? That there was a conspiracy afoot whose cruel end was to put the maximum strain on his already aggravated emotions. He calmed down a little and at the next break in the action I looked to see how he was doing. Leaning against the railing for support, his head was sunk into his arms, his eyes shut. He had been standing for over three hours and he looked so old and tired that Boston might have inflicted a bushel of goals upon him without lifting him out of his weariness. He spat on the concrete, slowly drew himself up, focused on the arena where he expected, demanded, so much pleasure and received, instead, so much torment.

Fifty-five minutes of hockey had swept by. Two periods and the space of two intermissions, the third period winding to a close; it was a long and taxing evening for my father but a fleeting one for myself. My animosity toward the Canadiens had all but disappeared. I was even mildly sympathetic to their frantic labours though unwilling to indulge their need to win, which was becoming the more hysterical as the prospect of defeat became the more likely. Defeat was a just reproof, would make them better, more thoughtful men.

And as Ferguson charged down the ice alone, hugging the left-wing boards, his head down, I smiled a superior parental smile. I was alongside Dallas Smith who was perfectly positioned to block any direct move Fergy might make for the goal. He had skated himself into a bad angle, could do nothing but swipe angrily at the puck which was on its end and about to bounce free. Smith moved to block the shot with a poke-check but it skipped by his stick, fluttered weakly in the air, what little momentum it had rapidly diminishing, its death throes a malicious parody of Fergy's efforts. It bounced to about ten feet from Cheevers. And Cheevers, conscientious to the last, playing them, weak and strong alike, with the same nervous care, fell to his knees to block it with his body. The puck took another harmless skip and Cheevers readied to gather it in. Warily, he followed it bouncing directly before him, then, impossible, finding an opening where surely there was none, it skittered through his pads and concluded its ugly little dance into the net. The Forum erupted in the predictable roar, my father's bellows joined to it. He unleashed a gleeful wallop across my spine. I jerked about, eyes blazing in anger. My father was already sheepish, aware that moments before he was fretting and fuming, more or less intent on depriving me of the pleasure I might have taken in my triumph. But he had tasted blood and had a prophet's certainty that the night would yet be his. He reined himself in and as the cheering died, tossed a pitying accolade in Cheevers' direction. "Really, it's a shame, wasn't so much a mistake as just one of those things, Cheevers deserved his shutout, he's played such a strong game." No way I'd let that remark pass: "He's done nothing because he hasn't had a single difficult shot. Till now Canadiens haven't been in this fucking game. Fifty-five minutes of total domination and only two goals to show for it, then that asshole Ferguson scores on a fucking freak shot!" My father would pursue the matter no further. He had seen this sort of intemperance before. Admittedly, his own words might have unwittingly added fuel. Perhaps he should have said nothing. I apologized sulkily and he trotted out something to the effect that he could understand, though of course it was only a game.

The game was delayed while the rink attendant swept up the debris thrown in celebration of the goal. I had convinced myself that it was a terribly unjust goal and that my father should understand and at least share the truth of that conviction. But we had always seen these matters differently, even when aligned.

The first Grey Cup football game I ever saw, I watched with my father on a neighbour's television. In those days the west was always the underdog, the east an almost routine winner. I was born in the west so my loyalty lay there. I had lived all my seven years in the east but had already developed a notion of my exile, even believing in a second birth and a second life so that I might relive those same years in the west. My father too supported the western challenger, the Winnipeg Blue Bombers. The pain of losing had not yet become insupportable to him and besides, everyone else in the room was cheering for the Hamilton Tiger Cats so he felt that I needed some aid and comfort. So Winnipeg played beautifully, gave promise of winning, but were behind by a touchdown with the game almost over. They mounted a last stirring drive, Indian Jack Jacobs moving them downfield on his golden passing arm. With time for just one more play, the ball on the Hamilton three-yard line, Jacobs dropped back to pass, floated the ball into the flat for his favourite receiver, Tom Casey. But Lou Kusserow, Hamilton defensive back, had anticipated the play, and the moment the ball arrived he hit Casey a jarring tackle. The ball popped in the air and fell to the ground. Incomplete. Rejoicing all around me; for me an instant of bewilderment and then as I understood what had happened, I wept unchecked. As we got up to leave, my father insisted I dry my eyes, thank our host. I performed this duty as best I could but was unable to shake the sobs from my voice. Our host, an old man who took things easily, smiled, tousled my hair, suggested I wait till next year, it'd be my turn then. I wasn't interested in next year. As the door closed behind us, I burst into tears again, repeating over and over, "Is that ever dirty!" My father suggested we take a walk together and took me by the hand. I made a fist with my free hand, rubbed at the tears that continued to flow. What was dirty he wanted to know. That Winnipeg

lost, that ... that ... that the referee hadn't called interference on the last play. "Did you see interference?" my
father asked. Yes, I had. This falsehood assuaged my
feelings some and eventually it would be as though
Winnipeg had not lost. Rather, malign action had stolen
the game. My father began to explain that while you
might not agree with the referees you still had to abide
by their decisions, that they were usually better placed
than you were to make the calls. Obviously I could not
adjust my sights to this view, my bitterness rose within
me as strong as ever, it was still *dirty*. No, my father was
sure it wasn't dirty, he could understand how unhappy
I was, but dirty it wasn't. To say it was dirty was to miss
the point. And he would illustrate that point. He could
recall a disappointment of his as great as my own.

He was playing in a championship basketball game.
His team were the underdogs but had carried their
favoured opponents to the series limit. Slowly, pains-
takingly, he described the last game, his team's glorious,
climactic fight, countering their opponents' height
advantage with excellent outside shooting, free-wheeling
playmaking and a tight, tenacious defence. Gradually,
the bitter taste dissolved. I listened, rapt, forgetful of the
moral of the story, certain my father's team was going to
come through with the miraculous upset, my father
himself the architect of victory. And, sure enough, with
but two seconds remaining, his team down by two points,
my father was fouled in the act of shooting. Yes, he
would make the shots, would send his team on to a
smashing overtime win. He stepped to the line, com-
posed, sure of himself. *Swish*. He makes the first shot,
I knew he would. He steps back, takes a deep breath,
receives the ball from the referee, bounces it once,

bounces it twice, eyes the basket, crouches ever so slightly, balances the ball between his shooting hand, the left hand, and the cup formed by the palm of his right hand, rocks backward lightly, pumps once, pumps twice, his arm flicks forward to its full extension, his hand releases the ball, it flies from his fingertips, arches toward the net. *Swish!* The game is tied; I dance a little jig of joy. But the referee is shaking his head, his arms signalling no score, my father's left foot is on the foul line. As suddenly as it shone through, my joy was clouded over, I was myself again, angry, bitter, cheated. I ventured to put words to this new catastrophe: "Is that ever dirty!" My father, his artistry all for naught, displeased with this embittered obstinacy, took up the hand he had released in telling his story and dragged home his doubly aggrieved, unregenerate son.

The game resumed, the Canadiens going at it every man for himself, the little method in their play abandoned to the wings of a mad, disorderly flight. At such times in the Forum, the deep roar characteristic of a crowd of about 18,000 persons, mostly men, disappears, transformed into shrill, bird-like screams. For some reason it rarely fails to unnerve either me or my team. But Boston could survive, Boston had Orr to take charge of the game, see his team through this crisis, restore them to themselves; for their nerves had overcome them, the discipline had gone from their game.

But Orr, though he had not panicked, seemed confused, unwilling to accept the reversal in Boston's fortunes. He wanted to continue playing the game he was playing that had bewitched Montreal. I sensed that Orr was too young not to regret what could not be undone. He too was disturbed by the injustice of Fergy's goal, the image of that goal was eating away at all of us. Orr's preoccupation grew fatally; he was playing himself out of his own game and into the hands of the Canadiens. He lost confidence in his teammates, who without confidence in themselves, were in a hurry to shift the entire burden to his shoulders. Orr, who by drawing a teammate within his orbit could raise that player's game, was failing to distribute his skills. But what was most astonishing to see was Orr himself playing ineffectively, even badly.

Time seemed to be in Boston's favour, but time was not going to let the Bruins off the hook. And despite the senseless character of Montreal's game, players colliding with one another and themselves, two and three teammates chasing the same puck, wild shots careening into corners of the rink, it was evident the Canadiens were not about to make any self-defeating mistakes. It would be left to Boston to do that.

With less than a minute to play, Vachon, the Montreal goalie, raced off the ice and was replaced by a sixth attacker. The Canadiens were pressing deep in the Bruins' end with only one defenceman, J.C. Tremblay, back at the blue line. The puck, perilously close to the net, squirted free to Bruin winger, Ken Hodge, halfway between his goal and the blue line. In this situation he has two good alternatives before him. He can play the puck into the centre ice area, where even if Tremblay gets to it first the Canadiens will be faced with the difficult task of regrouping outside the Boston zone before reorganizing their attack. Or he can choose to carry the puck; if Tremblay is foolhardy enough to meet him inside the blue line the odds are overwhelmingly in favour of Hodge getting by him and having a clear path to the empty goal. If Tremblay retreats in the hope that a teammate will get back to help out, Hodge still has a good scoring chance. Even if he doesn't score, Boston retains possession of the puck and precious seconds and territory are gained. But Hodge had long since ceased to deliberate. The puck no sooner reached his stick than it left it, heedlessly swept down the ice behind the Montreal goal. Icing. All that Montreal needed. From the ensuing face-off Beliveau knocked the puck into the Boston goalmouth where Serge Savard, the sixth attacker, deflected it past Cheevers. The Orr check that sprawled Savard into the net was too late and only made Savard the more heroic. The programs rained down from the stands again, the Canadiens' players streamed over the boards to join the widening circle of joy. Cheevers skated from his goal to the Boston bench. And Orr, who was down on both knees, after raising himself to one skate, suddenly hurled his stick against the glass behind the Boston goal. His anger was that much greater that it fell unbroken to the ice.

The period ended, another intermission to be waited out before the Canadiens would deliver the overtime death blow. I told my father to hold my place while I took a walk. I did not ask if there was anything I could get him, and when I turned my back on him, it was with the consciousness that I could hurt him only by hurting myself. And the pain that was strangling me so obscured my vision that I failed to see that my father was so tired he had not noticed me leave his side. His immediate rejuvenation would be borne on the stick that fired the winning goal. Our mutually inflicted wounds could only be healed face to face, not as we were, side by side. I wanted to turn back, fight my way to my father, tear out my morbid thoughts as I moved along with the crowd. I had lost my reasons for coming to the game and the purposes for which I'd hoped to misuse it. I stood in line for a hotdog, the air heavy with cigarette smoke, the odour of grease, the stench of spilt beer. I did not want a hotdog, I seemed to have lost my will, was carried in the sluggish tide of the surrounding crowd. Everyone was more cheerful than I, their lively chatter contrasting with the fetid mouths from which it issued. They would gorge themselves in this inter-mission, belch contentedly, give up what little alertness remained to them. On this evening they were certain they could look to their team to satisfy their needs. I felt I owed it to the Bruins to be the best prepared person in the building. I pulled out of the hotdog line, pushed my way to the fringes of the crowd, stopped short: I knew that the outcome was not entirely beyond my determination but I had assumed I need only give voice to the Bruins' cause, pray exceedingly hard or lend them my sharp eyes. But that was not enough. I was baffled, something else was required and at this time, whatever it was, I lacked it. I made my way back to my father, slowly, in a vacant stroll killing what remained of the intermission. The best I could do was to give up my hopes but they never left me. My father, a wiser fan than I, his back to the railing, was sitting cross-legged on his coat on the concrete floor. He must have forgotten he had spat on that very spot.

He looked up and smiled a dog-tired smile. I extended my hand and helped him to his feet. He replaced his coat on the railing, drew himself up, rubbed his hands vigorously: "Now we'll get 'em!" We were both pos-sessed of the same truth; we had arrived at it from opposite directions. But I could not suffer resignedly what I knew must happen, I must continue to hope against hope. I was intent upon the Bruins as they took the ice, my eyes at the ends of their stalks: absolute concentration might override the fear and trembling. I was this unchanging bundle of intense concentration through the 20 or 30 seconds the overtime lasted. Each mistake the Bruins made, bringing them nearer the end, did not call forth the usual curse or gasp but merely caused me to blink. The Bruins lost the face-off. Blink. The Canadiens shot the puck into the Bruins' zone, Orr lost it as he carried back to mid-ice. Blink. The Canadiens brought it back over the Bruins' blue line: Orr failed to poke-check it away. Blink. But when Ralph Backstrom picked up the puck and from a position of about twenty feet out, whipped it past Orr, who had gone to his knees to block the shot, past Cheevers on the stick side and into the net that billowed with its force, I did not blink, but stared ever harder, certain the game was not over, that all these acts were reversible, that my father's cries of triumph would cease ringing in my ears.

an excerpt from the novel

Bus Ride

Don Gutteridge

The snow came down upon the village that night as it
had for the last seven days. Not continuously of course.
At unexpected moments it would cease and there would
be sun again, blinding and new, or sudden stars, startling
in the brilliant dark. Then mysteriously, snow again,
coming out of nowhere, and everywhere: humped over
window-sills; drifted against walls, fences, doors; rings
around trees and hydro poles; filling up the ruts, paths,
roadways, even footsteps made only an hour before.

And like the night in question, there was no wind
driving it in from the frozen Lake. It fell, unaided, with
the soft profusion of its own weight, straight down, in
perfect verticals, as if it would not bend even with the
urgent turning of the earth under it. And so thick that
night the Bridge was only a broken shadow through it,
and you could not see the Lake standing on the shore-
line, or the dark ridge of the forests to the north and the
east, or the bright lights of the country across the River,
or the City which lay to the south. Its falling was almost
imperceptible—that kind of snowfall which seems,

looking up at it, as if it's moving up and down at the same time, like miniature galaxies expanding and contracting, continuously adrift and directionless. It *was* falling, though, as you could see if you watched it crawl perceptibly up your window-pane, shutting the room, the house, in. Day or night, it did not matter.

The first sign that not all villagers were occupied in this sort of ocular activity was the noise. Muffled by the snow but distinguishable: shouts, cries, groans, squeals, mass exhalations of indrawn breath, mass inhalations of rather soggy night-air. Sounds of excitation? Terror? Triumph?

Then the lights. Blinking up through the down-falling snow, a great ring of them. And in the larger ring of illumination thrown by them, the first bumpy outlines of a rectangle. It is clear now that both the bumpy outline and the noise emanate from a common source—human beings, villagers to be precise. Gathered in this incipient rectangle, three or four deep, and venting their breath (with certain vocalizations of rage, frustration, ecstasy) towards a series of rapidly moving shadowy figures.

Here at last underneath the lights and looking crosswise through the snow you will recognize an open-air hockey rink, surrounded by bleachers, now filled with cheeks, toques, gesticulating hands. And on the somewhat snowy ice the usual complement of hockey players making the gestures and moves appropriate to the intricate rules of that game—with an awkward gracefulness, a rough-edged fluidity. (Though admittedly a bit more awkward than graceful, here, almost two hundred miles from Maple Leaf Gardens).

Strange, you might think, to find almost the whole

population out on a Friday night like this one, with the village beseiged by snow, windows buried, the very doors blocked. But in truth they were: grocer, butcher, druggist, policeman (the only one), housewives, young-wives, dock-workers, day-labourers from the pool room, a foreman from the Refinery, the Reeve and those who voted for him, and some who didn't—young or old, wet or dry, you could not find a larger single gathering of villagers anywhere else except at Church on a Sunday morning, and since there were three houses where God dwelt (or visited on Sabbath) it was not nearly as unanimous a conclave as Friday night at the hockey rink. And one suspected, along with a certain trinity of clerics, the level of devotion was not so high nor so deep as it was here, with the score three to nothing in favour of the hometown Flyers and less than two minutes to play.

Despite the comfort of an assured triumph over the deservedly despised enemy, there remained in the air an unusual tension. Most of the several hundred pairs of eyes were not trained upon the puck nor the players who swooped awkwardly around it, but rather upon two players who only occasionally came in contact with it. Indeed, most of their vocal encouragement, somewhat strained after fifty-eight minutes and three spectacular goals, was now directed toward two of the twelve players on the ice.

"Watch it, Bill, watch it!"

"Don't take any crap from that guy!"

"Oooh...! did you see that? Brute! Brute!" (A decidedly feminine voice.)

"Get the Yank!"

"Board him!"

"Kill him!"

Bus Ride

The Yankee player alluded to *was* a huge brute of a
player, all shoulders and hips, craggy face, black arro-
gance in the eyes, with the distinctly un-Yankee name of
Danulchuck. How this alien came to play for the Wanderers from Landsend was still a smouldering mystery
in the village, and his unamerican name did little to
diminish the anxieties of the local fans. That he was
American was condemnation enough: the foreign
flavour of his appellation merely intensified the mystery
and thus the level of resentment. And never was the
resentment so deep as it was at the moment: with
Danulchuck cruising the ice like a bear in full stride,
with an ambling ferocious elegance — his prey in sight.

The prey provided a suitable contrast: slim but muscu-
larly so, and tall: moving gracefully on skates that were
mere extensions of the leg. And speed, muscular speed,
and quickness, as he darted with apparent ease — here,
there, just beyond the reach of the cumbersome lunges
of the bearish Danulchuck. Now and then a blur of light
brown hair, a flash of blue eyes wary but not fearful.
Certainly not scared. If this were prey it was a kind who
seemed secure in his swiftness, seeking pleasure in the
quick strides of escape so that, for a moment, the partisan
lookers-on were not sure who was pursuing, who was
pursued. Just moments before this same striding had
brought the Friday night village crowd to its communal
feet (for the third time) — speed and elegance generating
more power than beauty, but the thrust of energy in
control, endlessly practised muscular movements
(which led the local sportswriter to call him a "natural").

This natural — the local fans knew him as Bill — had
just scored his third goal of the night, had virtually won
the game and tied the series single-handed. All of which

may seem hyperbolic when viewed from this distance and this age—of T.V. hockey and commercialized enthusiasm. But it is not exaggerating to say that during the two-minute standing ovation (most of them stood anyway since there were no seats, but the ovation was genuine) accorded to their hero, the people of the Point came alive—individually and collectively—as they did on few other occasions. (Six years later when the bells began to ring out again over Europe there was dancing in the streets of the Point and a triumphal tolling of bells, but for now this triumph would do very nicely). For this was their team and their boys: Bill's father worked at the Refinery, MacDonald was the druggist's son, Murphy the butcher's boy, and so on. So the victory was to be shared, the triumph communal. And in the sharing and the spontaneous approbation of their applause, all the petty human divisiveness, the pain of ordinary days, the long dream-distorted nights, the memories of Wars on far-away ground, the half-healed scars—all that divides us from each other and ourselves faded with the blending voice, the harmony of the universal cheer. The momentary shout of triumph which gives, however illusory or fleeting, a sense of fusion and permanence. There was meaning in it. And if they did not know it they felt it.

How lucky, you think? To be the object of such praise, the source of this omni-healing enthusiasm? To be chosen not only hero of the hour, but 'saviour' of your people? To be nineteen years old: with strength and power and grace? To feel the praise of your peers and your elders come down upon you like a blessing? But you (lucky or unlucky) are not Bill Underhill.

Bus Ride

Oh he was feeling the weight of that applause all right.
He yearned for it. Every time he guided the black disk to
its assigned destiny, he would wait, not breathing in or
out, every muscle rigid, until the first wave of their
cheering struck him like a bodycheck and even his
bones vibrated with their mutual joy. Nevertheless, at
this moment, he had only two thoughts running through
his head—not in parallel, but alternately: *Watch out for
Danulchuck,* and *I want out of this!*

Now the first one we might have expected. After all,
the Landsend Wanderers had lost the game, but not the
series, and so all that could be reasonably gained from
this Friday evening's combat was to stop (injure, maim,
harass, embarrass) the Flyers' star winger, the one who
had scored three goals against them. In that way he
would be less likely to score three more next Saturday
at Landsend, they reasoned. Or if they could make him
lose face with his own fans a sort of Pyrrhic victory
might yet be salvaged. Bill, of course, had discovered
this reasoning for himself and knew that Danulchuck,
though awkward and slow, was the natural killer among
the Wanderers. And though he himself was tall and
strong, he had not honed these muscles for the purpose
of brawling. Besides, Danulchuck had forty pounds on
him and swung his stick recklessly—"like a berserk
bruin with an assful of bees" (Old Charlie's epithet?)

Thus the peculiar tension alluded to earlier, as the
fans, complacent in victory, nonetheless had to watch
apprehensively as bear and his prey did their ritual
dance beyond the regular circumnavigations of the game
now winding down toward the final whistle. Thus far
it had been no contest. Bill stuck to his position, made
his plays, stayed out of corners, and when in danger,

turned on the nervous speed which had become his trademark. Much to the delight of the fans who cheered each miss and near-miss. This was even better than goals, than winning, than sending the team off to the finals at the Gardens. They were delirious, intoxicated with victory beyond even *their* simple belief. To be blunt, they were drinking themselves silly on this last Friday, this last home-game of the year, with the snow coming down like a shroud around them and their village.

"Get Danulchuck! Get Danulchuck!" Male voices, in unison, more or less.

"Back to Michigan! Back to Michigan!" Descant, very feminine.

"You play better on your ass, Danulchuck!" (Old Charlie?)

The second thought running through Bill's mind, even at this point (Danulchuck *had*, as intimated, just slid thirty feet across the blue-line on both posteriors), is more difficult to explain. A nineteen-year-old about to be canonized by his elders does not normally cry, however silently, 'I want out of this!' But this sentence had been running like a continuous exclamation point through Bill's mind since the beginning of the game. It had been a thought long before it took shape as a sentence, growing, as it were, syntactically more articulate during the past few weeks, this longest of winters. Like most human thoughts when they finally give birth to the words, the phrase, the sentence toward which they are continuously striving, this one surprised its maker even more than is usual. To Bill, as to those now cheering him in their drunken delirium, there seemed no reason why he should indeed 'want out!'

But he did.

When the game first began he had thought it merely a natural reaction to the tension. After all, they were losing the series; he had played well (according to the County Reporter) but several marks below his reputation. So for a minute he had resented and feared the cheering which greeted his first appearance on the ice. It was precisely at that point that the sentence had burst, fully-formed and grammatically unequivocal, from his brain. He had assumed it would dissolve with his first goal, the reassuring praise of applause. It didn't. Even though he had scored unassisted on the first shift. The applause was no help either, though the vibrations still hummed in his bones. He looked helplessly up at the falling flakes, everywhere, on all sides, and the sound of applause seemed like the snow itself, coming down unendingly, with a smothering and terrible inevitability, cutting him off like the village. A desolate peninsula. Every bone in him rang like a tuning fork: 'I want *out* of this!'

Nor was it any different when he scored the second goal and the third and realized with his worshippers that the game was won, the series tied. True, 'Watch out for Danulchuck' had forced its thoughtful way in, but was at best a minor theme. He wanted out, out of this rink, this village; and knew now he had wanted out for a long time. What terrified him even more was that this feeling was accompanied by no sense of shame or regret. It was there, and he wanted it.

In fact, there had been only one moment during the entire game when the old feeling had come back. His third goal. The hat trick. Scored on one of his patented end-to-end rushes. The constantly falling snow had slowed the ice considerably and hampered Bill's stickhandling, but half-way through the third period they stopped the play and cleared the ice so it was smooth. Bill wanted to rush, to cradle the puck as it was meant to, to hold his strides in the familiar, long-rehearsed pattern. He felt new power gathering in his legs, flowing up into his arms, wrists, stick. The puck lay in front of him: suddenly obedient. Around his own net: half a dozen red jerseys blurred in the snow. That other net barely visible. When it went well it was like a dance. A shift to the right, all power channelled to that side, bursting back to the left, and the red jerseys, it seemed, merely playing their part in the intricate dance. One, down on his knees, unbelieving: a second, too clever, tangled in his own amazed skates. The speed was there now: red-line, three more jerseys behind him; the puck jumping to his muscled command. Net in sight, waiting, its role assured. Old feeling coming back; as if he could fly—skates like a breeze on the ice, speed alone would do it, would carry him up and over, he was rising, floating with the puck, into or over the goal, above the smothering applause, the suffocating snow, he was above it all, knowing the puck had found its own way, the applause secure, but high and floating now through the snow which had a beginning after all, here, high over it, floating and free with a peace shared only by a quiet cold audience of stars.

Such moments are reserved for our dreams. And we are probably poaching on Bill's private preserve, for it will be evident by now that the puck did go in the net, and Bill, rather than flying over the defence, simply skated past them and blasted a shot so powerful the Wanderers' goalie didn't move (on home-ice he would have made a suitable gesture, but why bother, here?)

Bus Ride

The first wave of anticipated applause, however, did not come, for young Bill, moving so fast, faster than anyone had seen him skate, seemed unable to stop, almost (they said after) as if he were in a trance, until the endboards kindly untranced him. As soon as he stood up, shaken but unmarked, the cheers poured down from the heights of the five rows of bleachers.

Dream or reality, illusion or not, Bill *had* been flying, the old feeling in him. The exhilaration that only power and speed and youth can give. It was the reason, he had always thought, for those late afternoons on the marsh-ice below the River, for the Saturday mornings, winter and summer, shooting pucks at potato sacking till hand and eye become one motion, one will. And when there was no one to play against him, he would take a beaten-up kitchen chair and push it before him, hour after hour, till the calve-muscles ached and the ankle-bones rebelled long before his desire gave way and he limped home hurting all over. But dreaming of applause falling endlessly like snow around him; dreaming, too, of a real arena where every shift, every glistening shot, was rewarded with cheers, was recorded and sent winging on air-waves over all the snows of all this country's towns and hamlets.

As always he had waited for the crowd's reward, even this bumptious hometown crowd, hoping that the familiar feeling would remain. But the end-boards had jarred it loose, for the snow was coming down harder now, mingling with the applause and the fading cheers. Then the inner voice: 'I want out of this! Away from *them*, from *him* (Danulchuck? father?), from *her*, yes, even her (mother? Penny?)' And, for a second, a twinge of shame. For which he was grateful.

But as we have noted that was the only moment during the game in which this second thought was not uppermost in his mind. Bill was beginning perhaps to recognize how close he *was* to getting out, yet at the same time was proportionately close to being trapped here *forever*. In a sense, hockey had been a way *in* — success, approval, local fame — and could now be a way *out*. For everyone knew a scout from the Leafs was in the stands — no one had actually seen him yet, but the rumour was too persistent to be anything but true. And why not? Had not the Flyers, led by their star winger, won the C Championship last year? Were they not moved up to and contending for the title of the B League? Everyone, and particularly Bill, knew the provincial final would be played in Maple Leaf Gardens where every other seat was occupied by a National League scout. The big time. And at some point over the course of this endless winter he had realized he was moving inevitably toward it. Toward that arena which none of the boys had ever seen except in their mind's eye- boyish imaginations fed only by a famous voice riding the radio waves across the hills, the valleys, the vast plains, to every village in every corner of the land, even to this last point where the water began.

If the scout were not here tonight, he would be there next Saturday for the final, or, failing that, for the play-offs in the Gardens. He *would* be there, so it was important for Bill to play well, for the team to make it. How puzzling, then, that the familiar exhilaration did not overwhelm him, despite his three goals and flying skates. The louder they cheered, the more he wanted out of it all. The snow fell impartially on both.

"Look out, Bill!"

"Ooooh, my Goooood!" Female fear. Thrill of danger. Sexual sound.

A near-miss that time. Danulchuck just grazing his quarry, jolting the end-boards with a furiously unintentional bodycheck.

The crowd cheered his accuracy. To the Echo.

Bill didn't hear it, vaguely felt the body lunge past him. (There are times when thought becomes the swiftest, all-encompassing kind of action, even to those whose flesh habitually sucks the brain outward to the nerve-ends, the consuming muscle. Thoughts with the power of voices: wafted like radio waves unimpeded through the high air, carrying his name into strange spaces beyond the lakes, the mountains even, to the bordering seas.)

At this point, another, more familiar kind of action took place—Danulchuck's thwarted, avenging elbow found relief at last against our hero's thoughtful brow. Then the fleshy thud of a stick butt-ended against bone. Bill saw or heard none of this. Pain flashed through him, he was falling, he was on his knees, struggling to get up, a fire on the left side of his head. And here, on the smudged ice, a patch of blood, a scarlet badge of defeat oozing into the snow, spreading and visible. His blood. Sudden shame. He stayed on his knees, dizzy, not wanting to get up.

There was no external reason for this fear, for the beleaguered referee (a neutral from the City) and his linesmen were endeavouring to keep the blue-shirted Flyers from skinning alive the avenging bear (now somewhat subdued and much less awesome). The crowd was attempting to assist them.

"Skin him alive!"

"Kill the bastard!"

"Cut out his Yankee guts!"

In fact they were becoming almost nasty and not a little dangerous, for Bill had struggled shakily to his skates, blood streaming down his left cheek, the scarlet pool at his feet widening, so that even those in the fifth row at the far end could see it despite the encompassing snow.

"Are you all right, Bill?" Baker's voice. Concerned. Genuine. He resented it.

"I'm all right. I'm all right. C'mon, let go of my arm, you guys."

"Christ, that's a helluva cut!" MacDonald. What a stupid remark. He was like that.

"I'm okay. I can skate. Okay? So lay off—

"All right, for Christ's sake!"

"We'll get him, Billy. Don't worry." Baker meant it.

Meanwhile, the referee had given up the idea of getting Danulchuck into the penalty box. In fact, he had given up continuing the game—only forty seconds remained—because the crowd was turning nasty. Redmond, the intemperate grocer, was trying to get over the boards to assist the referee. Only his own drunkenness and the desperate clutchings of his more temperate (i.e. sober) wife, preventing him from doing so. Danulchuck was surrounded by red jerseys at the north end, taking verbal blows with as much grace and goodwill as his terror would allow. The exit to the dressing room was at the south end, however, and the main problem for the referee was how to get the Wanderers and their beleaguered bruin to it before the villagers decided to participate in the game en masse. One could see him glancing helplessly around for the half-dozen constables normally required for the operation-at-hand. What he found was a solitary Chief, one Michael Piersall, who at that moment was standing on top of the boards beside the penalty box (where he normally sat, feeling at home no doubt) with a most unconstabulary expression on his face. From which issued forth an unbroken string of polite compliments directed at the gathering of red jerseys. Law and order are relative commodities, a fact which, despite his apparent lack of sophistication, was well understood by the Chief.

"Kill him! Kill him!" In unison now. The true rhythm of rage.

"Let Piersall at him!"

The dozen or so Landsend fans had quietly slipped through the snow to their cars.

What ultimately saved Danulchuck from immolation or worse, was his victim. At the precise moment when this Christian mass was about to re-enact its oldest ritual, the victim found his skating legs, and, shaking off any help from his teammates, began to skate wobbily towards the players' bench. The blood was stopped now. But the wound, bright and visible, drew all eyes toward it. The rage changed dramatically to a renewal of the cheering, stronger, more passionate, more sustained and genuine than before. For another minute the old unity was there again, intact, the fallen hero revived, the brand of his triumph brilliantly visible.

This time, Bill felt it too: the shared pride. And underneath, a whelming sense of shame, of regret, for a loss not yet really lost, but somehow gone, before the event. For the moment this wound would serve as the badge of his loyalty, this pain as proof of his worth, deserving of adoration. But what lay beyond the moment?

Although not exactly sharing in this adoration, Danulchuck and his red-sweatered comrades took advantage of it by slinking out the south end to the protective cover of their dressing room in the shanty. No one noticed or cared. And though there was some brave talk of staying around until the enemy should re-emerge to board their bus, the plot never materialized. By the time the Flyers had been cheered, one by one as they left the ice, the rage had dissipated, swallowed as it usually is by the insatiable human appetite for joy.

So, within minutes, the bleachers and the rink, which had held this congregation of villagers spellbound for two hours, emptied themselves. Clumps of people, shadowy in the continuing snow, dispersed to their separate private places, dissolved slowly into white blurs. Several lingered yet outside the shanty. Small, female figures. The only movement, that of the omni-present snow.

The Wanderers have long since filed out to their bus. It has found the road some way, moving off into the blinding storm, north along the Lake to Landsend.

The bleachers are bare. Not a footprint remains. The rink a hollow rectangle once more. The snow comes down, covering the boards, the nets, washing out the blue-lines, the red-line. Every sign of human motion blotted out by this soft, insistent, immaculate falling.

Only the keenest of eyes, looking straight down through the vertical maelstrom, could discern a tiny crimson spot, fringed with white and fading with each second—like the slow bleaching of a scar.

an excerpt from the novel

The Loved and The Lost

Morley Callaghan

At the Forum the sustained roaring echoing along the streets compelled Catherine to take his arm and go plunging into the cavernous corridors and up the flights of stairs, half running with the other late stragglers. The fact that he had been late and had come offering apologies had made her feel important to him. All week she had been wanting him to ask her to forgive him for some breach in their intimacy which she couldn't define; now she liked the way they were rushing up the stairs together. A fine blue homespun woollen scarf embroidered in pink and yellow trailed over the shoulder of her beaver coat. "Hey, not so fast! I'm out of breath," she gasped.

"Where were you this afternoon, Jim?" she asked, reaching for his hand at the turn.

"Well," he said, hesitating, "what time?"

"About four o'clock, when I phoned." They began to ascend the second flight of stairs.

"Oh, I must have been downstairs having a drink," he lied.

That it should be necessary to lie shocked him and made him realize how false his relationship with her had

become. And soon she would learn of his relationship
with Peggy. Wolgast had walked in on him; it meant that
word about him and Peggy had probably already got
around, and soon Catherine would hear of it. Everybody
would know about it. It was happening too soon. He and
Peggy were not yet ready; they couldn't as yet be truly
together. They would be dragged into the open while
everyone was against them. If word did get around to
the Carvers and they rejected him and he lost his job,
well, he could take it. If it had to happen—to hell with
them—let it happen. He had made his choice. It would
be all right if he had Peggy. As yet, though, he didn't
have her. Maybe he would never be able to count on her
love. If that were so and he lost the Carvers and his job,
and with his university post gone too, he would be left
with nothing. His life would be ruined. It frightened
him, and his head began to sweat.

Their seats opposite the Ranger blue line were in the
centre of the section, and they had a little luck; as they
started along the row, mumbling apologies, the Canadiens
threatened the Ranger goal, everybody stood up and
they got to their seats between a stout florid French
Canadian in a brown overcoat who was eating a bag of
peanuts and a short French Canadian priest with a pale
bony face. The roaring came like waves rising, falling,
breaking, and always in motion. "Oh, that Richard!"
Catherine screamed, pounding McAlpine's shoulder.
"Who says he isn't the best right winger in the business?
Look at him go!" Then the play shifted to the Canadien
end, the lines were changed and the roaring subsided,
with the background of gigantic humming always there.
Behind them, three rows up, a fight broke out. A fair-
haired boy in a leather jacket started swinging wildly at

a prosperous-looking middle-aged man in a hard hat. They couldn't reach each other and flailed the air. So the fair boy grabbed the brim of the prosperous citizen's hard hat and jerked it down over his eyes. Everybody laughed.

McAlpine remained standing, apparently waiting for the fight to break out again, but really gazing at the rows of grinning, exuberant faces. They would all be with Malone. They would all agree that Wolgast, too, no matter what he was, had really spoken for them.

They were fairly prosperous people, for the very poor didn't have the money to go to hockey games. Some of the men wore fur caps and coonskin coats; others, pink-faced and freshly shaven, wore hard hats; but most of them had on snap-brimmed fedoras. The women in their fur coats huddled happily together with their men, row on row, the rich men looking like rich men, and doctors and lawyers with their wives, and the merchants and the salaried workers and the prosperous union men. They came from all the districts around the mountain; they came from wealthy Westmount and solid respectable French Outremont and from the Jewish shops along St. Catherine, and of course a few Negroes from St. Antoine would be in the cheap seats. There they were, citizens of the second biggest French-speaking city in the world, their faces rising row on row, French faces, American faces, Canadian faces, Jewish faces, all yelling in a grand chorus; they had found a way of sitting together, yelling together, living together, too, and though Milton Rogers could shrug and say, "Our society stinks," even he had his place in this House of All Nations, such as the one they had in Paris, and liked it. And Wolgast! Wolgast, their bouncer, would whisper as he grabbed

Peggy to throw her out, "You goddamned amateur. Don't give me that tenderness and goodness routine. Our cheapest whores have lots of that stuff to throw around too."

"Look! Look!" Catherine screamed, tugging at his arm. The sea of faces rose around him, and it was rising around Peggy too; the waves washed over both of them.

"Hey, you in the hat! Sit down, you bum," somebody shouted at him.

"Sit down or go home!"

"Jim, Jim," Catherine said. "What's the matter with you?"

"Hit him on the head! Sit down! You're a better door than a window!"

"Hey, you! Get out of the way!"

"For heaven's sake, Jim," Catherine called, grabbing at his arm. As he sat down she screamed, "Oh, look, look, look!"

A beautiful passing play had been set in motion by the Canadien goalie. Blocking a shot, he passed the puck to a defence man on the right who sent a long pass across the ice to a forward who raced up into position, circled and feinted his check out of position, then shot another long pass forward across the ice to a wing coming up fast from behind the blue line. The wing trapped it neatly, swerved in on the defence, shifted to the right, then back-handed a pass to the trailing Canadien centre coming in fast on the defence, now split wide open. He faked his shot to the lower right corner; the goalie sprawled for it, did the splits, and the centre calmly lifted the puck over his prone body.

"They score! They score!" Catherine cried ecstatically. "Oh, it was beautiful, Jim, wasn't it? What a pretty pattern! It's just like the ballet, isn't it?''

In the din his answer couldn't be heard. The florid man with the bag of peanuts sitting beside McAlpine, leaping to his feet, emptied the bag on McAlpine's coat, then slapped him on the back and hugged him, and the French Canadian priest, both hands raised in rapture, burst into eloquent French. Everybody was filled with a fine laughing happiness. But McAlpine, staring at the ice in a dream, thought, ''Yes, Catherine's right. A beautiful pattern. Anything that breaks up the pattern is bad. And Peggy breaks up the pattern.''

The siren sounded, and they crowded out into the crush of people seeking hot dogs and coffee. Soon they were all jammed together, shoulder to shoulder, swaying back and forth, unable to get near the coffee counter. Catherine saw two of her Junior League friends and she called to them. McAlpine found himself thrust chest to chest against the thin bony-faced French Canadian priest who had been sitting near him. The priest, who came only up to his shoulder, wore his hat square on the top of his head. His elbow was digging hard into Mc-Alpine's ribs.

''Nice game,'' he said politely with a slight accent.

''Not bad.''

''But the way the game is played these days, I don't like it. No?''

''It's skate, skate, skate,'' McAlpine agreed. ''A long pass, and skate into position.''

''Like watching moves on a checkerboard. No?''

''That's true,'' McAlpine said. The priest had a homely, intelligent face. Surely he was the one man who at least would have a professional interest in an amateur like Peggy. It would be good to talk to him and get his professional understanding and not feel so completely alone. But no! In the end he would line up with his flock and Wolgast. "When I was a kid they had those beautiful short passing combination plays. It used to look wonderful."

"It's a different game today," the priest agreed. "It's still all combination. But some of them can't hold on to the puck."

"That Richard can at least do that."

"From the blue line in. Yes."

"With great drive," McAlpine said. He was certain the priest would be against them too. Sure! Get her into a confessional with him: "I confess to the Almighty God and to thee, father. I confess to having no sense of discrimination. I confess to not keeping my love for the right ones. I confess to bringing out the worst in people and turning one man against another. Why do I bring no peace to anybody, father?"... "My dear child, it's complicated. You must not be a nuisance. Guard yourself against the opinion that those who stand for law and order are always at war with those who stand for—well, this uncontrolled tenderness and goodness of yours. Examine it carefully, my dear child, in the light of the greater harmony. St. Augustine would say—"

"It's the coldest night of the year," the priest said vaguely, feeling he no longer had McAlpine's interest.

"How cold can it get around here?" McAlpine asked. And then the siren sounded, ending the intermission, and Catherine, who had been pushed four feet away from him, called, "This way Jim," and they went back to their seats.

In the corner to the left of the Canadiens goal a Ranger forward was blocked out and held against the boards by a Canadien defenceman, who cleared the puck up the ice. The Ranger forward, skating past the defenceman, turned and slashed at him, breaking the stick across his shoulder. The official didn't see it. The play was at the other end of the ice. The defenceman who had been slashed spun around crazily on his skates, dropped to his knees, and circled around holding his neck. The crowd screamed. The other Canadien defenceman, dropping his stick and gloves, charged at the Ranger forward and started swinging. The Ranger forward backed away, his stick up, trying to protect himself. The official, stopping the play, made frantic motions at the fist-swinging defenceman, waving him off the ice. Another Ranger forward came out of nowhere and dived at the defenceman and tackled him; then all the players converged on one another, each one picking an opponent in the widening huddle, fists swinging, gloves and sticks littering the ice. Some of the players fenced with their sticks. The crowd howled in glee. The referee finally separated the players and handed out penalties. He gave a major penalty to the Canadien defenceman who had first dropped his stick to attack the Ranger forward who had really precipitated the brawl; he gave a minor to the Ranger who had dived at this defenceman and tackled him. And the forward who had broken his stick over the defenceman's shoulder, the instigator, the real culprit, was permitted to escape. He skated around lazily, an indifferent innocent.

"What about him?" the priest asked Catherine as he pointed at the Ranger. "Yes, what about him? Look at the fake innocent," Catherine cried. She thrust out her arm accusingly. Ten thousand others stood up, pointed and screamed indignantly, "Hey, what about him? Why don't you give *him* a penalty?" The Ranger skated nonchalantly to the bench to get a new stick. His air of innocence was infuriating, yet the referee, the blind fool, was deceived by it. The players on the Canadian bench, all standing up, slapped their sticks on the boards, screamed at the referee, and pointed. The referee, his hands on his hips, went right on ignoring the angry booing. He proposed to face off the puck.

"Boo-boo-boo!" Catherine yelled, her handsome face twisted, her eyes glazed with indignation. "He's letting him go scot-free. The one who started the whole thing."

The stout French Canadian, who had been standing up shouting imprecations in bewilderingly rapid French, suddenly broke into English. Twelve thousand people were also screaming, but by shifting to English he imagined he would get the referee to listen to him. His jaw trembled, his eyes rolled back in their sockets, he was ready to weep; then his face became red and swollen, and he cried out passionately, "Blind man! Idiot! All night you are a blind man! A thief, a cheat! You're despicable—go on back home, go out and die! I spit on you!" He cupped his hands around his mouth and let out a gigantic moan.

The ice was now a small white space at the bottom of a great black pit where sacrificial figures writhed, and on the vast slopes of the pit a maniacal white-faced mob shrieked at the one with the innocent air who had broken the rules, and the one who tolerated the offence. It was a yapping frenzied roaring. Short and choppy above the sound of horns, whistles, and bells, the stout French Canadian pounded McAlpine's shoulder; he jumped up on his own seat, he reached down and tore off his rubbers and hurled them at the ice. A shower of rubbers came from all sections of the arena and littered the ice as the players ducked and backed away. Hats sailed in wide arcs above the ice and floated down.

"They've all gone crazy," McAlpine muttered to Catherine. "Just a crazy howling mob." Their fury shocked him. Only a few moments ago he had imagined himself and Peggy facing the hostility of these people. Aside from the rule book, that player was guilty, he thought. I'm sure Peggy's innocent. That's the difference.

Someone in the row behind grabbed at McAlpine's hat and sent it sailing over the ice. His hands went up to his bare head and he whirled around belligerently.

"Jim, Jim, what's the matter with you?" Catherine cried, and she laughed.

"What's the matter with *me*?" he asked indignantly.

"Nobody's got anything against you, Jim. The way you're going on you'd think you were rooting for the visiting team. Aren't you with us?"

"What? Why do you say that?"

"Why quarrel with the home crowd?"

"I'm not," he muttered. "It was my hat. What am I going to do for a hat?"

"Oh, what's a hat at a time like this? Maybe you can get it afterwards. Ah, look," she cried, pointing to the referee, who was skating toward the Ranger bench to have a conversation with the coach. "Now we'll see." The coach beckoned to the fugitive, who came over to the bench, and the referee, tapping him on the shoulder, raising his arm dramatically, pointed to the penalty bench. But only a two-minute penalty, mind you! Oh, the fantastic ineptitude of the authorities! The pitiful mockery of justice! But everybody was pacified, and the boys with the snow ploughs came out to clean the debris from the ice.

The game was played out with the Canadiens keeping their lead and winning by two goals. McAlpine made little jokes about recovering his hat. On the way out he agreed with Catherine he would have no chance of finding the hat and he might as well forget about it. They had the good luck to get a taxi at the stand across the street.

In the taxi, with the excitement of the game all gone, they were really facing each other for the first time since McAlpine had acknowledged to himself the falseness of their relationship. Now he accepted with relief the fact that he might soon be revealed to her in a fantastic light. Well, to hell with them all!

an excerpt from the novel

Two Solitudes

Hugh MacLennan

Leaning on her elbow beside him, Heather bent and looked close at his face. His eyes were closed and his lips slightly parted. She wanted to touch his hair and find out how it felt, particularly where it was a shade lighter and softer on the top of his head. Already faint lines showed at the corners of his eyes. It was strange to have him so quiet now, after all the talking he had done in her studio. She guessed it was more natural for him to be silent than otherwise. All his strength seemed to be held in leash. There was a scar on his left thigh, another on his chest; when he rolled over on to his stomach another appeared on the lower part of his back. She traced it with her finger.

"How did you get that?"

"Hockey."

"All of them?"

"Yes."

"It's a good thing you stopped playing."

"That's not why I stopped."

"Why did you?"

"It took too much out of me." He rolled over onto his back again. "After every game I was like a limp rag. And before every game I'd have to tighten myself up. You're useless unless you start nervous."

"You love hockey, don't you, Paul?"

"I used to." He shaded his eyes with his hands, his face wrinkling from the low-hanging sun. "Some winters I felt as if I lived in the Forum. I knew every scratch on the paint along the boards. There was one long gash near the south penalty box I used to touch before every game, and remember how it was made."

"How was it?"

"Eddie Shore kicked his skate into it once when he was sore."

"Were you superstitious?"

He looked at her from under nearly closed eyelids. "I was about hockey."

She touched the scar on his chest and then took her finger away quickly. "How did you happen to do it — play hockey like that, I mean?"

"Because I needed the money."

"No — I mean, why hockey and not something else?"

He thought a moment. "I guess it was the first professional game I ever saw. I was sixteen. Joliat, Morenz and Boucher were playing. After that I was willing to slave eight hours a day training just on the chance of being half as good as they were." He reached up and stroked her hair. "But now I'm an old man, and at the best I was never even a quarter as good."

"Now you're very, very serious."

"I know. Much too much so."

She grinned down at him, liking the rhythm of his moving fingers on her head, warm with the sense of him. Some men who seemed gentle enough were clumsy with their hands, but Paul whose body looked hard, was tender even through his finger-tips.

"I wonder if you'd like Daffy now," she said. "She's a natural blonde."

"What makes you think I like blondes?"

"She's tall and willowy, and she has skin like honey in the sun." When he made no reply she added, "And her figure is luscious. It looks as if it would melt in a man's arms."

"It must be a full-time job, being Daffy."

Heather laughed. "And she has a perfectly dreadful husband. I'm rather sorry for him, but not very much. Daphne says he rapes her."

"Is that possible?"

"Don't be horrid!"

"I meant, is it a physically possible thing to do? I've often wondered."

He sat up and they crouched on the sand looking at each other, the moment poised between them like a bubble, and then he jumped up and ran into the water, charging it so hard he tripped and went down with a splash. Heather watched him stroking out to deep water. He dove once and came up blowing, cruised a little, then crawled back and ran up the beach and dropped down on the warm earth beside her. She sat and looked at the rise and fall of his chest.

"I wish I knew more about hockey," she said. "Mother's never thought it quite proper for me to go to the Forum. Alan used to take me sometimes. I've never seen anything more beautiful; not a single ugly movement on the ice."

"Morenz, Joliat, Gagnon, Jackson, Smith—the whole lot of them are about the best artists this country ever turned out."

"Hooley Smith sent a man into the boards almost on top of me once. Without thinking what I was doing I booed him for it."

"That shows you didn't appreciate him. He did it beautifully and you never noticed."

She got up and walked to the car and he watched her as she returned with the sandwiches and beer. She put her bottles at the edge of the water, making them secure with small stones. Then she came back and stood over him. "Did you get into fights and get penalties?"

"Not if I could help it."

"I wish I'd seen you play."

"Too late now. My hockey days are definitely over."

(with thanks to Bob McKeown/Michael Boland's "Les Canadiens")

The Return of Aurel Joliat

David Gowdey

The winter I lived in Ottawa was a long one. The snow that began to fall in October stayed on the ground through April and into the middle of May. I was compiling records on the gold rush at the Public Archives, clipping articles, sifting old photographs, giving them labels and order. As I worked the contours of the past began to form, and a separate vein of memory became apparent. Perhaps it would be mined by another researcher, or perhaps it would remain undiscovered.

I was in the habit in those days of skating to work along the Rideau Canal. The natural ice of the canal was cleared before dawn by city workers with shovels and pushcart ice machines, and each morning thousands like me would escape the commute by skating. It was a fine way to begin a day, though when it snowed heavily overnight, which was often, the skate was impossible until well after nine.

For me, working more or less on my own time, the days after a snowfall were best. I would start out under a blue sky, street shoes in a pack on my back, the clean air speeding into my system, blowing away the cobwebs. I would take the most circuitous route, gliding alongside the other stragglers, the unemployed, college students, school-kids taking the morning off, housewives running errands.

On days when the ice was slow, if I'd started early I'd head over to a stretch on Carlton Street which offered a wealth of cheap amusements. For thirty cents I lingered over a third coffee in Passalalpi's, and for the price of a morning paper I could read a sheaf of magazines in Stan's Bytown Variety. A dollar-fifty bought a full treatment shave at Twitchell's Barber Pole—3 Barbers 3—and for two dollars Twitchell would throw in a trim, allowing me another precious half hour before the decisions about the past began.

More often than I would have thought I found myself at Twitchell's. The third partner had evidently departed: his chair remained vacant at the end of the room while the other two, Twitchell and Lamontagne, dealt with the flow of customers. Twitchell had a brushcut and dark horn-rimmed glasses, while Lamontagne's hair was longer and sleek. Lamontagne favoured a wide assortment of red, blue and green tinted liquids on the counter in front of his chair. I only once saw a bottle ever put to use—a green one, used as a preshave—but they gave his area a more festive flavour than Twitchell's, and a haircut from him seemed somehow less drastic. Twitchell shunned the bottles completely, content to use only a small tin of talcum powder, and then only when asked.

The small rituals of the place drew men back week after week at ages when the need for constant hair attention had long since disappeared. We basked in the luxury of our heads being touched, of the talk of sports and Canadian politicians, in the smell of the alcohol-laden lotions and the heat of the steaming towels.

It was on one of these morning that I first met Aurel Joliat. I didn't know it at the time but the small man with thin legs in the corner of the room had been one of hockey's greatest stars in the 1920s. He had played Gehrig to Morenz's Ruth with the first great Canadiens teams, flitting past the cheerful roughnecks of the ten team NHL. Joliat hadn't been as fast as Morenz, but he was tricky and very agile, with a great ability to accelerate while turning. The two had raced through the league together, changing the face of the game.

That morning Joliat sat forward in his chair, his elbows on his knees. He looked like a horse trainer, or a dog handler, someone who'd spent much of his life around animals. He spoke about the racetrack, a horse he'd had running—I first had the impression that he owned it himself. Joliat had been there when I arrived. He waved his hand without looking at me, motioning me to go ahead of him so that he could continue to talk. He spoke half in French, half in English, for the benefit of both the barbers, who each spoke only a little of the other's language.

I had my trim, listened, contemplated the bottled colours and Joliat's reflection in the mirror. Finally he checked the weather outside, said his goodbyes, put on his coat and left. Lamontagne made sure that I knew who he was.

"He wasn't a scorer like Morenz?" I asked.

"He was great himself without Morenz—but he missed him when he was gone." Morenz of course had died, in the legend from a broken heart, ten days after a severely fractured leg had ended his hockey career. His body had lain in state at center ice of the Forum—the arena, packed to capacity, observed an eerie total silence as twenty thousand people paid their respects, waiting together soundlessly for a last chance to experience Morenz's spell. Joliat had played another year before retiring.

"He would look around him for someone to pass to," said Twitchell, "but no one could keep up with him."

After that morning I started to notice Joliat skating on the canal. Lamontagne told me that he was there every morning, but somehow I'd always missed him before. He was certainly conspicuous enough, an eighty-year-old man with a hockey stick, pushing a puck in front of him, sometimes in a red Canadiens sweater and always with the cap he'd worn on the ice throughout his career. Once I brought a stick along with me and skated quite near him, hanging back a little—I'm sure he knew I was there but he wasn't yet ready to pass.

The next day I was out on the ice early, skating by myself in a driving wind, shooting a puck and sprinting after it. Joliat, skates over his shoulders, stood on the shore for a long time, smoking a cigarette. Finally he put his skates on and joined me, waving his stick for the puck. We spoke little, passing back and forth, until the puck disappeared in a deep snowdrift and we called it quits for the day.

As we sat together drawing the snow from our blades he mentioned that he'd soon have to get into shape. He was going back to Montreal into the Forum for a salute to the Canadiens that month. The game would be on a Saturday night, hockey night, and would be televised across the country. The Rocket would be there, Harvey, Blake, Dickie Moore, all the stars still left from the most dominant teams in sports history. It would be the largest tribute to the team ever mounted, and they wanted him to be last on the ice.

I was committed to staying in Ottawa that Saturday— I wished it could have been otherwise. As it was I had to break away early, racing to a tavern along icy roads to catch the beginning of the game. The bar was crowded but a seat opened up and gratefully I squeezed myself in. Dick Irvin and Danny Gallivan were still filling time— "this historic event"—and although Molson's no longer owned the team I ordered a Molson's Canadian.

My heart sped up, my breathing grew quick—it was like a playoff game against the Flyers. The Canadiens of old were introduced and at the bar we all applauded. The names and faces meant the same thing to all of us— the tribal legend was being told once again.

Finally the camera focussed on the corner doors at the end of the ice. Claude Mouton on the P.A. gave the introduction in two languages, and in the passageway appeared Joliat. Wearing his cap he came bounding down the ramp, growing visible to more and more of the crowd who greeted him with a roar.

He leapt down onto the ice and made several strides across the face-off circle. The ovation continued to grow. He was carrying a puck in his glove and began to throw it, but suddenly found himself too close to the boards— he tried to swerve away, lost his balance and tumbled.

It seemed as if the voice of the crowd had knocked him over. People laughed and cheered, then cheered again, as he shook off the Buffalo player who helped him to his feet and broke away pushing the puck across the blueline, his eyes pointed straight ahead. "They made 'em tough when they made this man," said Danny Gallivan.

My throat tightened as the cheering for him surged, the crowd larger than any he had ever played before, and he seemed to swell with pride crossing center ice. He began to focus intently on the goalie, Gump Worsley, at the far end. He swept near the red carpet where the old-timers stood, Moore, Richard, Beliveau, nearer, too near, skidded against it, tried to run across to keep his balance, lost it, tumbled again onto his shoulder, somersaulted over on the ice.

This time no one helped him up, but it looked like Doug Harvey might have said something to him, and after a moment of pain he broke into a grin. He set his cap straight, picked up the puck and again he set off, this time more cautiously, with Harvey trailing behind.

He looked like he might lose possession for a moment but he recovered on his turn and cut across the goalmouth—Worsley went down and he swept it into the net.

The crowd laughed and cheered for a final time. He tore off his cap and waved to them, both arms flung into the air. Again he neared the fateful carpet, but Harvey and Toe Blake grabbed him under the arms. He stood there once more in the center of the Forum, where Howie Morenz had lain in state forty-five years before, where he'd taken face-offs and held the Stanley Cup, and the cheering rained down, the Canadiens surrounded him, Larry Robinson tapped him on the shin-pads with his stick.

I don't remember if the Canadiens won. I played pick-up hockey after the game, and later we went back to the bar. Everyone talked about other things. The days and nights passed and my work went quickly, but I didn't see Joliat all week.

The next Saturday Canadiens were away, so we got the Toronto game instead. They lost. That night, we were at the rink early, and the other goalie didn't show — we skated, passed the puck too often, didn't shoot until we had to. The game was listless, maybe from watching the Leafs. We all went home early from the bar. I tried to stay up to do some work, but the energy level never reached critical mass and I ended up falling asleep.

But I woke up suddenly in the middle of the night. The snow shifted outside and I walked to the window, gradually clearing my eyes. From the dark room I looked out onto the canal, and in the distance I noticed a skater approaching, down the miles of open ice.

He was pushing a puck in front of him, and I saw as he drew nearer that he was wearing a cap. It was Joliat. Tonight there was nothing in his way, no boards, no players, no carpet. He drove towards me, labouring a little, clouds of breath vanishing over his shoulder. He was skating as fast as he could. The wind rushed in, roaring in his ears like a crowd, and he swept down the ice past me going full tilt, the way he had always desired.

Other titles in the Polestar Sports Library include:

Fuhr On Goaltending
Grant Fuhr and Bob Mummery
The world's best goalie shares his secrets in this
comprehensive illustrated how-to manual for both
goaltenders and goalscorers. *$16.95*

Country On Ice
Doug Beardsley
From shinny on the pond to Gretzky on the fly, from
hockey's roots to the big business of the NHL,
Country On Ice is a *must read* for all lovers of the game.
$19.95

On Fire: The Dramatic Rise of the Calgary Flames
Eric Duhatschek and Steve Simmons
Two respected hockey writers chronicle the Calgary
Flames and their recent surge to prominence. *$6.95*

Available from your favourite bookstore, or write:
POLESTAR PRESS, R.R. 1, WINLAW, B.C., V0G 2J0 604-226-7670

Printed in Canada